LOVE LIKE A DOG

Anne Calcagno

CreateSpace
Charleston, S.C.

Also by Anne Calcagno

Pray For Yourself & other stories

For anyone who has ever loved a dog,
especially a misunderstood one.

First edition, June 2010
Second edition, October 2010

Copyright © 2010 Anne Calcagno

ISBN-10: 1-452-83498-9
EAN: 978-1-452-83498-6

Library of Congress Control #: 2010905912

Front & back cover design: Les Vogt
Cover photo by Julie Eisenhower
Author photo by Leo Fitzpatrick

All cruelty springs from weakness.
Seneca

LOVE LIKE A DOG

I started first grade with the house keys on a shoelace around my neck. When the bell rang, I plodded home in a stream of kids, some with moms, dissolving as we veered onto different streets. Crossing guards in orange vests guided us with gigantic red stop signs through traffic lights and across Ridge Avenue. Six houses east, I climbed the seven stairs up to the porch of our narrow white stucco house. The porch was flanked by a drab stretch of bare yard. A driveway funneled into the unused one-car garage.

The house was so quiet it felt sharp, like it might carve into me and eat me alive. I reheated pizza in the toaster over. I pulled my homework sheets from my backpack, and sharpened my pencils. When I finished, I set the dinner table. Then I watched cartoons, and waited. Dad's firm order was: "You stay *in*side, buddy. Streets aren't safe." He'd lifted my chin to make sure we were eye to eye and repeated, "Stay *in*side."

Dad was the Manager at Happy Mart five blocks away. One late evening, he went out back to toss the day's spoiled produce into the Dumpsters. One lid wasn't closed, as it was supposed to be, to keep out varmints and smell. That angered Dad. He flung in the box of produce and slammed down the lid. The Dumpster started rocking. He thought he'd caught a raccoon. But when he looked in, a half-grown dog stared back. Dad called the produce man, Jim. "Can a dog jump this high?" The Dumpster was as tall as a man's armpits.

Jim said, well, it looked like a pit bull, and he had heard some of them were jumpers, but he'd also heard some people dumped their dogs, even purebreds, when they tired of them. "Poor thing's starving. Ugly, too."

The unfortunate pup was splattered with coffee grounds and wilted greens, but he tilted his head cockily at Dad. "That cracked me up," Dad said, "covered with rot, still trying to look charming. Anyway, it was too late to drop him off at an animal shelter." Dad made a leash out of rope, and hosed him down in the alley. He put him in our garage with an old blanket and a bowl of water, which is where I found him the next morning, before I left for school, after reading Dad's note: *Look in the garage.* Barely slitting the door open, I peered in. I saw this dog with big paws, his black nose going up and down, trying to smell me. He gave a tiny whine that seemed to want to reach me. I put two fingers in. He licked them. A new kind of joy thudded in me before I closed the door and ran to school.

The dog was white with black spots, with a particularly big spot centered on his right eye. I named him Bull's Eye. He didn't crap or pee once in that garage. Someone had thought to train him.

Or so we thought, until we brought him inside, where we discovered he had a hankering for chair legs. He'd lie down, all calm-like, under a kitchen chair; we'd almost forget him. Pretty soon his jaw would be wrapped around a leg, quietly, fiercely, chewing. Even after Dad yanked the chair high like he might land it on Bull's Eye, Bull's Eye just backed away bewildered. The next day he started in again on a new tasty leg, concentrated on his pleasure. He was stubborn.

I selected a couple of chair-leg thick old branches on the way back from school, but he just lay down on those, guarding them. He was drawn to chairs.

Dad shook his head, "Sorry, bud, he's got to go. He's eating us out of our damn furniture."

"Please daddy, he doesn't know."

"You buying us new chairs, are you? I worked for those."

Dad brought a big ham hock bone from Happy Mart, and that helped. Except for, when we weren't looking, he buried it between the couch pillows. Dad sat down and just as suddenly jumped up, his fist curled around the moist pink bone, before he threw it on the floor. "Now he's ruining the couch. He's too much damn trouble."

When Dad came home from work, Bull's Eye licked him like he was homemade gravy, showing Dad he was all genuine crazy love. He got to stay a little longer.

"Oh, you begged to keep him," Dad told me later. "You had that kid's dream of a dog sleeping at the foot of your bed. Got to me, too, how he'd been thrown out same as garbage." Mom left us when I was three, so I guess Dad felt an obstinate kind of kinship.

Dad lay down the conditions. "Feed him when you get home. Wash the bowls. Tie him up outside to crap, then you throw his business into the big garbage can. Get back inside." He couldn't sleep on my bed. "Dirk, he's lying around all day, wiping up the floor."

A couple of months later, I was shooting hoops alone in the driveway. Which I shouldn't have been, but it was the first really warm sunny day. And I was allowed to step out to pet Bull's Eye who was now usually tied between the laundry line poles outside. He couldn't run loose in our yard because it was still only half fenced. He slid back and forth along his chain, following my bouncing basketball, occasionally barking. I noticed how he was getting broader, growing nice and big. I was practicing some moves, when a car drove up our cracked driveway. It was spring, the ground was muddy, didn't have much grass. I grabbed my ball and moved over, my sneakers squishing. In Chicago, with all the apartment buildings and congestion, people use the few available driveways to turn around. But this guy stopped and parked. It was quiet, most everyone gone in the early afternoon, and no kids on our block. He struggled to climb out, his butt weighing like ten sacks of potatoes. He smiled, "We're all going to be wearing shorts soon, aren't we?"

I tried to remember if I knew him, but I couldn't think from where. Dad didn't socialize much.

"You want a Coke? I got a six-pack." I shrugged. Leaning against his car, he handed me a can, "I love this stuff," he said. "So are you on a basketball team?"

I shook my head. Bull's Eye lay flat with his head on his paws, staring at us. "You want to go for a drive to the Lake and run around in the sand? You look like you have good strong legs." I stared down at my scrawny knees, startled by what he saw.

"No thanks."

"I can see you're bored. Me, too. Come on, I won't tell on you. We can keep a secret, right?"

"No."

"Really?" He lifted his heavy self straight up and walked over. He put his hand under my chin, lifted it and looked at me funny. Then he glanced around us, where there was nothing happening but the quiet of the street. Suddenly, he yanked me by my free arm and, dragging me, pulled me toward his trunk, which he'd all at once popped open. I tried to yell but his fist pushed into my mouth, and I could taste my blood choking me. He lifted me up, my basketball fell, and must have rolled between his feet because this set him off-balance, and one of his arms flew loose. I started kicking and screaming and biting his fingers. That's when Bull's Eye came, yanking one of the poles out of the ground, leaping for that guy's neck. He ripped the whole laundry line out, and clamped on this guy. It was like Bull's Eye could fly. The guy let go of me and grabbed Bull's Eye, trying to yank him off, but Bull's Eye's body and teeth grabbed him. Like Bull's Eye was half tarantula. I was screaming and throwing my ball at the man, so he'd let go of Bull's Eye. I thought the man might pull out a gun and shoot him. So I grabbed Bull's Eye's back legs and I pulled. I clutched him so hard, still screaming at the man, when Bull's Eye popped loose. That creep ran to his car and screeched away, leaving blood all over our driveway.

I phoned Dad half-out of my mind, and he came home immediately. He walked right to the kitchen counter and filled a bowl for Bull's Eye with a lump of fresh ground sirloin. He ruffled my hair and his eyes actually got wet. He muttered, "I'm sorry, buddy. Somebody should be here looking out for you." He stared out the kitchen window, looking far off. "Damn your mother."

At the police station, based on the license plate color, they suggested the guy came from out of state. They promised to put out a notice to all Chicago hospitals for a man with dog bites on his face. "That's a hell of a loyal dog you got," they complimented Bull's Eye. My gift from the God of Lonely Boys.

Now Bull's Eye could sleep at the foot of my bed on a blue blanket from Goodwill. He'd never go away now, because I needed a bodyguard. Dad started practicing commands: "Sit!" "Stay!" "Gimme paw!" He cut the fat off his steak for Bull's Eye. Bull's Eye began to change us.

When Mom walked out, I was three and a half. Dad was thirty-four. Dad said the police searched grimly with flashlights and dogs. She had vanished without a note. A few days later, Mom had telephoned, "Call off the police, Russ," she said, "I won't be coming back. Let me go." The line went dead.

Dad couldn't speak. He locked himself in the bedroom, didn't relent when I sobbed and banged frantically on his door. Says I fell asleep curled against the door; made him feel like shit. I clung to him any chance I got. He patted my fingers, muttering, "Don't say her name. Just don't."

Once, I had wandered away from Mom in a department store. The aisles transformed into a maze, long miles of blinding lights and revolving racks. I couldn't think of what to do but keep walking and walking. Until a clerk urgently swept me up, "Your mommy's frantic!"

Clutching me, Mom sobbed, "I thought you were gone! Never *ever* do that! Ever! Always hold my hand."

The nights continued to pass without her hands returning to tuck me in or to wash my hair or to tickle me under my shirt. I missed her soft cheeks I used to pat between my hands.

Dad began dropping me off at Mrs. Morrissey's home day care every morning at seven-thirty. Eight other kids, aged two to five, ran around Mrs. M.'s basement, where a neon carpet glared the alphabet, and a slide the shape of an elephant absorbed our energy. She disliked tattle-tales: "If I didn't see it, I don't want to hear about it." Sitting cross-legged in a big blue dress, she yelled out colors and numbers we repeated, surrounding her in a circle. Then she ran around, preparing snacks and lunches, applying band-aids, wiping her sweaty forehead. Many days, I let her busy basement spin around me. Until the mothers came to pick up their children – it was always mothers rushing over to their precious children.

I was almost always last to be picked up, and, on occasion, ate my supper with Mrs. Morrissey and her two plump high school girls who alternately doted on and ignored me. Dad was tired when he arrived. "I've worked all day. I can't do it all night, too, Dirk. Soon as we're home, get on your pajamas."

It was a sign of Dad's healing that he went back to talking. First, he furiously threw out every single remaining sign of Mom. In the evening, before supper, a can of beer in hand, Dad turned the TV to wrestling, boxing, baseball, or car racing, "Been pandering to customers all day. I need a jolt of real men." He propped his sock-covered feet on the shiny coffee table, and settled into our saggy plaid couch, which he'd recently covered with a green blanket for appearance's sake, the blanket tightly tucked under every pillow. He pulled me down on the couch next to him, and tousled my hair; "You know I have to be tough on you because we're two men alone, right? I can't risk you screwing up." He laughed, "You look too damn much like me!"

I nodded, safe in his grip. I was big for my age, but small inside his thick hug.

Flinging mashed potatoes at my dinner plate, burying the fish sticks and peas, slamming down a greasy burger or ladling lumpy stew, Dad talked. "People told me to put you in foster care. How many men'd raise a three year old? But I don't like quitters. I do what has to be done.

"It's you and me, buddy. I never could stand my family. Bunch of alcoholics, repeating the same sad stories to each other and any one. Lucky great-Uncle Terence couldn't stand most of

6

them either. Which is why he willed this house to me when he passed. You would think your mom would've at least appreciated the house."

"She didn't?"

Dad put down his knife and fork and surveyed our narrow wood-paneled kitchen. "Hell, who knows?" His broad forearms flexed as he pushed against the table's edge. His eyes tightened like fists, "I always fell for quiet girls. They LISTENED. Your mama, Estelle, had big wide watching eyes. But I didn't predict how she would catch a grain of sand inside her. Thinking she surrounded some secret pearl. She got bigger and bigger. I thought she was just big with you, Dirk. But you – turns out – you weren't the pearl she was after. She was unnatural for a woman."

"Why, daddy?"

"Most times a woman runs away, she brings her kid." Dad let that hang in the air, then smacked both hands on the table, standing up. "But that's the way our cookie crumbled, bud." He left his plate for me to clear. He sat in the living room, flicking the TV remote until he caught a sports channel. It was at this point, when there was a sudden pause to everything, that his hands sometimes rose, covering his face. He'd sit a long time, the volume blaring, clutching his own face. At times, his shoulders shook. Then my feet all but stuck to the floor, my heart pounding.

Dad claims I necessitated a huge labor of love, but I know I wasn't even in school yet, maybe five, when I started putting myself to bed. I was scared stiff to do anything but sleep through the night. If I had woken at an ungodly hour facing the jaws of darkness, I would have let myself be devoured rather than wake Dad.

Now Bull's Eye took to plopping himself on the floor between us in the evenings, watching the TV intently, in between chewing his old bone. Dad shook his head, "This pooch understands wrestling! I thought their eyes were different and they couldn't see like us. Amazing."

What Dad did not know about dogs – and pit bulls in particular – irked and intrigued him. One Saturday early, Dad said, "We're going to the library. That one on Clark Street."

Where we'd never been. He held my hand all the way there, giving it a happy squeeze now and again. I concentrated hard on this, our public connection, warm sweat building in my hand, as we maneuvered our way through stoplights, around curbside vendors in the parking lots, and people riding bikes on sidewalks. The local library was cramped, gray and sad. You stared through dusty windows at the jammed traffic outside. Dad got us a library card. I watched him speak to the skinny librarian. She grew enthusiastic and he walked off with her to a long shelf devoted to dog books. He gestured for me. Dad finally settled on three volumes crammed with photos and drawings of dogs. We walked home energetically. At the kitchen table Dad plopped down the books, and began his research, reading aloud, almost forgetting to leave for his Saturday shift. I never wanted the morning to end.

"Listen here: *The American Pit Bull Terrier can jump a six-foot fence if motivated.* Maybe that's how Bull's Eye got into the Dumpster. *It's rarely a good idea to have two males play together.* What should I do about you two?" Dad poked me in the ribs. "*Contrary to popular belief, the pit-bull is very human-friendly, and is not naturally aggressive toward humans. It is a very athletic breed, strong, quick, agile, never willing to quit, very loyal and eager to please.*" Dad loved that the American Pit Bull Terrier came to the U.S. as the dog of the common man, of farmers and miners. Furthermore, most writers called pit bulls "working" dogs, and hard work was exactly what Dad defined himself by.

"Look at this! There's a picture of Helen Keller with her pit-bull. They're even good with the handicapped." Dad did not generally appreciate injured or impaired people. He'd been furious when Happy Mart was required to re-build its entrance to accommodate wheelchairs. But he seemed to think Helen Keller reflected well on Bull's Eye.

Bull's Eye watched us grow excited. His head turned from me to Dad and back, then finally rested on his paws. "They like to play with something called springpoles. If you hang a tire or an animal hide high on a tree branch they'll leap at it for hours. Listen to this: *A disproportionately large number of pit bulls are able to climb trees.*" He slapped his palm on his knee, and laughed out loud. "I'll be damned."

We brought Bull's Eye to a vet named Dr. Lance for a check-up and shots. Eager to make a new acquaintance, Bull's Eye bounced side to side. We ordered: "Sit! Made the vet laugh, as Bull's Eye tried to solve the predicament of plopping his butt down on his out of control wagging tail. "I'd say, he's ten, maybe eleven months old. Young," Dr. Lance told us. "Put aluminum foil around the chair legs. They hate chewing that. Or hot pepper sauce." I chose a red bone shaped tag for his new collar.

Before, the loneliness had been like an ice pick landing on me.

Now, when Dad got home, we had something important between us. As time passed, he assigned me more tasks. And the more we did, the better Bull's Eye behaved at home. Mostly, I had to walk Bull's Eye. I learned to hold the end of the leash by my side, giving it a quick yank if Bull's Eye pulled. Dad showed me how to grab up his poop with a grocery bag, which was gross but city law. Dad said, "Hey, love is sticking around someone else's shit." He jabbed his finger into my shoulder, "Believe me, I know." Back at home, I brushed Bull's Eye short fur, though he hardly shed. Just that he liked it so much, going still as a marble statue with concentration. I couldn't wait to get home from school. We lived on Chase, eight blocks of downward tilt to Lake Michigan. Walking Bull's Eye, I discovered the names of our neighborhood streets: Birchwood, Fargo, Jarvis, Sherwin, Touhy. Gradually, I recognized the faces of people who liked dogs. And others who frowned and crossed the street. We lived in a city where streets ran miles into distances I did not know. Out of work guys hung out afternoons in the alleys or by Pottawatomie Park, leaning on their cars, blasting music, revving their engines. One guy shouted, "He game? Come here, boy. Sell him. Pay you fifty." His front gold tooth leered.

I squeaked, "He's my pet," and hurried away. In front of our house, I told Bull's Eye, "You're mine. Forever."

Would mom have liked a dog? She might not have, what with all the extra responsibility entailed. Perhaps all situations had checks and balances. With her, I might not have had Bull's Eye. How I wished to show him to her. He always cocked his head when he looked at you, as if you were puzzling and he was trying hard to find the right answer. I felt fearless with him.

9

True, I had to be on total alert in the streets, because he could leap off the line like a muscle car if he saw a squirrel. He *could* pull me right across the street, if I didn't tighten his leash right fast. Mom would not like that. Yet Bull's Eye's mostly obedient behavior made it clear someone had started to train him. Before we took over.

The baths Dad had insisted on nightly cleaned Bull's Eye right up. He got white as milk, and black as ink. His broad shoulders and torso became silky smooth. His nose shone like it was polished. Hands-down, his favorite game was tug-of-war. Dad brought home coils of thick rope, which he knotted at both ends. I held one end; Bull's Eye tugged on the other. He could fling me to the ground with his yank. Then he came over, looking puzzled, and licked me, until I got up and tugged again, while Dad yelled, laughing, "Get him, buddy!"

After supper, Dad liked to read aloud: *"Pit bulls fulfill their natures through demanding tasks, challenges of skill."* Dad grinned: *"Meek and mild potential owners should forget this breed.* Damn straight!" Neither of us knew exactly what kind of challenges Bull's Eye was supposed to experience. Dad patted a spot on the couch next to him for me. He put his arm around me, and tickled me hard and quick. I squirmed, "Stop it!" Dad laughed.

Dad paused, "When your mom was pregnant, we used to sit here like this. She'd roll up her shirt and we'd watch you kick. Free entertainment! Little Jonah in that whale belly. Every day, I brought home fresh cut red steaks. Got her all the ice cream in the world. Thought things were going good." He stared at the floor. "Dirk, grab the bull by the horns. You got to wrestle your way through life."

I could hardly remember Mom and Dad together. Watching me somersault in her belly, had Mom been happy?

In the one picture I rescued of Mom, black and white, hidden under the lining of a drawer, she leans against the front door frame. Her arms look so skinny, the way they're crossed, her dark curls blown by a breeze and caught in a shaft of sunlight. Her eyes are dark and round and alert like beetles. Mine are sharp blue like Dad's. But his brows protrude, chiseled like barriers. My brows melt into the slope of my forehead so my eyes stare with a wideness that didn't come from Dad. It's this look of being on alert that makes me hers. I try to believe she really had to leave us. Otherwise, she's a monster.

May 4th, I turned eight. Dad presented me with a bicycle. A gleaming new Schwinn. I choked up. He said, "Don't blubber. I didn't buy it just for you. You're going to keep Bull's Eye in shape."

Dad showed me how to push off, while looking straight ahead at my destination. I fell again and again onto the sidewalk. I waited for him to yell in exasperation, but he didn't. He was oddly patient, relaxed. And we had to keep stopping to let people pass by with their groceries and stuff. Each time, he held the seat, as I sputtered a few feet down the block. Then he tricked me; still running alongside, he let go, and I went five yards solo. After that I could manage five, then ten, then fifteen yards. I felt like an eagle, with the wind rushing at my head, and my feet clutching the pedals like talons. I could ride a two-wheeler!

"When you're ready, Bull's Eye will become your partner. You'll hold his leash as you ride, and your legs and his will grow real strong."

For weeks, we worked on that. Dad taught Bull's Eye's to run three to four feet away, so we wouldn't tangle and crash. Practicing this, I discovered that Michael, from my class, and his older brother Bill, lived three blocks west. Most days, when school let out, we crossed Ridge together because his mom didn't come to pick them up. Michael asked if I liked sports, and I shrugged, "Yeah, mostly though it's stuff with my dog."

"Dang, I'm always after my mom for a dog, but she says no way."

When school ended in June, I rode to his house, trailing Bull's Eye. Only, his mom wouldn't stand me there. "He can't mess here," she pointed at their lawn. Then she pointed at Bull's Eye, "Who gives their kid a pit bull? Insane!" She scowled, her arms clamping, a resistant fold. Michael said, "Maybe I can come to your house."

I nodded, "Sure."

Anne Calcagno

Some kids called me Dirk-n-Dog, seeing me ride around, but it was nothing. A few of us had dogs and there was something extra about us. I'd never known anything like that before. I'd never let go.

Our budget was tight; Dad drilled that through my head. "Not because I don't work hard." He deserved more. "But do I give up?" In our cold unfinished basement, Dad had installed weight lifting equipment and an exercise bike, all scored from the Salvation Army. When Dad wasn't watching TV, or polishing his shoes, or sweeping the floors, he worked out. Unless he called me down, I hung at the top of the steps as he grunted below.

Some nights, he lectured while he pedaled, "You're no man if you let yourself turn into a jelly donut some waitress could squish." He indicated the firmness of his thighs. "Got it?" I nodded. "Now a woman should have a little softness. She should cushion you. She shouldn't be practically a stick like your mom. Estelle had no give, just those startled eyes that bored into you like you'd jumped out from behind a tree, damn her."

He paused, "Dirk, come here. Let's teach you how to lift weights." He bent my knees and put his hand in the middle of my back before he handed me two of his dumbbells. "Keep your legs apart and your back straight to do curls." His eyes softened, as they did sometimes, "Estelle broke our hearts. But she can't break our backs, right?"

When it was warm on the weekends, the sky fresh as new paint, we stepped out of our cramped home to give Bull's Eye a long walk. He tore into the open, straining his leash, his white haunches rippling. Dad firmly corrected him. One day, we walked all the way to Indian Boundary Park. There, a pond with mallard ducks tooling around nearly drove Bull's Eye mad with desire. Finally tired of Bull's Eye's insatiable lunges toward the water, Dad started heading back, when a tall balding man in a yellow polo shirt, stopped us. "Your pit's gorgeous," he said. "Do you train him for weight pulls?"

Dad eyed the man suspiciously. He hated confrontation with things he did not know. "No."

"You don't compete with him? He's game, isn't he?"

"What?"

"Jumps? Agility? Weight pulls? — "

"Why? Is this for money?"

"Yeah, but for me it's more to know how much heart my girl's got. That's the wow factor. The heart. Love of the game. Pits are naturals."

Dad looked tense, but attentive. The man petted Bull's Eye admiringly. "If you're interested, I'll put you on to some weight pull newsletters. He like catching a Frisbee? Pulling a tire? He looks in great shape. He'd have lots of fun. Here's my number. I'm Jack Gray."

After the man left, Dad fumed, "What the hell was he talking about?" But he proudly rotated his biceps, staring down at Bull's Eye.

Dad eventually phoned Jack. Before long, he was receiving newsletters about pulling equipment and meet dates. He bought a big red Frisbee. Bull's Eye vaulted right up into the sky to get it. He rose five, six, and then seven feet into the air. Glistening from his own effort, Dad shook his head, amazed; "I swear he's part bird."

In school, I counted the long tedious hours. I sat silent, my thoughts blocks away. My head bowed at my desk or surveying the floor, teachers paid me little mind. Other kids seemed different, always organizing games, full of noise. I did my assignments and avoided any fuss. Sometimes, the curly-haired homeroom teacher studied me with pity or confusion. I shuffled papers in my desk to look busy, silently urging her to go away with her chagrin, "Dirk, would you like to stay in and talk?"

"No, ma'am."

What I hated were holidays. Dad wasn't big on Halloween or Thanksgiving. And then there was Mother's Day, with its stupid paper flower projects, poems and note cards. My teacher saying, "Make it for your daddy, honey." After the colors they gave me to work with were pink and purple.

I counted the minutes until two forty-five when the dismissal bell rang and I could escape. I rushed home, hooked up Bull's Eye's leash and grabbed my bike. We rounded block after block going straight into the wind. Later, I fed him and let him out to do his business. Then we lay on my bed, me whispering in his right black ear. I plowed a brush, drawing long skinny trails through his white belly and throat, while he flung his legs in the air, better to relish the pleasure. Then I traced spirals inside his back's black spots, his eyes closed in concentration. When Dad wasn't home, I even played dog, on all fours, barking at him to chase me, which Bull's Eye thought tremendous. Dad mentioned Mom less and less. To push the thought of her away, I buried my nose into Bull's Eye shoulder, inhaling his briny smell.

Dad was on fire about disinfectant. He kept Happy Mart spotless, which was a point of pride with him. Its floors gleamed. Fruits and vegetables were lined in perfect rows or stacked in inviting pyramids. Customers loved this, but it made our house a place where my sweatshirt draped over a chair or forgotten pencils strewn on the table spelled doom. I kept to my room mostly, the bed made, my puzzles and books of mazes neatly lined on the bookshelf. I counted fifty-seven floorboards in my room. Three cracks scurried up one wall. The bathroom floor tiles were in a grid of twenty-one squares by thirteen, with two tiles out of place in an off color that troubled me; someone had broken the pattern.

One Saturday, Dad got inspired to totally disinfect the house, pouring out the Pine-sol. He scrubbed the floors with white vinegar, then waxed them, then washed the windows. Carrying a water-filled bucket and a bottle of Mr. Clean, I climbed up and down the stepladder, dousing tile grout with a thick soapy sponge. Then I had to polish the tiles, using a *slightly* damp rag, which I dragged across their square surfaces. They shone. No one I ever heard about washed their walls unless they were trying to sell their house without paying for a paint job.

"My brother nearly peed in his pants when I got the house from Uncle Terrence." My eyes bugged out; who was his brother? "Not that we'd been close. He never forgave me, like I up and deceived him. Went ballistic. My cousins, too, who weren't Terrence's kids mind you, because he had none, put up a mean ass stink. But I was the only one who hadn't had a scrape with the law, hadn't been in juvie. Uncle Terrence appreciated that. Screw the rest." The walls around me took on history. I would've liked an uncle. "What's ours is ours, boy." Dad pulled me to him in a quick hug.

Dad wiped crumbs off the Formica counter as soon as he buttered his toast. I had to do the same. If my glass left a circle of milk, I got a cuff in the head. I cleaned while swallowing my grape jelly and toast. I didn't like thinking Dad could walk in, raising his voice, "You're not expecting me to clean up after you, are you?"

"No sir."

"Damn straight. Let it be said we are men who take care of their own shit." He paused, and leaned close, "And here's what. We look after each other. You don't see me out drinking with pretty ladies. Lucky for you, I'm devoted."

The recent *Pit Bull Works* newsletter listed a wheeled pull: "Harder work than any rail pull." We were learning that dogs existed with an inherent drive to pull tremendous loads. To test them, numerous pull types, varied in their rules and requirements, had been devised. People traveled far to show off and compare their astonishing feats.

"We gotta go to see this." Dad decided, "Know what it is." He phoned Jack Gray, who said he'd be competing his bitch, Fiery, in Indiana.

On the last Saturday in October, we woke at dawn, headed for Indiana. Me and Bull's Eye conked out on the back seat, Bull's Eye snoring in my lap. Two hours later, Dad was curving down a gravel road deep inside farm acreage, far on the outskirts of South Bend. In a makeshift parking lot, more than fifty cars settled into rows. People bustled back and forth, carrying coolers, picnic baskets, grills, and chairs. Many dogs remained waiting in their crates, either in their cars or in the holding area. A few were being walked. We didn't own a crate yet. We walked Bull's Eye down the main path a short ways.

Shadowed by a row of enormous blue spruces, a stretch of newly raked and packed dirt quietly announced the competition site. Bales of hay bordered it on either side. At one end, a big empty wooden cart waited. Next to it, a pick-up truck was piled high with forty-pound bags of the sponsor's dog food, *Buddy-o!* Barking filled the air. Bull's Eye growled uneasily. Dad whacked his nose, "Stop it."

A large sign read:

$10 TO ENTER YOUR DOG.
NO PAPERS OR PEDIGREES REQUIRED.
IWPA SPONSORED.
TROPHIES!

Behind another pick-up truck with a weight scale, dogs lined up with their owners. Huskies, Boston Terriers, Pit Bulls, various mutts. Upon being signaled, each dog had to stand over a square of carpet. A pulley cinched the carpet round the dog's belly, lifting the dog into the air, legs dangling, while the pick-up driver shouted out each dog's registering weight, "Twenty-five! Forty-two! Sixty-seven!" Weight determined the dog's pull classification and competing group. A twenty-pound Patterdale Terrier might start at one hundred and sixty pounds, eight times his weight. But a seventy-pound dog had to start with a lot more.

The MC spoke through a bullhorn, "Folks, the empty cart alone weighs two hundred pounds." A bag of dog food was ceremoniously loaded onto the cart: "We now officially start. Opening at 240 pounds!" On the sidelines, people of all ages, struck quiet in anticipation. Small terriers were starting. Some young large dogs whose owners wanted them to build confidence would join, too, competing in the separate "novice" category. We watched the first Boston terrier being led to the dirt chute. The owner mumbled something, and the dog went stock-still.

The man reached for the ring that would harness his dog to the cart. He clicked it on and instantly the dog started pulling like his butt was on fire. His owner ran ahead to the finish line, turning around to face his dog, calling, "Georgie, pull! Pull! Pull!" His fists pumping up and down with each "Pull!" Georgie had to drag the cart sixteen feet in less than a minute to be eligible for a subsequent load. But he became stuck, veered to one side, then back to the center. Suddenly, he unstuck himself and gained momentum. He lowered his head like he wanted his small thick stubborn black forehead to touch the ground, and pulled 240 pounds clear across the line. His owner jumped over to release the harness. He rubbed Georgie's ears, sweet-talking him. The crowd clapped.

"Next!" the organizer ordered. A woman with a Welsh Corgi lined up, and the pull began all over again.

People on the outskirts of the pull sold drinks from their home coolers. One guy held up a Bud Lite, "Gotta love Spuds." He waved the can at us.

"Can I get a soda, Dad?"

"Shhh! Not now!"

The smell of grilling meat floated around us. These comfortable people oppressed Dad with their ease, their familiarity. Meanwhile, Bull's Eye shivered with excitement, his eyes darting, his skinny black tail wagging. He lifted his paws up and down in some anticipatory dance.

Soon, Jack, the man we'd met at Indian Boundary Park, approached the chute with his brindled female pit bull, Fiery. They were competing in the under-sixty-pound category, Fiery having weighed in at a light forty-three pounds. Fiery stared intently at Jack. He clicked on the harness, it pressed into her chest, she bore down, moving that cart like it was loaded with marshmallows. From beyond the finish line, Jack urged in a low calm strict voice, "You go, girl. Go. Girl. Go." Her sinuous shoulder and leg muscles rippled. Dad whistled, "Pure beauty, isn't she?"

Over the course of the day, Fiery went fourteen mesmerizing rounds. Her tongue lolled eventually, but her glare remained tireless. She won in her category for dragging 760 pounds, almost seventeen times her body weight.

Dad shook Jack's hand, "I've never seen such a thing. She's terrific!"

"Got you hooked?" Jack smiled, his cheeks red from all the excitement in the hours outdoors. "She earned eight more points, and look at my trophy." He swiveled the silvery vase, reflecting the late afternoon sun. Jack petted Bull's Eye, who'd started licking him affectionately. Soon, Bull's Eye moved closer to Fiery, sniffing her butt. She raised her nose warily, but let him approach. "He's one fine-looking boy. If he does well, builds a reputation, you could sire him. That's where the money is."

"Fine event," Dad said. "Very, very fine."

Jack squeezed my shoulder, winking, "You like this?"

"Yessir." I watched him. It was odd how a stranger had appeared out of nowhere, and suddenly we were following him. I couldn't wait to tie something heavy to Bull's Eye's collar just to see.

The sun was low and orange in the sky when we left. Bull's Eye dozed off, plopping his big black and white head in my lap. Dad didn't speak, driving past dry brown fields and ramshackle houses. One old barn featured a huge painted sign: "The Best Tranquillizer is a Clear Conscience." Ideas tumbled into Dad's brain.

At the hardware store, Dad bought rope, a coil, and an extra thick bike tire for a springpole, which he hung on the craggy maple that leaned over our yard. He wanted to see if Bull's Eye would not only jump like with Frisbees, but really hold on. And Bull's Eye did; he flew right up like a missile, pausing in mid-air before twisting his big head and agile body in a firm lunge at the dangling tire. He landed back on earth on his hind legs clinging hard to the tire, pulling against the springpole's upward pull. "Yowee, boy!" Dad clapped his hands.

Dad had learned that, to truly see if your dog would last through a weight pull, you did preparatory strength training. We went to pet stores for ideas but they didn't carry info on training pits. Even when we used proper breed names – American Staffordshire Terrier, American Pit Bull Terrier–

clerks eyed us like we'd crapped on the floor. "Ignorant idiots," Dad countered. "Prejudiced. They want stupid frou-frou dogs, and screw the true blue collar breed." He glared at me: "You understand what's going on?"

I didn't.

"You see sweet strong goofy Bull's Eye; but others see a monster. Once people believe something, it's majorly hard to change their minds. Here's the rub, bud; once upon a time, like in old England, say, you're a butcher, you need a dog or two fearless and loyal enough to wear a bull forty times that dog's size, so you, the butcher, can kill it to sell the meat. On your own, you'd get gored. This crazy tenacious dog does anything you ask of him. At home, he looks after your children. In city slums, pits kept a home clear and safe of rats or mice. One story tells of a pit intentionally caged with 100 rats that killed them all. Problem is, people got into this as entertainment. Fought the dogs, circus-like, people sitting around, betting. Pits went against bears, badgers, then against each other. Dog fighting got them the killer reputation. If they'd killed their own species, next it'd be your kids. Which wasn't true. People forget how pits were famous for their loyalty and devotion. Now stores want pretty dogs, useless ornaments. Temperamentless, is what. We got a lot of history on our side. We're going to raise us a good working dog, like he was meant to be."

The more difficult the search, the more Dad egged himself on. He wrote away for new books not sold in stores. Soon he was reading: *Put Your Pit In a Pull, Weight Training for Pit Pulls, The Guide to Weight Pull Success.* "It's not just muscle, it's confidence you've got to build, " Dad reported. "What you can't force is the desire in them."

My after-school tasks grew harder. Dad taped a schedule on the refrigerator; some days we had to ride a mile, other days, two or three. This took a lot of patience and control because Bull's Eye and me had to stop at every one of about ten intersections, checking for cars, until we reached Loyola Park, where the path ran smooth and free along the lake. Dad had shown me how to throw the Frisbee at a high demanding angle in the back yard for at least half an hour, after the rides, to build Bull's Eye's hind leg reflexes. At one point, Dad clutched my chin in his callused palm: "Don't you dare check *anything* off before you've completed it."

"No way, Dad."

"Just doing a little pre-emptive strike."

On the one-mile days, I had to hurry back for Bull's Eye's new harness work. I tied milk jugs filled with gravel to the harness and counted on his pulling this heavy racket back and forth across the yard, low to the ground, at least thirty times. When he lagged, I had to cheer him on. I gave him plenty of water. I knew when the hands on the clock told me to feed him: five o'clock p.m. I was nine years old, handling these responsibilities. Dad and Bull's Eye expected this. I was needed. This was worth everything. To have shirked my part was unthinkable.

Bull's Eye loved orders, keen to each task, eager to serve, swelling Dad with pride. And I'd been sprung from house prison, those former days when I lived alone, inside counting tiles and floorboards. The world, with my dog in it, was a far better place.

"Guess what else?" Dad jawed on over supper one evening. "The U.S. Marines got a bully breed type mascot, a bulldog. Our best and toughest men, bud."

Our worldview that focused on pit bulls opened up to so much else. This dog *was* America. RCA had marketed its gramophone through Nipper, the pit bull terrier searching for its master's voice. Our Great War's propaganda posters had draped a pit bull mascot in red, white and blue, with the words, "I'm neutral but I'm not scared of any of them." Dad, like other boys, had bought Buster Brown shoes, stepping onto Tige, the durable insole pit bull. The Lil' Rascals had Petey. And, of course, Helen Keller had her pit bull. Dad and I belonged to something historical we'd never known before. We felt smart and important because a lot of people did not know all that we now did. Dad taught me, and I listened. And I loved him for loving our dog who was the world to me.

Then the temperature dropped down to single digits, and it became too bitter and icy to ride. For Christmas, Dad unveiled a huge box. Together, we opened up a giant kit for constructing a dog treadmill, "This'll keep away the fat." He smacked his hands. "We can't suddenly stop building his stamina." He handed me brand new five and ten pound weights, tied with green and red ribbon. "Buddy, and you gotta strengthen those skinny arms. You look like E.T."

During that cold winter, the three of us descended every evening into the basement to push our bodies. A black cassette player cranked up Bruce Springsteen, John Mellencamp, the Rolling Stones. I warbled along. Bull's Eye was too busy running hard to care that I was tone deaf.

Dad sometimes blurted things like, "Your mom should see what we're up to, huh?"

I had no idea what to reply.

"She wasn't given to patience, Dirk. Didn't give a man much opportunity to try and learn her. Shit, she hardly knew herself." Dad shook his head. His recollections agitated me. I wished he wouldn't talk about her. She hadn't given either of us much of a chance. Yet whenever he brought her up, I spun with questions I couldn't block; "Why did she leave?"

"Hah, that's the $64,000 question. Hell. How was I supposed to do something, when she wouldn't say *nada*? Yeah, she said I didn't listen, that was her complaint, she said it hurt her. But she hardly ever spoke, just stared at me like a goddamn owl. You know how many married people don't listen? What the hell! Big deal. What she was, was selfish. Over delicate, that's what. My providing for her and you, that wasn't good enough for Estelle."

I wished I'd shut my mouth, every time.

Finally, late that spring, the weather turned mildly warm. Dad drove us to Foster Beach, "Time to test him on newly packed sand. The water's edge is perfect." We were alone on a cool stretch of off-season Lake Michigan, Bull's Eye running wild in big circles. The water a dark deep blue, a few puffy clouds tracing the sky like giddy balloons. Dad grabbed our pull-wagon out of the car trunk. I helped him load on an old car tire. Leashed to it, trailing in the sand, were short heavy planks and metal weights. Dad found a flat spot, where he drew a start and finish line. He called Bull's Eye over. He harnessed him. Bull's Eye stopped his mania to watch Dad devotedly. Dad shouted, "Click the harness to the wagon." Then Dad started shouting,

"Pull boy! Bull's Eye! Pull!" Bull's Eye hunkered down and that cart began to move, slow and noisy at first, then faster, more determined, and then Bull's Eye was over the finish line, and still going. "Whoa, whoa!" Dad threw his arms around him, rubbing his shoulders. He plunked onto the sand, shaking his head, "Dirk, he just moved three hundred pounds." Bull's Eye's black tail wagged. Dad added another fifty pounds, which Bull's Eye pulled like the sand was oiled. Dad was yelling, "You're it, boy. It!" Bull's Eye weighed fifty-one pounds and by the end, he'd pulled everything Dad had brought, over four hundred pounds.

Dad announced, "We're competing him!" He yanked me in a big sloppy hug. "After I get you the biggest ice cream money can buy." He let Bull's Eye run free and glad, and we stood there grinning.

And so Dad registered Bull's Eye for his first weight pull. An ADBA weight-pull competition in southern Illinois, specifically for pits, scheduled for mid-July.

I got suntanned a dark brown riding my bike every afternoon with Bull's Eye. "You're a real Indian," Dad teased. He didn't care what color I turned, as long as I kept Bull's Eye strong.

But by the end of June, Dad was so wound up he was near exploding, "Bull's Eye is what they call a prodigy! Came out of nowhere and extraordinary. A freak of nature!" He studied Bull's Eye. Then he smacked his round white butt, so that Bull's Eye looked up startled. "You *better* be good in a real competition."

On July fifteenth, I woke up ready to puke. Dad warned Bull's Eye, "Don't fail me." He stuck his finger in my face, "You better have been doing all you were supposed to." The possibility that I could jinx Bull's Eye or that Bull's Eye might wimp out had me biting my nails. It was like Dad thought Bull's Eye was tied to him by an umbilical cord. My lips were zipped, Dad ready for any excuse to pitch a fit. We took off with a full tank, and a cooler stuffed with sandwiches, a pound of ground sirloin, and lots of water.

Leaving the bulging curve of Chicago, me and Bull's Eye
stretched out on the vinyl back seat, staring at the skyscrapers,
industrial warehouses, huge housing projects darkened by
burned out windows.   Gigantic billboards made colorful
promises.   Bull's Eye whimpered, excited, then eventually
quieted.   I woke up somewhere in the middle of Illinois to
countryside flat as a sheet of cardboard.

Foot leaden on the accelerator, Dad was doing the nine-hour
drive in a day, with a couple of short stops for Bull's Eye. We
skimmed the flat blade of Illinois, my head vibrating groggily on
Bull's Eye back, watching the treetops zoom past like green
brushstrokes. By early evening, the ground around us began to
lift and fall, hills building on one another. We crossed a river
and arrived at our destination, the outskirts of Carbondale. A
dog-friendly motel had been recommended by the ADBA,
though we seemed to be the only dog people there. Tiny white
cabins scattered through a small grove of evergreens.

Dad sat on the edge of his bed, rubbing his neck, eyes bleary,
griping about being tired, but we had to walk Bull's Eye. "Don't
want his muscles cramping tomorrow." At the end of our walk, I
grabbed a big stick and let Bull's Eye tug and pull. When I
tired, he placed the stick between his paws, staring intently, as if
to say: *It's ours. Aren't I perfect? Don't I give you everything?* Dad
filled up a bowl with sirloin for Bull's Eye. We ate sandwiches,
and collapsed.

Six-thirty in the morning, and Dad was shaking me, not of
the mind that boys needed much sleep. "Up, up, we've got to
get Bull's Eye used to this hillbilly heat."

At *Baba's Diner*, Dad drank four cups of coffee, repeating,
"Hurry up, hurry up." As I shoveled down my syrupy pancakes.
The weigh-in wasn't for another two hours.

Dad drove stiff-backed, following the map to the opposite side
of town. We were looking for an Elks Lodge. Bull's eye stuck his
big white head enthusiastically out the window, as if willing to
help. Finally we reached the parking lot already filling busily
with cars. A large board faced arrivals:

WELCOME TO SOUTH SUMMERTIME'S
ADBA WEIGHT-PULL MEET!
(And by the way: Love Your Pit. We do.)

An empty railroad cart rested at the far end of a chute with metal tracks. A large stack of cement blocks piled next to it. Men wearing wife-beaters and women in spaghetti strap tops settled their kids down on the lawn. Others walked their pits, all sizes and colors. My T-shirt stuck to my back. Dad wiped his face with a rag. We heard the echo of the Course Marshall announcing the weighing in. A line formed. When it was Bull's Eye's turn to swing up on the carpet square, his brown eyes wide, he placed in the under-sixty pound category.

Some competitors considered the rail pull easier because the tracks kept a dog from pulling off course, but the sheer size of the rail car was daunting, and most dogs would be expected to start with heavier loads.

The sidelines buzzed with conversations. A guy in a smudged baseball hat bragged, "I once seen this black pit drag 1,600 pounds. She was small to boot."

His friend with a thick black beard said, "I don't know why my dumb dog won't try harder."

"You're too lazy to train regular, Bobby. I seen you at the bar every evening, for Chrissake." He removed his baseball hat to wipe his sweaty scalp, then slapped it back on.

"Not everyone has a right little girlfriend to keep him busy, douche bag."

"Look for this pit called White Fang. He'll win for sure. I seen him before."

Bobby nodded.

I listened, intent on Bull's Eye, sweat sliding down my nose. *You've got to do this, boy. Please, please.*

This was a different crowd than before; less organized, more red-eyed as if the air stung. The judges sat behind a table with papers and notepads held down by stones. Soon, the pull began, as before with the small or novice pit bulls going first, followed gradually by larger ones. All we could think about was the under-sixty category. We watched a small young male pit straining to see the cart to which he'd just been hitched. Unable to turn, he sat bewildered on his haunches, looking for his owner. When his owner urged, "Come! Come here!" the pit rose half-heartedly, before stepping off the chute as if he thought he could leave, thus disqualifying. Some people had barely trained their dogs. They expected the pull to happen by instinct.

Bull's Eye started at 350 pounds, the weight set to gain in fifty-pound increments. Soon, a competing bitch struggled and disqualified at the 450-pound mark. Dad's excitement increased.

I watched Bull's Eye pull five hundred and fifty pounds of cement blocks. Then six hundred. By six hundred and fifty pounds, I could hardly think, my brain like a thousand flags fluttering. Dad walked over and tousled my hair, his touch rough and harried. "Cross your fingers, Dirk. He's got to stay in the zone." His face and arms tanned brass-color, his steely blue eyes shining, his temples moistened by the heat; I loved him.

Bull's Eye's coat was now gray and sleek from being rubbed down with water, his black ringed eye focused on Dad. He needed to pull 700 pounds. Again, they approached the chute, and Bull's Eye waited for that harness to click. And he took off, his front legs digging like fork prongs, his back legs tilted at a hard forty-five degree angle. He moved eight feet. Then he stopped. Dad cried, "Pull! Pull!" But Bull's Eye wouldn't budge. He tried to sit but the harness made that difficult, then he tried to lie down. My head hurt. Dad shouted, "Don't you give up! You pull! You do, Bull's Eye!" And Bull's Eye lifted himself up with a jolt. He pulled through, but the timer had gone off. Yet, according to the rules, he was allowed a second chance. Dad flashed me the thumbs-up sign, keeping his temper.

"This here's the one to root for: White Fang," the talkative guy with the baseball hat was back, poking his friend's shoulder. He pointed his beer toward the cart: "Watch this."

White Fang saw the harness and bent his legs squat as a crocodile. When his harnessed ring clicked, Fang dragged those 700 pounds so effortlessly you would've thought the rails were greased. His owner had stood silent at the finish line, hands stuffed his jeans pockets, his eyes the beacon. The crowd cheered. My eyes nearly popped out.

Suddenly, a frenzy of barking erupted. Men hurried toward the noise, shouting. Hesitant, I followed the commotion. On a patch of dirt at the edge of the parking lot, a muscular blue-gray pit had his jaws clamped on the head of a little red pit, dragging him, blood spraying like fireworks over the dirt. Four guys jumped in, working to separate them, blood splattering from the red dog onto their hands and shirts, while they yanked on the blue's hind legs, then his collar. My stomach flipped up my breakfast; clutching my intestines, I heaved onto the grass. A heavyset bearded guy shoved a stick into the blue pit's mouth, yelling, "Release! Now!" Twisting and turning this stick until he finally popped him loose. He heaved the blue dog away into a crate into his pick-up, followed by the injured pit's owner who screamed: "Get your dog out of here! You know the goddamned rules!" The bearded guy looked unmoved.

The Marshall and two others ran to keep the men apart. The Marshall yelled, "Can't you read the goddamn signs? The flyers? No dog fighting! No dog-aggressive dogs!"

The big-bellied guy shrugged, "He got a little excited."

"Get out!"

"You pussies never seen a game pit?"

The air lodged like a rock in my throat.

"I'm calling the police!" the Marshall hissed.

Big Belly scowled and lurched away, dragging his dog. "Pansy pits!" he shouted. He fired up his pick-up.

I dry heaved. Spit dribbled down my chin. All at once, Dad's hand was firmly patting my back, "Fighting, huh?" He wiped my face with his handkerchief. "Bad stuff. I told you about this, remember, there's people who think that's entertainment. You avoid them. But, listen, the ear bleeds a lot; that's mostly what you saw. The red pitty'll be fine in a day or two." He put his hand on my shoulder, "Come on."

"Back to the pull, people!" The Marshall blared, "We're not letting some low-class ruin everything our dogs have worked for."

Back at the rails, in the increasing heat, people swatted at the biting horse flies. On the grass nearby, kids poured water on their heads, and ran in circles. The judge, the timekeeper and the Marshall had wrapped their heads in wet bandannas. The Marshall continued, "We deeply apologize for that unwarranted situation. May we remind everyone: dog-aggressive dogs are strictly prohibited."

I felt tears coming on and pretended I was wiping away my sweat. Bobby turned to his baseball friend and smiled, "I would've liked to see me more of a fight." His fingers played inside his beard.

I dabbed my liquefying face with my T-shirt. Dad wasn't eating or drinking. Bull's Eye entered his second round. His brow furrowed, the harness ring clicked, and Dad yelled, "Pull! Bull's Eye! Pull!" Bull's Eye rolled the 700 pounds like a train on schedule. Dad fell on his knees and hugged him. I was jumping up and down. Bull's Eye looked over his shoulder to where I was leaping, his head tilted, like he was again trying to figure out the puzzle of this life he'd fallen into.

An hour later, with the weight at 850 pounds, another pit bull named Bronco pulled the load in forty seconds when it took Bull's Eye fifty-two. Then at 900 pounds, Bull's Eye didn't make it. Yet Dad was euphoric, "He has that drive. Gameness! I can't force that. He's got the gift." Bull's Eye got a huge juicy bone. While he chomped contentedly, I sat on the ground next to him, rubbing his strong wet flanks, this body I adored.

Other handlers chatted with Dad, impressed Dad hadn't even tried the Novice category, this being Bull's Eye's first event. "Found him in a Dumpster, too," Dad said. "Talent ready and waiting. One man's garbage is another guy's treasure."

Instead of recoiling from these strangers, Dad's shoulders opened broad and swaggering. The men mentioned dietary supplements, training techniques, swim practices, and upcoming pull dates. Dad did not have friends, no one who came over, phoned, or crossed the street regularly to talk to him. We lived a closed life, the two of us, with Dad refusing to see his relatives, and everyone in Mom's family gone dead to us. I didn't want us to be so isolated. I thought of how Bull's Eye was leading us to change. He was my guardian. I was his brother. The responsibility I faced was not just to condition him, but to save him from anything that might limit him or us. I was nine and I saw what being responsible was in a new way. To be both servant and guide. My love for Bull's Eye leapt and spun like a wild song.

Dad believed education was like compulsory military draft; "No point in complaining." I slipped through school doing the minimum. My classmates shared the language of Pac-Man, Pong, Atari, like a cult. I rarely had the necessary items. Those few times I'd proudly brought foil-wrapped cards, I was greeted with impatience, "You gonna trade or not?"

"Sure."

"Sure you *have* anything?"

Michael was the only one who ever explained anything like I was worth his time. Though he wasn't much for sitting still; he was usually running, tossing a baseball, or playing Dodge. Which left me with gobs of floating time at school. My teacher's mournful glances announced there was something sorry about me. I wanted to crawl out of my skin. To forget about them all, I bent my head. I picked up a book. Before too long, I was reading anything and everything. The sneering faces, my heavy hours, started flying by.

My habit, when Mrs. Harris, my teacher, drew the continent of North America, or listed spelling words related to "scientific experimentation," or dictated the dates and locations of major Civil War battles, had been to stare out the window at the parking lot and the trees limbs blowing about. It wasn't that there was a world of wonder out there, but wonder certainly wasn't with Mrs. Harris. I squirmed through her paces. But, gradually, I also got to thinking about how I wasn't inspired, not even as much as Bull's Eye, whose ears pricked up daily, everything thrilling to him. Dad and I were *his* school. And he was magnificent in his discipline. What about *me*? I wondered if you actually chose discipline might it be like a special power. *Self-determination.* When I got this idea, it stuck. I started taking extra time, made colored borders on the United States map we had to outline. I offered Mrs. Harris more than one-word replies. Easiest was acing the math tests; I liked clean fractions and measurements, percentages and decimals. Mrs. Harris rested her hand gently on my shoulder, "You make me so proud." My cheeks burned, and I shifted uneasily in my chair. Bull's Eye had rewired my brain.

I nabbed some books recommended by the school librarian, about boys who owned dogs: *Shiloh, Henry Huggins, Rigsby.* Sometimes, I imagined myself like them, a character in a book, growing adventures.

And then there was home. In the kitchen, I flattened my hand in front of Bull's Eye's shiny black nose and ordered, "Sit. Stay!" He froze, still as stone. I filled his bowls with food and water. He could not budge an inch or I had to remove his bowls for half an hour. I said, "Now!" Then he ate. After, I called "Place!" and he quickly lay down. Bull's Eye needed to perform these same orders instantly for Dad, or we got into trouble.

Bull's Eye learned to be patient as my increasing homework crept into our afternoons. He stopped nudging my knee with his nose. Not until I cried, "Atta boy, out now!" did we throw ourselves down the porch steps, charging the streets, bike-bound, our leg muscles pumping the blocks. I explored new streets. Whether you turned east or west, Ridge Avenue marked the high ground. I bicycled up to Ridge, then down Chase or Sherwin or Jarlath, a boy tracing the northeast ribs of Chicago, memorizing the worst sidewalk cracks, and where tree roots distorted the cement into clutches of carbuncles. I knew which curbs made my bike fly, and which alleys engaged the most traffic. Bull's Eye charged along devotedly. I almost always stopped by Michael's house, just to say hi. He was crazy for Bull's Eye, even if his mom wasn't. He hugged him, revved him up in a game of tag.

I told Michael how Bull's Eye had saved me from that abductor creep. He went quiet, and I got embarrassed and climbed back onto my bike, ready to hurry away. But Michael spoke. "He would've died for you. That's loyalty. People aren't so brave, not most. Man, wish I had that."

"He knows you. He'd do it for you, too."

Michael grinned, "All right then."

And so with Bull's Eye, I saw I had something to give.

I watched owners, especially old women, walking disobedient yappy dogs. Those dogs had become weird on overeating and lack of control. People created ridiculous relationships. But not me and Bull's Eye. I lifted my hand, palm up, and he rose off his haunches. I turned my hand, palm parallel to the ground, and he flattened himself down. He was so good. Extraordinary.

I brought my report card home with As and Bs. Dad laughed, "I see you got your teacher fooled." I nodded. I couldn't explain myself. "Your mom fooled her teachers, too."

"She was smart?"

"Not by me." Dad scowled. "Would you say so?"

How could I? He scruffed up my hair, "Maybe some day you'll get clever enough to pay all my bills."

"Yessir."

Summer came and soon people hung out late into the long evenings on their porches or at Pottawatomie Park, or in the parking lot of Felix's Drugstore, car radios blasting. The humid air warmed up like wax melting on my skin. New families had moved into other narrow houses on Chase, spilling out surprising numbers of people, families extending into grandparents and uncles and uncles' girlfriends and little kids. Spanish, Vietnamese and Polish ran up and down the sidewalks. The more I paid attention, the more the world grew, my head no longer the biggest universe. Staring around, I had to watch not to crash Bull's Eye and me into a pole.

Michael had been insisting, "So when can I see a weight-pull? I've never seen dog sports." He didn't need to convince *me*. Traveling alone with Dad was like being caged with a badger, though Dad called it *jitters*.

I suggested, "Michael could help carry stuff."

"The two of you'll behave?" I shook my head. "We'll try. One time." He lifted one finger in front of my face. "*Once.*"

And so one night when the heat lay heavy and scratchy as wool, Michael slept over. We rose groggy to a light pink sky. Dad directed us where to put things, urging, "Hurry!" He pointed the car toward Michigan. Bull's Eye's ears pricked up; he *knew.* Miles and miles slipped under our wheels, us going catatonic from the silence. Then Michael waved to some people. We started singing out the window at everyone we passed. We nearly wet ourselves laughing, until Dad ordered us to shut up. But finally, finally, hours later, we were at our site, people pulling or carrying their crates across the noisy parking lot. Michael nudged me in the ribs.

"Everything out of the car! Now!" Dad commanded. "Walk Bull' Eye!"

Michael's face just about split from smiling. He talked a mile a minute: "Does Bull's Eye have bad days? I mean, can you tell if he's good and ready? Do you know any people here? Seen any of these dogs before? Do they ever get into fights, the dogs? What do you do?"

"Michael, jeez. Shut up."

He jammed his middle finger into my stomach, "Dickhead."

"Imagine tying a harness on Mr. Proce." Our balding gym teacher. "Heart attack central." Michael lunged side to side like a frantic Godzilla. We fell to the ground writhing, clutching our throats, our feet stuck straight up the air, flailing with gusto.

"Hell of a lot of help I get," Dad suddenly stood over us, big head eclipsing the sun. "Hurry up. Cool off Bull's Eye." Made serious, we moistened two washcloths with melting cooler ice. We rubbed Bull's Eye down. "Lickety split, you goofs."

Then it was time; dogs weighed & categorized, this a competition for bigger dogs, with more weight. Everyone lined up along the chute. The first Husky lifted his white and gray head before he tilted his long nose, narrowing his eyes. You could imagine him fighting a snowstorm, the wind knifing him, his unwavering sense of direction. The crowd grew anxious, as it did when the dog worked. Then cheering erupted as, 40 seconds later, the Husky charged across the finish.

"Does it ever break their bones?" Michael asked.

"They can stop and give up. I've never seen one injured."

Dad muttered, "We're screwed." He led Bull's Eye to the cart's 600 pounds. Bull's Eye looked fresh, sniffing the air for opportunity. My eyes widened and Michael went still as a telephone pole. Bull's Eye took off like a rocket. I heard birds twittering in the trees people were so quiet. Bull's Eye's muscles rippled, and, at 36 seconds, he crossed the finish line. Dad fell on his knees, hugging him like there was no tomorrow.

"Get him a treat!" Dad ordered, as he moved Bull's Eye away to some grass to rest. I rushed over with a piece of beef jerky, and kissed his big stubborn head. A round woman in a pink shirt walked over to Dad. Dad smiled at her, intent, walking Bull's Eye closer to her. Smiling back, she massaged Bull's Eye's spine. They pointed at Bull's Eye, didn't acknowledge me.

Fast forward. Bull's Eye was now hooked up to 1,150 pounds. Half way through, though, he stopped. Dad was about to have a stroke: "What? Not now! Pull! Pull!" A man in a stained short-sleeved shirt said, "End of that pit." Michael and I pressed closer, aching. Bull's Eye cocked his head, enough to see me without anyone realizing. He gave me that look he always did when he was trying to figure out the answer, and suddenly he crouched and pulled all the way to the end. Michael moaned, "Wow-wow-wow!"

Bull's Eye had pulled over half a ton, more than twenty-two times his weight, in 58 seconds. Michael yanked a bystander's sleeve, "He pulled for Dirk!"

"Right-o, boy."

It wasn't much later that the loudspeaker claimed: "First place is awarded to Bull's Eye, four-year-old pit bull from Chicago, Illinois." People applauded and shook Dad's hand. Michael and I grinned like idiots. The lady in the pink shirt reappeared, chatting away.

Before we headed home, Dad bought an order of fries, totally spoiling Bull's Eye, and giant milkshakes for us. Bull's Eye looked at us like he was saying, *I'm pretty wonderful, yeah, admit it.* The passenger seat held a huge silver-plated trophy. Michael and I sang horrible songs and made funny faces at people we passed. We couldn't irritate Dad. Bull's Eye thumped his tail on the seat, adding his own rhythm.

A few days later, the phone rang. Our phone sat silent so many days in a row it was more like a rock stuck to the table. "Well hello, hon, you must be Russ's son," a woman's voice cooed. "You tell him Nellie called, won't you? I understand you love pit bulls, babe?"

"I train Bull's Eye." My skin prickled, going numb.

"And what a good job you've done. Would you like to train a puppy?"

"Can't say." I wanted to drop the phone. I wasn't used to calls.

"Baby, tell your Daddy I called."

When I did that evening, Dad went all smiles. "Isn't that nice? If I breed Bull's Eye to her, she'll give me a pup from her bitch's litter. If we get a good pulling girl out of that, when she's older and ready, we'll breed her to Bull's Eye – that's called double-cross breeding – we'll start our own dog line."

"But we keep Bull's Eye?"

"Hell yes, he's our golden goose! *If* I get a squeaky clean bill of health from the vet." Dad scoured the kitchen counters energetically with Comet. "It's not unusual for the ladies to flirt, but Nellie's got that something more I need. And she's not damn quiet." She'd looked about Dad's age, with reddish-blond hair, and elongated silky brown eyes. "She's not a perfect beauty," Dad explained. "A bit round, got some wear and tear from life. But a real pretty face. And energetic, positive, like she's connected, and she's sharing."

Bull's Eye was mine, though, mine. He shouldn't be part of any deal. He was going to get whisked away to Nellie's. And then? Dad was seeing Bull's Eye like he was a fill-in-the-blank. Still, this wasn't the kind of thing I could say to him without his face and ears going maroon, his finger pointing me to my room.

Now, he chatted on the phone in the evenings with Nellie, stretching the cord while he vigorously dusted the tops of the kitchen cabinets, or knifed out crumbs from between the stove and the cabinets.

Then one Saturday, Dad left to deliver Bull's Eye to Nellie's bitch; "Not a sight for young eyes." I lay on my barren bed, feeling sick, counting the floor slats, the quilted squares of my blanket, how many strands of hair I could grasp between my thumb and forefinger. The hours clumped by, leaden weights. The old dogless silence returned. It had always been lying in wait. I blamed Nellie, and her stupid plans for the future.

"Bingo!" Dad exclaimed, opening the front door. Bull's Eye ran over, slathering me with kisses, fussing busily. Dad observed: "You use an inbred dog for type breeding but an outcross to obtain an athlete."

"Which is Bull's Eye?"

"He's unrelated, so he's an outcross, bud."

It all seemed so enervating and irrelevant.

I now learned about Phase Two. "Listen up; we're going to build a solid six-foot high fence. That's our job for the summer, enclosing the yard. Keep our business private."

Over the next few nights, Dad drove back and forth to Menard's. He unloaded twenty four-by-four studs into the garage. They'd frame the fence. Next, he delivered fence sections, the slatted wood piled on his Chevy like a stack of square pancakes. He lugged in a fifty-pound bag of concrete mix. The garage overflowed.

All that summer, every long, light-filled, evening, we worked on erecting that fence. Dad plunged the post-hole digger, I stirred the cement, struggling to keep it from crusting. Dad dumped in cement, and positioned a stud. Bull's Eye ran back and forth along his chain, while the studs, clutched by cement, grew around him. Dad aligned the fencing, studying his level's bright green liquid. Then, he nailed each section, top to bottom, into the studs. It took weeks of evenings. Then, one day, the yard was finally surrounded and Dad fitted a latched gate. That evening we untied Bull's Eye and let him run amuck. Squirrels sprinted over the phone and electrical lines, maddening Bull' Eye underneath. He ran and ran, trying to get one to fall. Pleased, we chomped on hot dogs and chips.

When it got dark, Dad phoned Nellie and laughed a lot. I sulked. We'd hardly had time to train Bull's Eye lately.

We cleared the sawdust and scraps out of the garage. Dad packed up his tools. "Now we'll invite Nellie. We'll have us a real special barbeque."

It was the strangest thing, having someone over to our house. No one ever visited. First, we had to clean house. "I want my face shining at me from the kitchen floor," Dad planned as he waxed. Then he took a toothbrush to the metal sink fixtures, in the kitchen and bathroom, brushing every edge with precision. I madly surface-sprayed the counters with 409, after which Dad handed me a pile of newspapers and a bottle of blue Windex.

The day Nellie was coming, Dad had me take a bath in the middle of the afternoon and put on a new T-shirt. He shopped for red, white and blue napkins, and bought a big blue bowl for chips. He made a fuss over three fat T-bone steaks, and got me shucking ears of corn. He swaggered, clean-smelling in his laundered jeans and white T-shirt, squinting his sharp blue ice eyes. Bull's Eye moped from being left alone outside; Dad wanted the inside pristine. Dad yelled, "You liked going over to Nellie's though, didn't you? You rascal!" Bull's Eye tilted his head, doubtful and taxed.

Nellie arrived in a red Mustang convertible. I heard her stereo click off. I squinted through the peephole. Round, and golden-colored; her soft skin tanned, her hair reddish-gold, her strappy gold sandals shining. In tan khakis and a cream shirt. She smiled even before we opened our door. "Well hello, boys."

How tall and broad-shouldered Dad looked near her, bronzed from his labors outside, brushing back his thick blond hair. She eyed him with lash fluttering appreciation. Dad's sharp eyes wrinkled with satisfaction. "But where's Bull's Eye?" she asked me.

I dully pointed outside. Dad led her through the house to the back door to show off the fence. She oohed and aahed. Bull's Eye ran back and forth, a blur of black and white spots. Nellie cajoled, "You've trained him. Show me some tricks."

I disliked her interest in Bull's Eye. I didn't budge.

"Hey, step to it!" Dad snapped.

I stomped over to pick up a Frisbee. For Bull's Eye's sake, I'd do this. I tossed it at least six feet in the air: his body lunged like a torpedo and he snagged it. I did this twice and Nellie clapped.

"More," Dad ordered.

I showed how Bull's Eye obeyed "Sit," "Down," "Come," "Heel."

His tail wagged like mad when I brought him over to Nellie, who rubbed his ears and muscle-thick neck. She said, "I've got photos of my girls." Her girls weren't daughters, but three Am Staff Terriers and one American Pit Bull Terrier. Nellie pointed to the latter, "Here's Penny, Bull's Eye's new girlfriend, then Sandy, Betty, and Millicent. Like them?"

"They're beauties," Dad flattered.

Nellie touched my arm, "You're going to be a heart-breaker, aren't you?"

"Don't butter him up. I need to keep him in line." Dad scolded.

She winked, "Some men are *so* serious. Russ, he looks like *you*. Aren't that many smart and handsome men out there working with pit bulls. Seems to me we got a double lottery win here."

"Hah!"

Dad pulled out two chilled glasses and two Coors. He seated Nellie and poured her beer at the outdoor table. He doused the coals in the Weber Grill with lighter fluid. I shook potato chips into the blue bowl. I sat, swinging my legs, drinking a Coke, not knowing which way to look. Bull's Eye shoved a tug toy into my lap.

"How often do you see your mother, hon?" Nellie asked out of the blue.

My mouth gaped.

"Oh she's gone," Dad said. "Vanished into thin air. Not a thought for him. Heartless."

"I'm so sorry," Nellie stammered. "Russ, you never told me."

Dad shrugged. He tossed this fact up like it was weightless. Mom's abandonment of *me* was *my* business. I had burned a hole into my heart, trying to understand. I should get my forehead tattooed: LEFT BY MOM. Better than having it flung at me the second I forgot. Blabbermouth Nellie patted my hand. I snatched it away.

"Now he's sulking," Dad said.

"Sweetheart, it's my stupid fault," Nellie returned her hand over mine. "I'm very, very sorry."

I stomped inside. I turned on the TV. I glared at the screen, unfocused. I wanted Bull's Eye with me, but Dad kept him outside to show off. I considered crawling under the couch. It wasn't long before Dad called, "Want your steak cold? Get out here, Dirk."

I didn't budge. Unexpectedly, Nellie entered. She smiled but in a serious sort of way. "We'd really miss out if you didn't join us. Your dad's steaks look scrumptious. Strangers can say the wrong things even when they don't mean to. Please don't be mad at me. Please come out." I wasn't used to being talked to like this.

Dad forked over a steak. "Look who's come around."

"Each of my girls' birthdays I make steak. They love me for it!"

Dad shook his head, "They sound spoiled."

"They're my babies."

"Dirk, did I ever spoil you?" I looked away, still smarting. "We do things differently around here." Like he expected to receive an award.

"Nothing wrong with a little spoiling," Nellie mused.

The afternoon light had faded. A few late-blooming cicadas whirred and clicked. The blue of twilight rose over the roofs, spinning into our yard. Dad turned on the back porch light. With the slight drop in temperature, I felt a cool edge to my skin. The fence gave our small city yard importance. Neighbors on either side could no longer blankly stare in, unless they were tenants in the upper floors. Dad recounted the fence construction, shared theories on weight-pulls, analyzed Bull's Eye's skills. When Nellie interrupted with her views, Dad paused to listen. Bull's Eye's tail wagged. I cut off my bone and flung it through the air, and Bull's Eye leapt to the occasion, settling in to gnaw. Dad didn't bristle. Eventually, I returned inside, this time with Bull's Eye. Stupid old movies came on TV, so I went to my room. I built a tower of cards. I skimmed a book on space exploration. I started re-reading *Rascal*. I conked out.

The next morning, I munched Cheerios in the kitchen. Clickety footsteps approached. Before I could blink, Nellie was asking, "Sleep well? How does your Daddy drink his coffee?"

I almost fell off my chair. I pointed to the milk.

"I see you can look after yourself," she said.

"Are you moving in?" I just blurted out.

Nellie laughed. She took my chin in her cool velvety hand. "You're a good boy," she said. "There aren't too many of you. This is still your place, don't you worry." I indicated the coffee making stuff. I watched her fill the pot with water and unfold the white filter, spooning in the Folgers, with ease and efficiency, before clicking the red *on* button. She sat across from me, "Tell me about school."

After that, every time she came over, she knew what to do and did it. I wondered each time if she was coming to stay. She was always cheery, asking about my favorite books or TV programs or Bull's Eye. I sighed with relief when the door shut behind her.

One evening, before Dad got home, Nellie rang the bell. Bull's Eye ran back and forth in the yard, barking, excited as always at the prospect of a visitor. "Wait big boy," Nellie called out. She carried in a small travel crate. "Dirk, your Dad's made a good choice," Nellie said. "You get to play with her first." Placing the crate on the floor, she opened the little gate. "This is Delilah." A bewildered puppy scrambled out. My heart hopped up and down. Delilah was small enough to cup in my hands. She had a carnival quality: multi-colored spots, white, black, but mostly brindled brown. Her tiny brown tail stuck up like an antenna; she glanced eagerly left and right, sniffing. "You should start training her right away. It's harder to do when they're little and unruly. But she'll be so much smarter for it. You like her?"

"Yeah!" I got on my knees. Delilah ran into my lap.

Nellie whispered, "Wow, she's going to be crazy about you."

"Not like my mom, huh?"

Nellie grabbed both my hands. I felt handcuffed; my heart quickly locked in my chest. Nellie looked very serious, "We got off to an awkward start, you and me. It was my mistake, honey. But listen to me. People leave the ones they love for reasons too difficult to explain. Your mother's heart probably breaks every morning when she wakes up, and sees you are not with her. Something else was hurting her and she had to take care of that. Grown-ups are like that. They have big corners of hurt they have to take care of. Even while they still love you. There is no way your mother did not love a sweetheart like you. I promise, promise you."

Though she couldn't, really. Did most women talk in this way that made you feel gooey and half outside yourself?

Delilah was jumping on my foot, pulling at my sneaker laces. My eyes were burning and I didn't want to cry. Nellie could not possibly know who loved me. She said. "I could be the same age as your mother, so I know."

Thinking of the photo I cherished, I was sure my mother was not as old. But it was Nellie I wanted to believe.

"He's an unneutered male, honey," Nellie elaborated. "Jealous in his territory. We don't know what he'd do." Nellie and I were in the kitchen, Dad at Happy Mart, our eyes on Bull's Eye, watching Delilah totter into the room. First, Bull's Eye went stiff as a tree trunk. He growled low, and Delilah flung herself on her back, displaying her belly, her submission, ears flat. He leaned over her, asserting his size. Then his tail wagged. He pawed the ground from side to side, head lowered, nudging her. Delilah was an eighth his size, silly-looking with her colored spots and tiny flapping ears. She tentatively sniffed him, and licked his big bent head. He smelled her butt. Only when she neared his bowl, did he flash his teeth and knock her down. She scampered away. He didn't need to do that again.

Within days, Delilah had clearly accepted him as the Alpha dog. If he wasn't nudging her, she was following him. Now we had two friendly pit bulls. I was in heaven. They both curled up on my bed.

Nellie checked in daily by phone or in person. "You'll have the urge to spoil her. So cute, so tiny. But she's got too much darn spunk. It'll serve her well, if it doesn't get the best of her. You've got to be *firm*."

Discipline nourished character, we agreed. But Nellie believed dogs had souls, something Dad never mentioned. "A truly disciplined dog doesn't just execute commands. She anticipates them. And, in a complicated situation, she'll weigh the options. Remember this." Nellie showed her girls off in conformations, beauty shows for breeds. "Their temperaments woo the judges. My girls react to the moment, creating that extra spark." The dogs were her life and most of her stories.

Nellie brought out something extra in Dad, too. More and more, I woke to her sipping coffee in Dad's bathrobe, shaking her head, "Look at my wonderful boys." Dad's sharp eyes watched us with ease.

Nellie advised, "Throw Delilah balls. See how fast she learns that by bringing one back, she gets to chase it again. Pits aren't retrievers, but she may want to perform."

Delilah's spots grew wider as she filled out; we could see her mom's brindle taking over, the dark stripes growing prominent. But one big spot on her chest, another on her belly and an elegant stripe down her nose glowed with Bull's Eye's white. Our vet, Dr. Lance, complimented her health, and inoculated her against rabies and distemper. Like Bull's Eye, Delilah tilted her head as if I were straining her credulity, making her wait to play. We nicknamed her Dee. The first time I clicked on a leash, inside the house, she spun and spun, making herself dizzy, toppling. Then she reached around and tried to eat it. When I tried to walk her, she clamped on the leash, and hung on for dear life. I pulled her; she sat on her haunches and tugged back, pleased with this new combat adventure. It took a hard squirt from my water pistol to startle and stop her. Sometimes Bull's Eye ran over, in the middle of our play-training, and tipped her over. She pummeled him, still on her back, nipping his ears, unwilling to consider defeat. In her circus, he and I were the supporting cast. When I presented her with a rope pull, she yanked with the frenzy of a tiny Godzilla.

Dad became inspired to build kennels in the yard. "I'll position them in the shade, up against the fence, visible from the back door. We're doing this professional, serious." In his drawing plans, one kennel would be double-sized, "For the lactating bitch. With Delilah's pedigree and Bull's Eye's awards, their puppies'll fetch a fine price. We'll start benefiting."

"We're not benefiting?"

"Think ahead, kiddo. Want to live in the same place, same way, your whole life? Zero to zero? Not me." He elaborated, "This is still America. You can make a dent if you've got balls." He yanked his crotch, chuckling. "People pay for studs. Even more for puppies."

He shone with sweat and self-confidence. My stomach felt queasy.

Then, one night, just as I was drifting off, Dad loudly opened my door. "Hey! Hey! We didn't know better with Bull's Eye. Now we're doing this right." He lifted Delilah off my covers, saying, "I've been reading. She's got to learn her place, toughen up. You sleep."

He carried her out. I jumped up, following him through the yard to the garage, where he plonked her down. I argued, "I never read anything that said to leave a puppy alone at night!"

"You don't read as much as I do."

My face flushed. "Ask Nellie."

"This isn't *her* dog."

I stomped my foot, "It's a stupid idea."

Delilah pranced about, nosing things, hardly bigger than a bread loaf. Dad shoved his face into mine: "You don't dare disrespect me!"

I charged back to my bedroom, stripped my bedding, while Bull's Eye edged over sleepily on the mattress. I dragged it all to the garage.

Dad slammed the garage door behind me. "Be an idiot! But when the kennels are built, that's where they're sleeping." My legs and hands shook. I folded my blanket; one half to go beneath me, the other half for cover. It was only September, but the cement was an ice block. Delilah paraded up and down my chest, looking to nuzzle. She had a milky smell. She tugged on my pajama sleeve, fighting an imaginary rattlesnake. Until finally we fell asleep, her cold nose pressed into my armpit. I felt the quick tiny beat of her heart in the crook of my elbow, her paws pressing soft as marshmallows.

I slept like this for three nights. Dad and I avoided each other. On the fourth evening, Dad yanked me off the floor. "Listen!" He shook a book at my head:

It is a very bad idea to take a dog into your bedroom at night. The dog becomes so attached to you, it will be impossible to leave him alone without his howling. He will not sleep anywhere without you. Both owner and dog will experience unnecessary hardship. Obedience work becomes more challenging.

He clapped it shut in my face, "You're deforming her potential."

"She's a baby. You don't raise babies in garages."

"*You* seem to like it." He snatched up my bedding, "Anyway, you're *not* screwing up my investment." I followed, as he dumped everything back in a clump on my bed.

"You're wrong!"

His arm lifted fast, "I'll smack you." Stepping back, I fell on my bed. Delilah remained out there. I sat grabbing my knees, refusing to allow tears. I must stay strong for Delilah and Bull's Eye. Bull's Eye scratched on the other side of the door. He'd been out of the picture these past nights. He bounded into my arms, and I clutched him hard.

Nellie was visiting for the weekend and I planned to talk. She shook her head: "The dogs need a united front. This arguing is going to put them on edge. Leave Dee blankets, toys, and water. I would do it differently, but she's staying her spunky self. Let this be."

I closed myself in my room, disoriented, bitter. Nellie sided with Dad.

That night their voices spilled through the walls. Dad announced, "In this house, all creatures live by the same rules. No sissy dogs *or* boys."

Nellie shouted back, "You can't raise a dog in isolation. You'll never get the best out of her. She needs to adore you and trust you. What are you teaching Dirk? Not to love and protect his dogs?"

"Did *you* train Bull's Eye? See, this is how you women are. I share my life, and you think you *own* it. Damn you!"

Nellie's voice rose an octave, "*Caring* makes a dog strong, not weak. If you can't see that, you're blind."

"Did I *ask* for your opinion?"

"It's because you didn't ask, that I gave it." Nellie's voice quavered. She had to make Dad listen; who else? It was so important.

Dad yelled, "I don't want it!" Something, like a shoe, thumped hard against the wall. Next, there was awful silence. I lay frozen, ice crystallizing sharply in my heart.

In the morning, Nellie was gone.

Dad said he needed to clear the air, and get out of town. He entered Bull's Eye in a weight pull, last minute, on an upcoming weekend. It was overnight, so Delilah came, too. We packed Dad's blue Chevy: "Sixty-five miles an hour, it'll take four hours." We crated Bull's Eye in the back, worried he'd get too rambunctious with Delilah. He barked intermittently to remind us of his grand presence, while Dee romped free, dashing over my lap. After we escaped the city's grit, we zoomed past miles of yellow and green; thick oaks and elms, wide cornfields and unpopulated fields, everything both curious and dull. It was a mystery to me whether people who didn't live in a city got bored or felt freer.

Dad checked his watch obsessively, like he had a spastic tick in his neck. He turned on the country music station. Serenaded by twangs and fiddles, I felt our adventure become larger. But after awhile the glib DJ got on Dad's nerves. He snapped off the radio. He checked his watch, monitoring our speed.

In Sparta, outside of Grand Rapids, Dad located a run-down motel. Much later, when Dad was snoring loud, Bull's Eye and Dee snuck into my bed. Bull's Eye's head pressed on my belly, Dee's nose buried in my neck, wet and black and small.

"Hey!" Dad woke me, pointing at the window the dogs were glued to, transfixed, bright daylight pouring in.

We drove to the site. Dad raised his arm like a Nazi general, "Dee has to stay out of the way."

"What?"

"She's distracting."

Delilah couldn't believe her luck. As we walked, a foil wrapper on the ground unfolded its savory history, discarded corn on the cob saturated the air with buttery residue, a rumpled T-shirt became a toy she clamped on and hauled away. But I wanted to watch Bull's Eye's pull.

"A puppy!" Three girls about my age approached, clinging to each other, with tanned legs smooth as Creamsicles. A red-haired one leaned over, "She's sooo cute."

"Yes," I said, unable to think of another word. The girls stood around. It was weird. My hands got sweaty.

"She's licking me! It's adorable!" A butterscotch-skin girl giggled. I nodded doubtfully.

"You're sooo lucky! Bye-bye!" Much to my relief, they wiggled off like a giant jellyfish. But my adrenaline pumped. I liked something about how they'd made me feel. They'd been cute with sparkly tops and cut-off shorts. I felt older suddenly.

I trotted back to help Dad. "Look, Dirk, you know non-competing dogs aren't allowed in the sidelines. It's too hot to leave her for long in the car. You gotta stay with her, away from the pull." Delilah scampered about my feet, the white stripe of her nose pointing up like an arrow, while I glared at the wall of backs approaching the pull, seeking the dog that would most stun them. Our dogs weren't supposed to separate us. "Did you hear me?" Dad repeated. "Man up."

I marched off, turning around once to spit: "This is very wrong!"

After awhile, we lay in the grass, Dee's round white belly up, looking for a good scratch. Then we walked again, while I boiled and seethed. Dee's delight over her treasure-filled day only burned me. When the day finally fell into the afternoon, I heard the announcer call the final pull. I head Bull's Eye's name. I had to see. I scuttled to the sidelines, slyly hiding Dee behind me. Dad clicked on the harness. Bull's Eye bent his big black and white head, each muscle in his shoulders bulging, rising, moving clearly now, one, two, three, four, five, six, seven feet. Then he stopped, ears pricked, his head turning, keen to locate something that was not his pull, which turned out to be Delilah, all at once happily barking. The entire audience swiveled, and the judge yelled, "Interference! Pull disqualified!"

I bent my head, paralyzed, stunned. Delilah busily nosed the ground. Dad charged over with a bewildered Bull's Eye. He whacked my arm, drilled his index finger into my cheek. "What were you thinking?" People frowned.

My ears burned, "You should have let me watch!"

"Think! You could've crated Dee for ten minutes."

This hadn't occurred to me: "But you have the car keys!"

"I would have given them to you!"

"You said it was too hot."

"Not for ten minutes."

"He's mine, too! I train Bull's Eye."

"Yeah, good going."

Tears pushed like a flood behind my eyes. I bit my lip until I tasted blood, trying to stop myself from blubbering. Delilah and Bull's Eye licked each other effusively. Tossing our stuff into the trunk of the car, Dad was mute. He must have remembered Delilah's purpose. How she'd up the ante of his life. "You got to be more of a man. Be responsible for your actions. You want Bull's Eye to win?"

I nodded.

"Okay, we're on the same page. Because, otherwise, you shouldn't come."

My mouth fell open, trembling.

Michael dropped by a couple of days before school started: seventh grade. He'd been away most of the summer at baseball camp. My skinny white body was runty and lacking compared to his broad ruddiness. I envied his going to these great camps. He shrugged, "Sure the practices and games are cool, but you have to sleep in these scuzzy wood cabins surrounded by guys in their BVDs. They reek, man. And there's no one there who doesn't want to beat you out. One night I dreamt they were stabbing off my limbs, laughing like hyenas. You think baseball is worth this?" It wouldn't have been for me, but he was bitten with the game, magnetized by bases, mitts, bats, earned run averages.

School began. In social studies class, I recorded the world's growing urban population centers; so many places home to somebody, so many people it was hard to think about. Michael and I rode our bikes home together, flying off the curbs at every chance, rushing past Ridge Avenue's fire-breathing crossing guards. With sports practices not yet underway, Michael came over, too. We tossed Bull's Eye Frisbees, high and clean. Michael had rafts of friends, but he didn't stop coming by. Maybe it was Bull's Eye. Because Michael wanted a dog. Maybe it was because half the time he forgot his homework. He'd ride by before school, "Man, what was the math?"

"Page 139; decimal points." He'd scribble fast, while I ate Corn Flakes. Before we jumped on our bikes, pedaling like hell to make the bell.

Before long, my legs took to stretching out like elastic, snapping at my joints. At night, my knees and hipbones ached. Dad shrugged, "Growing pains. All usual." My arms sprouted blond wire-thick hair, and my voice cracked like falling tiles. More than ever, I hated talking. I hated mirrors. I bought big, baggy, loose clothes. Half the class still looked like kids. Me, I was a beanpole. I disliked anyone coming too near me. Mr. Moffit's Advanced Algebra class was what got me through. When I lost myself decoding problems, he said, "You're a born mathematician." He handed me harder problems. The more I could go inward, cogitating, the better. Evenings, after I ran the dogs, I devoured *Catcher in the Rye* and *Lord of the Flies*.

People moved in and out of the apartments around us, a constant stream of cars, deliveries, new commuters, and startling cries. Dad had transformed half the yard into a miniature kennel village that looked more like a block of prison cells. Each of six kennels surrounded by a four-foot high cyclone fence. The other half of the yard was plain dog-trampled, with Delilah and Bull's Eye chasing the trapeze-style squirrels zipping above them on the phone lines. Where the springpole hung from the old maple, the ground had been worn into a big smooth bowl.

With Nellie gone, Dad was back to talking through dinner. "This customer comes today to Happy Mart, hauling around a petition for Breed Specific Legislation. Today! Ban pit bulls! I said 'Not here you don't. I've got two great pits.' She starts in, 'You're harboring public menaces! Their jaws have locking power! Bred to kill!' I could've slapped her upside the head. People don't know what they're talking about. Locking power! That's a lie! How many breeds we got to remove before people figure out who's stupid? Confederates used Bloodhounds to nab runaway slaves. The Nazis got German shepherds and Dobermans to kill the Jews. The Japs got Akitas. Punish the deed not the breed!"

"Stupid breed terrorist!"

"Yeah!" Dad plopped down on the couch, rubbing Bull's Eye.

I played tug-of-war with Delilah. Her body was becoming longer and lean. "Dad, you think Bull's Eye would ever kill another dog?"

"Don't know. Pits'll do almost anything for their master. It's the owner's responsibility, right big boy?" Bull's Eye's tail wagged, thumping happily on the floor.

Dad studied Delilah. "You. You gonna be a good Mom?"

Dad resented Nellie's absence. "She didn't teach me the ropes like she promised. Breeding, you know."

"You hurt her."

"I did not. You mean the argument?"

"You yelled."

"For Chrissake. Know why I like dogs? You get mad, take a deep breath, and it's already over."

He didn't want to patch things up. Still, he was impatient to learn her skills. One night, he bowed his head, and called to invite her to dinner. "Told her I was sorry. What she wanted."

Our house had energy and enthusiasm when she was in it. I grinned like an idiot at her as she sat down, and quickly passed her the dishes. Nellie repeated firmly, "A bitch needs to be two years old to be bred safely."

"You women are always overprotective."

"Good breeding is not a stab in the dark. A male OR female breeder will tell you that. Want to weaken Delilah's hips? Have a litter of runts?"

"You didn't inform me this'd take forever."

"I didn't? And you haven't read anything on your own?" Nellie stood up, her hands at her hips, growing agitated.

"In fact, my books don't agree with you." He smirked.

"No reputable breeder would wait less than two years, Russ."

"Do you see anything happening? Besides you getting yourself overexcited?"

"Ideas can become facts, Russ. Then it's too late to change them."

"Well, nothing's happening."

Nellie shook her head stiffly.

When Nellie left shortly after dessert, Dad called me over, "Hear this: '*Some breeders believe that a bitch bred during her first heat will have an easier delivery as her hips are most elastic at this young age.*' See? Nellie doesn't know everything."

I muttered, "Neither do you."

"What's that?" Dad stuck his face in mine.

"Nothing," I capitulated.

"Damn straight," Dad growled. "You know nothing."

Somehow, Nellie was soon back to visiting, spoiling us with her cheerfulness and her ability to whip up a delicious spaghetti dinner or the most tender breaded pork chops. She and Dad had spats more often, but they made up pretty regularly now that Dad had his apology technique down. One source of tension was that Dad wanted her to help him find stud prospects for Bull's Eye; Nellie thought it better to wait. Dad debated whether to do it on his own, going back and forth. Still, our house almost seemed normal that seventh grade year. If a good life is achieving balance, maybe this was the point when we were at our zenith. Dad and I were one parallel line and Nellie was the other, heading beautifully aligned into the bright horizon.

With Delilah growing, Nellie over for dinners and nights, Bull's Eye mad passionate about pulling weights, and Delilah learning to drag her own tires, we'd forged a good tempo. Our proscribed routines, our unwavering training regimens barely differentiated with the seasons. Only my body veered from certitude, my limbs in a crazy dash to replicate a stringy reflection in a funhouse mirror.

I slouched in the back row of eighth grade, as Mr. Walker, our new teacher, announced we'd study historical American Literature. The class moaned. Me too. Then he stalked around the classroom, book in hand, reading in a loud tenor, chuckling with conviction. We started listening. He favored American humorists. You could stare out the window, but his voice swirled around you, wrapping you in the material. I dug him for loving his stuff so much. Mr. Walker assigned James Thurber. I lay on my back on the couch that afternoon, Bull's Eye snoring at my feet, Delilah chomping on a bone, reading Thurber's essay about his childhood with Rex, an American bull terrier. Rex loved swimming: *"He would bring back a stick to you if you did throw one in. He would even have brought back a piano."* To prove his claim, Thurber offered that Rex *had* brought home a chest of drawers: *"We first knew about his achievement when, deep in the night, we heard him trying to get the chest up onto the porch. It sounded as if two or three people were trying to tear the house down."*

I'd read writers who liked dogs, but the dogs were never pits, not charming, hilarious pits. What a wake-up call. I'd developed a defensive edge, watching people cross the street rather than let Bull's Eye and Dee near. I expected my ignoramus classmates to read Thurber and not get it; someone'd spout trash about pits, what with the media's constant rant about their being born to kill. Bull's Eye and Delilah sighed in contented oblivion.

The following day, I sat at my desk, attentive. Mr. Walker entered, and I shot over before he hardly opened his briefcase. "I've got pit bulls." My face burned like an oil slick. "They're all Thurber says they are. It's hysterics who try to ban the breed. They're wrong."

Mr. Walker nodded calmly, "All right then. I can't say they're my favorite dogs. But I'll trust your field research."

I swung around, prepared to defend my claim but no one was getting riled up on my account. Still, I said, too loudly: "A pit bull saved my life."

A shy girl named Violet, eyes big as billiard balls, asked, "But how?" Embarrassing me.

"Scared off a pervert." Hoots and hollers followed. I rolled my eyes. Michael studied me, alert. Knowing. Mr. Walker said, "Wow. We need that kind of dog." He opened his book: "So, so this seems to be a particularly American dog, scrappy, self-reliant, hey? But notice how the dog becomes complex in Thurber's hands; a character with history, personality, belief and dignity, right Dirk? This is why Thurber's humor resonates. He hasn't thinned reality and put us in a cartoon. A really great humorist makes you remember, in fact *insists*, that laughter is an awareness."

I listened to Mr. Walker, who had listened to me, who had brought Thurber to the class. Life tossed a person a lot of disappointments, but it also offered unexpected teachers. So far, my balance of losses to gains hadn't exactly totaled out fabulously. But someday? Mr. Walker made hope real.

Over mashed potatoes and chops, I informed Dad about Thurber. "Damn, if a pit's good enough for a big deal American writer, it sure as heck should do for the rest of America. Will this country ever get it?"

I told Bull's Eye and Dee: "You're in the literary anthologies!"

Mr. Walker copied Twain's "The Celebrated Jumping Frog of Calaveras County." He paused at my desk, "This is just for you, Dirk." Mark Twain, too, had immortalized the pit bull's comedic effect. Who would've thought?

One Friday evening, Dad arrived home with an old pull wagon and a can of red paint. He said, "Tomorrow, shine this up nice with a couple of coats."

"Why?"

He drilled in a large hook clasp: "This'll attach to the halter."

"For?"

He began lettering a square white board:

HAPPY'S DOOR–TO-DOOR SERVICE.

He looked up, "From now on, after school, bring Bull's Eye straight here. We'll change people's thinking. You'll deliver groceries at $3 per customer. After the wagon's paid off, you can keep the profits." He hooked his thumbs into his belt loops and stood up looking proud.

"Right, I'll get rich."

"No teenager of mine sits at home, not working—"

"Dog training?"

"My point. Bull's Eye gets pull-training and you get a job. It's perfect."

I argued, "But to carry in bags, I'll have to leave Bull's Eye tied up outside, alone."

"For a few minutes."

"I'll be the local joke. Do you know how stupid I'll look?" This was the last thing I wanted to do.

"Is that what your books are teaching you? Deliveries are beneath you, Mr. Lily White Hands? Or are you looking down on me? My offer isn't good enough, huh? You bite the hand that feeds you. Well, I can think up some consequences you won't like. Fight me on this."

I didn't see what options I had that wouldn't turn Dad ballistic. He needed me to make his idea work. Part of me saw his point; if people benefited from Bull's Eye, how could they refute his value? His capability. But why did I have to pay the price?

That October, November, and December, I traipsed us around Rogers Park over clumps of wet leaves, navigating around tightly parked cars, moving aside for edgy pedestrians. I tied Bull's Eye to lampposts when I hiked up to different apartment floors. I worried the whole climb, each and every time, with him out of sight. There were people who commandeered me the whole length of their apartment, demanding their bags be delivered way back to their kitchens. For three bucks. I felt like a complete idiot.

But Happy Mart shoppers quickly fell in love with our deliveries. For those without cars, our duo provided innovative relief. Dad got praised, and answered, "A pit bull's a working dog. Pure American grit. Meant to help."

Mrs. O'Neill always handed me a dog biscuit. Mr. Siemansko joked he'd start a competing service with his toy dogs the size of Bull's Eye's head. But others acted as if I might have stolen something out of their grocery bags, making me wait until they pulled everything out, checking each item against the receipt, hassling *me* about prices, while I panicked about Bull's Eye. What did they care? Put together, these people were what my social studies teacher called a "microcosm of the macrocosm." Too much of the time, they had me thinking most people were jerks.

Though this new routine offered nothing of our old joyous freedom, Bull's Eye acted cheerful. I tossed him Frisbees when we got home, but I also had homework and chores. Delilah was often frantic.

Michael said, "Girls will definitely go wild for a juicy-fruit delivery boy with his cute red wagon."

I flipped him the finger. "Want to take it up with Dad?"

Michael knew what a joke that would be. He shrugged, and punched me in the shoulder. If any girl from class saw me I'd be branded a total loser. "At least you've got Bull's Eye." He petted him, got his tail wagging like a metronome. "Your Dad'll never get rid of him if he makes money."

"He wasn't going to get rid of him."

"I'm just saying." Michael had asked me before if Dad ever tired of the dogs. Which made me anxious, as if Michael could envision something I was blind to.

"Dad thinks the wagon's a stroke of genius."

Gradually, winter piled pukey snow on the sidewalks, narrowing the streets into angry single-lanes. It wasn't until the wagon overturned because of an unplowed stretch of sidewalk, spilling groceries like marbles into the street, all of which Happy Mart had to replace free of charge, that Dad put a moratorium on the wagon until spring.

Nellie had disliked our being out in the dark on short winter days. "Of course, your Dad doesn't see reason until it smacks him in the head," she said. We laughed because we'd become allies. When he wasn't around, we felt easy liking each other. She'd bought me sturdy padded gloves for my deliveries. And a wool hat. "You know I stick around because I figure with Russ having a son as sweet as you, he's got to have goods I haven't uncovered yet, right? You're the clue." She pinched my earlobe, teasing, and I grinned.

Delilah had grown. She remained playful, but also newly conscious of herself, growing her sense of privacy and dignity. We doted on her when Dad wasn't watching. When he got home, she needed to be perfectly disciplined. If Dad gave her a command, and she faltered, I got a dirty look and Dee was sent to another room away from him so she'd experience his full displeasure. "She has to think she's incomplete without me. She has to know her place." He just didn't seem to get it that sometimes she was bursting with love and couldn't wait to feel his hand and presence. Delilah could make my heart do a double flip with her serious brown eyes seeking direction. But not Dad. That's why Nellie and I coddled her on the side; she deserved that much.

When it finally warmed, in early spring before lifeguards ruled the beaches, I brought the dogs to Loyola beach. Nellie met me on those couple of afternoons when she could get away from her job with the insurance company. I set Bull's Eye up dragging a weighted truck tire through the thickened sand.

Delilah pulled window weights I'd attached to her harness. Nellie had her own vision, "Teach her conformation. It builds performance pride. She'll love it."

"But how?"

Nellie said, "Watch me now. I'll work on *Ready*, followed by *Heel on Leash*."

With Delilah leashed, she whispered enthusiastically, "Ready!" Delilah stared. Nellie smiled, "Delilah, Heel." Nellie began to trot in a circle, yanking Delilah who at first balked, then zoomed ahead of Nellie, then balked. Delilah had to learn to keep an exactly even pace at Nellie's side. They looked comical trotting around. I laughed. Nellie ignored me; "She's getting it, even with you distracting her, you lout. She's wonderful. Try it again, baby." They repeated their trot-dance five or six times, Nellie slowing down, speeding up, Delilah only distracted when a runner shot by. Training was nothing new, but Nellie added the dimension of pacing and etiquette. Perhaps women were better at bringing out the dance in a situation. I thought about Mom's eyes in the photo, arresting and keen. Those eyes could make you do things, for sure. Following that gravitational pull improved life, I felt certain, like swinging in a waltz giddy with dependence. Nellie and I were still tentative square dancers, stepping back, hopping forward.

She asked Dad to let her teach me to prepare Delilah for conformation competitions.

"Prancing in beauty shows? MY dogs *work*." He glared, "Don't you try to turn Dirk into a faggot."

"Russ, that's totally ridiculous."

"Dirk works for *me*."

Nellie shrugged. She had a job, plus she traveled to shows with her girls a lot. There were long weeks I didn't see her. She wanted to do good by me, though. I saw that. I didn't pretend it didn't matter.

On another rare afternoon, Nellie relaxed with me on the cool sand. "Don't over-train Dee. Her bones are still forming, Dirk." We let the dogs romp loose. Lake Michigan was turquoise, with a dark blue strip ribboning the horizon. With no coastline in sight, the water seemed endless. In the Midwest, a guy has to pretend oceans. "What are you staring at?" Nellie poked me in the ribs.

"The Lake. This beach. No one's hardly ever here until summer. It's almost too big for just us. I mean, we're in a city, but here it feels like we're on an island."

Nellie rubbed my head, "I don't know how Russ bred a dreamer. It's the unlikeliest thing. But it sure makes you a sweetheart."

Had I sounded goofy, like I *was* a pansy? Maybe there was something wrong with me. I shook my head.

Michael had a knack for getting invited to parties. He'd run into me, "Hey, come on; come on, yeah, yeah." Because I didn't know what the hell I was supposed to do with myself, sometimes I went. "Loosen up," he advised. "That girl Melissa. With the orange top, that one. She's been eyeing you. Bet she'll make-out."

"Screw you."

"Yo, tense or what?"

"Who says I want her?"

"Yeah, and I hate baseball." By the end of a party, Michael was usually talking deep with some pretty girl. It wasn't even that he did all the things he said he was going to. He wasn't the jerk he pretended to be, which actually had to be why so many girls liked him; he swaggered but he was kind of sweet, a joker but too smart to really mess up. He told me, "You are some sad sack at a party. Dude, I don't know why I bother." I didn't know either. I was magnetized by the restless shifting under a girl's sweater, but paralyzed. Like I risked electrocution. I wasn't brave.

In fact, what with everything, I'd been seeing Michael less and less.

Delilah ran circles around Bull's Eye, teasing him to play, but by late evening he didn't budge. We were back to lugging Happy Mart deliveries. Getting tired, dragging that ridiculous cart all around Rogers Park.

Dad pored over his books on breeding. "She'll be a year old, this July, Dirk."

"You throwing her a party?"

"Yeah, a *birth*-day party, heh, heh."

"What are you talking about?"

"She's going to come into estrus, you know, get a period, be fertile. I'm not unprepared."

It was too weird to think about her discharging and bleeding, so I didn't. But Dad became Mr. Dog Anatomy, charting ovulation patterns, analyzing mating positions, getting Bull's Eye to stretch his paws over Delilah's back before Delilah quickly twisted back snapping, and Bull's Eye scrambled off. "Pity Bull's Eye's basically an inexperienced stud." Dad creeped me out.

One evening, weeks later, Nellie finally came over. While Dad showered, she cooked lamb chops melting in onions, and sprinkled the steaming broccoli with paprika. I set the table. The frying pan sizzled. She opened the cabinet to hand me napkins. Inside it, Dad had plunked two breeding books out of sight. Nellie asked, "Dirk, what are these?"

"They're Dad's." I didn't want to discuss animal positions.

"Put them on the kitchen table, will you?"

Dad entered wearing a close-fitting clean blue shirt buttoned tight against his well-formed muscles, hair combed and wet. "You smell good," Nellie said. Her onions were caramelizing the air.

Dad grinned, wrapping his arms around her, "Not as good as you, baby."

I turned on the TV in the living room to a re-run of "Miami Vice." Dad yelled, "Get away from that goddamned noise. Come back here."

Dinner was ready; the tantalizing speckled broccoli piled up like teeny Christmas trees, the lamb chops gleaming mahogany. We buttered the golden bread rolls. My mouth watered. "A toast to the chef," Dad raised his beer. I lifted my milk.

We savored our first scrumptious forkfuls. Nellie smiled and took a long sip of beer. But she was restless, "What are you reading these days, Russ?"

He glanced at the books, "I'd say you've figured it out."

"What are you discovering?"

"I'm educating myself. You took him off my hands last time. I hear half the time the owner has to help with breeding. Especially at first." Then he winked at Nellie, "Not like us old hands."

Nellie brushed him off with a wave of her hand, "Delilah won't be ready for a whole other year."

"You know that's a matter of opinion."

Nellie's voice cracked, "I didn't give you one of my puppies so you could hurt her. If the dam's too young, even if her body handles the delivery, which is questionable, she could freak out, even eat them. They need her. I hope you've read that far."

"Amazingly, I have."

I ate quickly, trying not to choke.

Nellie took another long drink of beer, clutching the glass in both hands. "If you don't keep your end of the bargain, I'll take Delilah back."

"I've been reading," Dad snapped. "Just reading! Dirk's not the only one allowed to have his nose buried in books."

"I know you, Russ. You don't listen to reason."

I bit into my lamb chop, closing my eyes, trying to drown them out by concentrating on the rich flavor, reminding myself that Mr. Walker taught us that opposing sensations could be perceived simultaneously, which was a truth writers sought to express.

Dad said, "You piss me off, not trusting me."

"You're too easy to piss off." Nellie's plate was untouched. Her face was pink, her temples were moist.

Dad shoveled down his supper. When he paused, he said, "You promised to help me stud Bull's Eye. You know I need the money. Why am I waiting on you like this?"

I asked, "Can I leave the table?"

Nellie snapped, "Damn it! Because puppies reflect the stud. A bad litter and you damage his reputation. Dee's, too. And for what? Discipline, Russ, is everything."

"You're telling me?"

Turning to me, shaking her head, she pointed at Dad, "Keep an eye on him."

"Great lamb, babe," Dad said. "Dirk, clean up."

I expected Nellie to leave, once again exasperated. But Dad pulled her to him on the couch to watch a late season basketball game. At first, she pushed him away coldly. But he whispered in her ear, and ran his fingers through her shiny bronze curls. He brought her another beer. He kissed her. He lifted her feet to his lap and tickled them, and a little smile broke. Then he slowly massaged her toes and heels. The dogs lay lazy on the floor, Delilah nestled into Bull's Eye's chest. Soon, we were yelling crazy at Notre Dame to beat Marquette.

I let the dogs out to smell the earth and do their business before I led them to their kennels. Back inside, the lights were off. I channel-surfed, raising the volume, sitting like a dope. They were in the bedroom, Dad probably right now removing Nellie's clothes. God, it embarrassed me. My disgust took the form of an awkward rising between my legs. Jesus. A scene of him pushing himself onto her lifted me in its talons and shook the crap out of me.

By July the days hung heavy as wet rags. Even the blowing fan simply stirred more hot air. Dad programmed a summer pull schedule. Suddenly, Delilah started licking her crotch fanatically. She turned skittish, rubbing her butt all over the floor. Bull's Eye flung himself onto Delilah. Delilah snapped and growled to send him the hell away. Bull's Eye started humping everything in sight, chairs, table legs, *my* leg, whining high and strangled. Dad undertook a thoroughly revolting examination of Delilah's genitals, "She's swelling! She's gone into proestrus. That's just before she gets fertile."

I didn't know: "How long will she be like this?"

"Give or take twenty days."

"That's awful."

"It's normal." Dad restricted Bull's Eye to the yard, admonishing, "Give the girl time." I felt enormous relief, grateful Dad had listened to Nellie. Nellie was out of town, visiting her parents in Florida. Dad brought home fresh sirloin, "Got to keep Dee strong." Delilah nervously licked and licked herself, going through panting fits, irritated by any of my attempts to be friendly.

Dad said, "Yeah, maybe a week." I thought I'd misunderstood how long she'd be in this condition. Sure enough, she soon went into estrus. Dad inspected her discharges, "See? Darker, browner now, it's the blood, that's ovulation, boy." Disgusting. Delilah looked wretched. I had to walk her on a short leash wearing a weird diaper Dad bought to protect her.

Bull's Eye and I still worked deliveries. When we returned, Bull's Eye sulked in the yard, pacing miserably back and forth, digging trenches in the dirt. One evening, Dad rubbed his hands and slapped me on the back, "Tomorrow's the party."

I refused to think about what he'd said. But tomorrow came. Dad put up a sign at Happy Mart:

NO DELIVERIES THIS WEEK

He said, "You're helping at home."

"What's my pay?" Always at his beck and call.

"Smart ass." He clenched his teeth and his jawline's tendons rose visibly. He must have considered whacking me upside the head. But he needed me. For my part, I obstinately ignored what was coming. He said, "Move the table against the wall. We need space. Mop the kitchen floor. We need hygiene." He walked out to the yard, and sprayed Bull's Eye with the water hose, sponged him down. I turned up my CD player, sweeping maniacally to *Nine-Inch Nails*.

The linoleum glowed, the chairs hung upside down on the kitchen table. Delilah lay near, cautiously studying our movements. Suddenly, Dad came up from behind me shouting at Bull's Eye, "Stop!" He shot away from Dad, bulldozing toward Delilah. She ran to me, crouched behind my legs, pressing against the wall. Bull's Eye pawed at her through my legs while I pushed him back yelling, "Hey! Hey! Sit!" Delilah growled. Bull's Eye managed to swerve, pushing his nose roughly against her withers, and became fully erect. Too weird. "Now what the hell?" Delilah glued her butt to the floor, baring her teeth.

"Close the doors!" Dad yelled. "Stand for him, girl," Dad cooed. "Come on."

My breathing labored, I said, "She doesn't have to do anything she doesn't want to."

"Oh yes she does. We don't have all night. Delilah. Come! Now!"

She rose very slowly, her tail between her legs, her head down. Disobeying Dad meant exacting his displeasure. She hunched her back, trying to drop her butt while moving toward him miserably. Bull's Eye charged, nearly toppling her over. "Get a grip, you idiot!" Dad shoved him aside. And reprimanded me, "Hold him back, will you?"

My mouth was wide open, but I couldn't speak. I clutched Bull's Eye, trying to find words. "What?"

"Get Bull's Eye behind her, so he can do what he has to without jumping on her sideways, damn fool!" Dad quickly positioned Delilah against his forward leg, clipping her to a leash, palm pressing firmly on the middle of her back.

I barely loosened my grip when Bull's Eye tore away, clambering onto her, frantic. My stomach churned, my eyes burned. He fell off because Delilah bucked hard. He scrambled back, getting re-oriented, his nails clicking and skidding on the linoleum. Bull's Eye had definitely lost his mind. "Delilah, Stay!" Dad yelled and gave her a hard correction, choking her. She hacked and coughed while he screamed at me, "*You* hold her. Give *me* Bull's Eye."

I didn't move. If Delilah had an advantage I wanted her to keep it. I stared, full of feeling. I was in her camp. Dad's hand came swatting hard, jolting my head sideways. He grabbed a clump of my t-shirt.

"She's terrified," I shouted. "She's too young!"

"No way, I got the only frigid bitch in Chi-town. She's going to learn. Grab her."

"If she doesn't receive him, something's wrong. Something's wrong."

"Do you really want her to get hurt? Is that what you want? Try me."

What was he talking about? Things would worsen if I didn't help? He seized Bull's Eye. I gripped Delilah's collar, keeping her close. She looked at me cowering, trembling. "Baby girl," I murmured. "It's okay."

"Face her butt to me. Lift her tail." Dad could barely control Bull's Eye, slathering and yanking. I wanted to rush

Delilah out the door. But I couldn't loosen a bitch in heat into the neighborhood. She was doomed. Delilah whimpered.

"If you can't do it, I'm muzzling her. I'll chain her down! I don't care how cut up she gets."

"Nellie will never speak to you again!"

For a moment, Dad stood suspended in time, arrested in a snapshot. "You're a boy. You know nothing. Women want a man. Oh, yeah. Not a wimp. They're scared, and won't tell you. Nellie'll act pissed. But she'll be proud, impressed. This is how it works. I learned once already about being too nice and agreeable."

Bile rose in my throat, "I don't think so."

"You want me chaining Dee to a pole? That what you've got to give?"

So I turned her. Dad directed Bull's Eye's lunge. Delilah tried to snap, but this time he penetrated her. Bull's Eye was spitting all over. He humped insanely. Jesus. Dad grabbed, then flung Bull's Eye's leg over Dee's back, and Bull's Eye went at it in a trance, the two of them facing in opposite directions, not like anything I'd ever imagined, Bull's Eye yowling, pushing like mad, Delilah frozen, grimacing, uttering one long keening cry. "God almighty -- " I blurted.

"It's perfect. He's finally locked in, a perfect-fit. Look at him go. " Dad rubbed his hands. I looked around, a stranger in this kitchen. The hideous strafing noises surrounded me.

I yelled, "You told Nellie you wouldn't do this!"

"Nope. She didn't listen to me."

"What if you're damaging Delilah?"

"You think they'll know what to do, hey, it's nature, and what the hell. But a bitch is unpredictable. I read this, how you might have to take command. Regular breeders have these wooden contraptions they lock a bitch into; so as she can't give them trouble. Even if she pitches a fit, it holds her. "

"She's too young!"

"How old do you think your mom was when she had you?" What did that have to do with anything? "She was sixteen, you dope, and you don't have *major* defects."

My face turned to fire. How could he talk about Mom here? He was deranged. I shouted, "Hell of a lot of good you did her, too!"

I got another whack in the head. "What kind of pussy are you?"

The truth was, I felt close to tears. I didn't want Bull's Eye making these monstrous yowls, didn't want Dee to be standing stock still like that, whining, helpless against her own condition. With me no ally. And Mom, sixteen? Maybe she saw life stretched a long ways out in front of her when I was three and she was nineteen. Maybe she saw the gain, only if she moved quickly. God. Bull's Eye screeched, and then, sighing and panting, he slithered off, collapsing momentarily like a sack of rocks. Delilah pulled quickly away, pressing into a corner, ears flattened, her brown eyes squinted, edgy. Dad led Bull's Eye outside. Delilah began licking herself vigorously. Dad announced, "We'll have to do this a couple more times to be sure she takes."

I had come to be born in this house, with this man, mating dogs when I would rather have been doing anything else. "Nellie's going to hate you. She'll take Delilah back." I was blathering.

"You don't listen, do you? And the only way Nellie's finding out anything for quite awhile, is if you tell her."

"You think she can't tell when a dog's pregnant?"

"It'll be too late by then. She'll be all worried about nurturing Delilah."

"I'm never doing that again. No way!" I ran out of the house, down the street, charging ahead mindless for a few blocks. I had no idea what I was doing. Tears of rage flew off my face. I stopped to wipe my cheeks with the back of my sleeve. I had to call Nellie. And if Delilah were pregnant, what would that do, except make Nellie angry for longer?

It wasn't easy, but I showed up at Michael's. I rang the bell. He leaned in the doorframe. "Where you been? No longer playing Lone Ranger?"

His dad waved from the living room couch, "Come in!" Michael shrugged and we walked into his kitchen. "Well? Play-station's set up; want to battle?"

"I suck."

"Wanna watch TV?"

"Nah."

"You look like shit," he said.

"Yeah." I couldn't speak. After awhile, with me being mute-boy, he became impatient, and led me to his room. He tossed me his sleeping bag, and left to play Tekken downstairs, sporadically whooping in victory.

When he came in later, he sat on his bed, hands dangled between his knees. "Look, it's cool," he said. "I'm sorry. Jesus, it's been awhile since we hung out. Hey, is Bull's Eye all right?"

I bit my lip, "Bull's Eye's fine. Thanks."

"So it's just you, man?"

"Yeah. It's me."

"My parents are pretty screwed up. Wound too tight."

"Parents suck royally."

He laughed and pointed: "Mr. Pissy Mood shows some attitude. Damn." It took me awhile to bring up the breeding. "Frickin' A. Your dad, man."

I slept at his place all week, didn't go near home. Nellie got back to town after that, serendipitously having missed the whole thing. A trick of fate. All I could think about was how I was party to what had tricked her. I couldn't even look Delilah in the eye.

Anne Calcagno

It was so damn hot, and Delilah was a slim brown and white-spotted girl, still growing, so the fact that she gathered some girth and slept double her usual didn't register with Nellie immediately. With every day that slipped by, the knot in my stomach tightened. If Delilah woke up in my room, swiveling her brown eyes on me, I cringed. I rubbed her silky ears; *sorry Dee, I'm so sorry.* What would Nellie say? I would change in her eyes. I'd played Dad's sidekick. That couldn't be taken back.

I could hardly look at Dad. I'd read his breeding books in a panic, too late to help Delilah. One guaranteed: *A bitch goes into heat when she is physically mature enough to handle pregnancy, and lactation.* Another said: *In the wild, males fight for dominance. Females accept the winner, ensuring the most vital genes. In a domestic setting, where breeding is being done for selective traits, human intervention is essential for control and success.* I had never wanted to be one of those humans, taking the laws of nature into my hands. Delilah's cries played in my head, her forced submission. It was over, but I could not forgive Dad, or myself, nor did I want to. The breeding books contradicted each other, written by different people with different drives. I prayed Dad was, at least, right about women.

That August, on the weekends, Nellie, Dad and I sat plastered to the plastic chairs outside, our glasses loaded with ice, waiting for the sun to sink. We didn't have air conditioning.

Inside, it was like a sauna. On this late Saturday, Dad was grilling brats. The smidgen of breeze felt like a blessing. The mosquitoes descended in battalion formation, though Nellie had brought citronella candles. Dad slapped his arm, his neck, and shook his head, "I told you those're worthless, except maybe to some fairy mosquitoes."

"It's the female that bites."

"That's got to be why they're so insistent, and you can't kill 'em." Dad pointed the greasy tongs at her.

Nellie ran her fingers through her dark gold hair, "I know people who swear by citronella."

"People believe what they want, doll."

We had some peaceful, oblivious moments, sitting there, me vaguely listening, squirting any blood-loaded mosquito that landed on my arm. I waited for the dark to inspire the fireflies. Their blinking drove Bull's Eye wild. We'd watch him charge in every direction, frantic to catch one, and we'd laugh. For now, Bull's Eye and Delilah lay on the grass panting, Bull's Eye's head plunked on Delilah's flank. They were friends again.

"You feed those two too much," Nellie said. "It's bad for their joints."

Dad rolled his eyes, "Like I don't train and weigh them regular. Thirty seconds on these brats."

Nellie suddenly slapped her ankle, "That's where the blood's so near the surface," she murmured to me. "I'm glad you've got socks on."

"Brats!" Dad yelled. The dogs' noses quivered. I swirled mustard on my brat bun, and grabbed a foil-encased corn on the cob. We settled our plates on the patio table. The dogs knew not to beg, but the temptation! Dad sat down, and said, "Actually we're letting Delilah eat more." Everything -- my hand raising my brat, Nellie shifting in her chair, Dad pressing his glass to his lips -- went into slow mo, while my heart beat a million times in one minute.

Nellie smiled, "By what theory?" I wanted to vanish.

Dad smiled back, "Guess."

Nellie's face went through some shifts; her brows bunching, her head tilting, resting her ear on her shoulder, her brown eyes widening, all within seconds. She took on a serious expression.

Her food lay untouched, her palms pressed flat on the table as if to balance herself. "An idea occurs to me, but it's so screwed up, it can't be. Right, Russ? You wouldn't be grinning, right?" The cicadas launched into a loud crescendo. The first firefly blinked, but Bull's Eye didn't see it as he sniffed the air. I bit into my brat. It felt enormous, fat on my tongue, gagging me. Nellie scowled. I would have given anything not to be in this moment. Nellie walked over to Delilah who lifted her head to lick her hand. Nellie rubbed her white throat and chest. Delilah stretched back, spreading herself open for a belly scratch, her hind legs flailing happily. "Her teats are swelling," Nellie said. "Her uterus is thick." Her face had gone very red; but I didn't think it was from the heat. Her eyes were shiny, hard as marbles.

Dad chomped on his corncob. He swilled his beer, flaunting his thirst-quenching arm.

"Fuck YOU!" Nellie shouted.

Bull's Eye and Delilah leapt, alert, watching Nellie with concern and fascination. My eyes bugged out; cold sweat seeped out my forehead. Nellie began to cry. She fell on her knees, clasping Delilah's neck, "Oh my baby girl. Jesus Christ. Oh, Jesus Christ. You *asshole!*" Tears slid down her face. "How could you do this to her? How could you do it to me?! We discussed this! You'll kill her!"

I was paralyzed, postponing my own reckoning.

"You're hysterical." Dad's calm was insulting. "She's healthy and normal."

"You can't see inside her, Russ. You can impregnate 10-year-old girls for Chrissake, but you don't do it! I told you. It's too much wear and tear on her developing hips, *and* on her psyche. A dam that's too small can die trying to deliver. And how can she know how to mother?"

"She's supposed to take classes?" Dad raised his eyebrow.

Nellie stood up. She approached Dad, who leaned back to advertise the length of his body. Her tears were skinning me raw. Her make-up ran down one cheek in a gray streak. In the blink of an eye, her hand flung up to the sky, and crashed down, slapping Dad.

"You bitch!" He grabbed Nellie's wrist.

"Stop it! Stop!" I grabbed Dad from behind, hanging on his waist, his chair, buckling to my knees as I tried to glue him down.

Dad flung me off, "Don't act like this is news to *you*. *Get* in the house."

He hissed at Nellie, "Don't you *ever* do that again. *Ever*."

Nellie sobbed, "I wish I never met you."

"It's too damn late for that, isn't it?" He opened the screen door, and pointed the dogs inside. They hurried in. He yelled, "Down!" Both dogs hit the kitchen floor.

Nellie wiped her face with the back of her hand. We'd forgotten to bring napkins outside. My feet heavy as anchors, I clumped over to her. "I'm so ashamed—"

"Sweet boy, oh honey." I didn't know where to put my hands. Comforting was a habit I didn't have.

"Now it's a love fest," Dad smirked.

"You're not a smart man," Nellie announced. "You'll never make it in this business."

"Right, Nellie, breeding takes so much sophistication." I cringed. He continued, "Your protectiveness is emotional bullshit. She's an animal, doing animal things. She's not a *child*. She's the picture of health."

"If you don't love what you're perpetuating, you'll never understand its potential. You'll miss the clues. Soon, people find out you're selling deficient dogs, dogs without temperament, half of what they could be. Smart buyers'll stay away. Then you'll have wasted years. Which is just what you deserve."

"Got a crystal ball, huh, Nellie? Truth is, I bred Bull's Eye to two other bitches since. You're the only one complaining."

He hadn't told me this. Not long after he'd bred Delilah, he'd gone to the Department of Motor Vehicles and splurged one hundred bucks on a license plate: **BULLS I**

He'd expounded on its multiple meanings, "First: I own pit **bulls**, Second: **Bull's Eye**'s our stud, and Third: I'm going to be the Number **One** breeder. Sharp, huh?" Like a license plate set the rules. Which was Nellie's point. Breeding took more than self-promotion. He should've grasped what she was saying, ambitious as he was.

Nellie stumbled inside and sank into a chair, her face in her hands. The silence hurt. The clock ticked. The air hung on my skin like a wet towel. I brought Nellie a glass of water. She asked, "When's Delilah due? How are you going to handle her delivery?"

Dad patted the table amiably, "I was hoping you'd help."

"I don't owe you that!"

"It wouldn't be for me, would it?"

Nellie's glance hopped from me to him, him to me. She stammered, "I'm going."

She stood up in a stiff mechanized way, distractedly searching for her purse, her hand rising to her forehead then patting her head, as if to hold it in place. I grabbed her purse from the entry table. Tears flowed down her cheeks, as I handed it over. I flinched, hearing the metal clang as she slammed the door.

Dad scratched his arm, and shook his head, "Just because someone tells you they're right, it doesn't mean that's so. I did my research. But I can't *make* her listen."

The dogs circled me, anxious and perplexed, "You betrayed her."

"She's going to come around, like I told you." But he pointed at me, "Don't ever go against me again! Now straighten up around here."

I pulled Bull's Eye to my side, whispering, "Hey, boy." I rubbed his big head, his one coal black ear. "Dad, who are you mating him to? When?"

"He's got a prize-winning record and they pay me cash." He headed for his bedroom.

My mouth had gone dry as sand. My head stung, my eyes burned. I sponged the dishes clean and swept the back deck. I had no idea what to do next.

Nellie did not return. In the mornings, Dad smacked his coffee cup down, poured himself a glass of water, and muttered. He didn't talk about her. Nellie's ideas and suggestions, all our moments sharing the dogs, had opened me up and sustained me. But when a woman got to know Dad, she left. Him *and* me.

Two weeks later, in the early afternoon, when Nellie knew Dad was at Happy Mart, she phoned. "Hey, Dirk," she said. "I've missed you."

"I wish I could take things back." I struggled to get the words out.

"Dirk, listen to me, you are not your Dad. However he used you, look where he's got me now." A small sob escaped her. "Hell, I know how he works." Dad's theory of women wasn't so great. "How is Delilah? I'm very worried."

"She kind of looks like a bathtub on legs."

Nellie sighed. "Feed her more, okay? Those pups absorb everything. And she still needs exercise; keep her in shape."

"Yeah, she's voracious."

"He hasn't taken her to the vet, has he? When does he figure she's due?"

"Maybe the third week in September."

"Be extra attentive with her."

"Of course, I promise."

She paused, taking a deep breath, "Dirk, I can't believe you're starting high school soon. Seth High, right?"

"Yeah, weird." Every time I thought about it I started sweating like I'd run a marathon.

"You're going to have extracurricular activities and distractions. But, this is such a critical stage for Dee. Please look after her."

"Nellie, you should come see her." This had popped out of my mouth. How to get Nellie back.

The pause on the other end of the line was short. "You're right."

On the appointed date, I darted out of Seth, jostling through the crowd of sluggards. I wanted to get home to have everything clean. And the dogs already walked. I'd never been impeded by the multiple school activities Nellie imagined, because I kept mostly to myself. I poured myself a cold glass of milk. Shortly after, Nellie rang the bell. "You're so smart. You hatched a plot for us." My face grew hot, thinking of my part in Delilah's predicament. I didn't feel smart.

Dee waddled over, wagging her tail enthusiastically. Nellie prodded Dee's flanks and belly, and checked under her tail.

"What do you think about my visiting one afternoon a week – after we sneak her to the vet?"

"Great." Dad was never home afternoons.

"Dirk, you're a real treasure, I hope you know. Are you growing taller by the week or what?"

Nellie had targeted what was messing me up lately. A treasure, hah! Being in my own skin was my latest nightmare. My legs were turning to stilts. Wiry hair sprouted from my legs, my armpits, my butt. My skin burst with zits though I washed my face plenty. There were days I could've walked around with a bag over my head. With four thousand students, Seth High at least provided indifference and anonymity.

If I saw Michael, it was usually at lunch, when he wasn't hanging with his team. He talked girls; "Man, it's not the cafeteria makes me hungry. Look at that juicy peach ass. Yeah, the spiky blonde. Ask her out."

"Right."

He laughed, "She's rad. Maybe she likes the intellectual type." I could barely get my footing and he'd play me for Casanova. He shook his head, "She won't talk to me."

"You're a scummy jock."

"Skinny-ass brainiac."

"I don't swagger around in a sweaty T-shirt, right."

"Impress her with a poem. Power of words and all that."

"Take care of your jock itch."

Even if I exasperated him, loyalty was real to Michael. He defined himself by loyalty, or we'd never have kept up. "You and me, we know where we stand, man." I didn't ask much. We'd met by chance way back when. But I knew chance could be built into a good long thing.

The only other guy I was tight with was Mr. Koreman, my crazy physics teacher. "Whew! You're analytical—" he tapped his skull in reference. "But you're willing to trust the unknown. You've got that extra. Faith, my man." I thanked the stars for his class. "A scientist is a believer," he said. "Going where others won't." Computations moved through him like symphonies, and he turned me into an instrument playing and penetrating this music. I felt grateful for how his requirements gave me unselfconscious moments full of occupation. He loved unreasonable questions. So I jumped in: a) "If for every action Newton guarantees us an equal and opposite reaction, why is it that two individuals of the same weight and size, doing the same activity, inevitably provoke variant reactions? Can we only measure the inanimate?" b) "If every object has its own natural frequency, why is sound so easily distorted? Is it hardest to attain what's most natural?" c) "So the pressure of the atmosphere, at ground level, would crush you, were it not for the fact that the fluids inside your body exert as much pressure as the air outside. In a case of severe dehydration, does external pressure kill you?"

I thought of my Dad, the pitiless skeptic.

Physics was the science of trust. It relied on the invisible. The unseen was interpreted through man-made models and diagrams. What was least visible could be most powerful. Think atoms. Think gravity. It made me consider that, if I'd sometimes believed Dad could crush me, perhaps he hadn't considered how my *will*, that energy stalker, would bear up to his.

Nellie arranged to visit Mondays. She brought vitamin supplements, yogurt, and steak, all traces of which we removed. She took Dee to her own vet, who, lucky for us, found her healthy. Delilah got slower and fatter, sporting plump pink teats. Nellie and I preoccupied ourselves, counting out the days and measuring her girth.

Dad checked out library books illustrating births. I asked, "What supplies do we need? What will she do?"

"She'll start to leak white stuff. She'll get jittery when she's 24 hours from delivery. We'll prep a closet for her, line it with newspapers."

"That's it?"

"You sound like Nellie."

"Right."

"This is what bitches do; they get pregnant, they deliver pups. It's not rocket science. Think about wild animals. Don't make a soap opera out of it."

"A bitch can die delivering."

"About as often as she's likely to deliver a two-headed pup, okay?"

I read these books though the pictures made me sick with the blood-soaked puppies squirting out. Every time I picked up a book, I wanted to run out and thump a basketball. I begged Nellie, "You have to, have to, be here."

Dee looked ready to explode. Nellie ruffled my hair, "Okay, I better call your Dad. I dread it."

That next evening, getting off the phone, Dad swaggered around the kitchen, "Told you Nellie'd come back. I *know* women." Deluded fool. "Women love babies. Present company excluded." He slapped me on the back.

"Yeah, you're a real comedian."

He raised his eyebrows, mocking.

Bull's Eye sniffed Delilah, solicitously obsessed. He licked her, stuck his nose to her butt, and followed her around, much to her annoyance. On the afternoon of September 23rd, I was hunched over, pursuing a convoluted Geometry problem, when Delilah entered my room panting and shaking. She'd probably taken a spin around the house and exhausted herself. But, half an hour later, she hadn't stopped panting. I called Dad who said, "Can't leave for awhile. Call Nellie."

Nellie murmured, "Stay calm. Rub her back if she'll let you. I'm heading over." Dad *had* emptied out the back hall closet and layered it with newspapers and an old blanket for Dee to have a whelping spot. I led her there, but she wanted to pace, room to room, shaking uncontrollably, while Bull's Eye followed close behind. I finally plonked down on the floor facing the closet, offering myself to her. She bared her teeth at Bull's Eye. I stuck him out in the yard with a bone, yelling, "Be good!" Delilah went into the closet, pawing at the blanket, biting and tearing. I phoned Nellie again, and got her answering machine. I started biting my fingernails. Delilah lay down. I rubbed her back, and her shaking slowed finally. I hoped I was helping.

Forty-five minutes later, the doorbell rang. "Take these things," Nellie ordered. Delilah threw herself at Nellie, and started yelping like never before, her paws pressed to Nellie's chest, trying to climb all over her as Nellie quickly took my place on the floor. I unpacked Nellie's cans of simulated bitch's milk, scissors, cotton balls, mineral oil, blankets, and more newspapers. "She's nervous," Nellie muttered. "She's in pain. Get a big bowl of warm water, clean rags and extra towels. We've got to soothe her." Delilah pushed herself up against Nellie, as if, if she could just flatten herself into Nellie's body, her own wouldn't hurt. She panted and panted. Nellie wiped her slowly with a warm wet rag. As we sat in front of the closet, an hour passed. "She's going to need both of us," Nellie said. "And where the hell is your father?"

"He can't leave work."

"He has no business breeding. Do you understand that?" I nodded. "When your dam's in labor, you *be* there!" Again, I nodded. "Asshole."

All of a sudden Delilah was bleeding. It was thick and dark and Delilah leapt up, madly circling herself, unable to quite lick herself clean because her girth prevented it. "It's okay," Nellie whispered. "Okay, okay, baby." Nellie buckled down on her hands and knees and scooped up the blood mess with newspapers, "Get a lined garbage can! And a bigger bowl with more water!" I ran. Nellie washed her down again. "Could've been an incomplete birth, Dirk. She's ripped herself. Oh, God." Time went by with nothing more happening, except that Delilah, half-draped on Nellie, panted without cease. All at once, she was up tearing again at the closet blanket, circling that small space. Nellie shouted, "You can see the birth coming!" Sure enough a dark bubble-lump swelled from Dee's behind. Nellie's hands hovered there, as Dee strained. Suddenly Delilah swung around, and the lump dropped in front of me. "Grab the puppy!" Nellie yelled. "We've got to clear away the placenta!"

I stared, incapacitated before this dark glob. Nellie's hand darted in front of me, grasping firmly. She pressed the puppy lump toward Delilah, who turned away. "She should bite off the placenta, and clean the pup. Damn." Dee started climbing onto Nellie again. "Stop it!" Nellie shouted. "Grab me another rag, Dirk. Focus! Keep Dee off of me a sec."

I pulled Delilah over, petting and sweet-talking to her. Nellie rubbed the pup energetically, then swabbed its nostrils with Q-tips, "Got to clear out the afterbirth. Breathe, baby, breathe!" Her rag sloughed off more dark mess, and a reddish-colored puppy emerged. "Dee's supposed to lick him to stimulate the vitals. Come on, mommy." But Delilah was up circling again. Nellie gently pulled her down on the newspapers and blanket to nurse the pup. "It'll get that colostrum flowing, girl, make the other babies come easier. Come on." But Delilah would not stay still, making it impossible for the puppy to latch on. Within minutes, Delilah contracted wildly again, another bubble-bulb straining from her. Nellie plopped down the first towel-wrapped puppy out of harm's way. "You can do this Dee," Nellie urged. "Go girl." Dee pushed and the next pup slid out, plopping into Nellie's hands. "Christ, it's bleeding. Get me some thread and needle! Hurry! Hurry!"

My stomach was Jell-O as I ran to the bathroom. I smashed into the door. I yanked every drawer open, looking for the old sewing kit I'd seen shoved out of the way once upon a time. Finally. "You took so long! Hold this puppy." Nellie shoved the squirming pink-nose into my hands. She darted the needle into a tear below the umbilical opening. Squirts of blood shot into my fingers. Nellie sutured, determined and efficient. She sighed, now talking into Delilah's ear, "Okay, okay, please feed your pups." But Delilah just wanted to climb all over Nellie. "We have to force her to nurse, Dirk. I'll roll her down, and lean on her, so you can place both puppies at her teats." I nodded. "Open their mouths just a tiny bit, right by the nipple, press them in!" She baby-talked to Dee. I concentrated by reciting odd numbers to myself: 1! 3! 5! 7! 9! 11! 13! 15! 17! "She's terrified," Nellie said. "The pain makes no sense to her. Your Dad was going to leave you alone to deal with this? I could kill him."

"Be my guest."

"Delilah better start accepting these puppies soon or we're in trouble. Are they latching on yet?"

I got the first little guy's mouth clamped onto a nipple, and he pummeled madly with his pink paws. I worked on the second one, the spotted girl. She was so small in my palm, warm and soft and slick. The way the pups' paws pushed while their eyes were shut in those tiny wrinkled faces snaking about for some orientation, it was something. "The girl's not getting it." Her head snuffled around lost, though I pressed her snout into the teat.

All at once, Dee took to huffing hard, and rose quickly, scattering the pups, "Watch she doesn't step on them," Nellie cried. "Quick! Hold them!"

She snatched the pups, shoving them at me. Sitting cross-legged, half-freaked, I cradled them, one to a hand, in the crook of my arm. Then I rested them on a towel, in the circle made by my lap, and stroked their small round backs and short skinny tails, continuing to clean them, my rubbing intended to fool them their mother was caring for them. I touched their paper-thin pointy nails. Delilah circled and panted. They were so perfect, so entire. The girl pup squeaked like a mouse, the boy nosed the air for the vanished teat. They made my eyes fill. This, them, the beginning of life. Cynicism or indifference here was absurd. These seconds appeared in high definition with miraculous precision, every one of my cells alert. I never wanted this to end. Dad should see these births and be shaken, made to wonder.

Nellie shouted, "Here's the next one!" And Delilah quivered and gasped and once again pressed out a new puppy. Nellie no longer waited for Delilah to lick the babies clean. She leapt into action herself, rubbing energetically, cleaning inside mouth and ears, checking for defects or damage. Again, we pulled Delilah down, shoving more fresh newspapers under her, while I hurried to get the pups nursing, their little pink mouths opening, seeking, seeking, with tiny flailing squeaks. "Stick your pinky in, then push each open mouth onto a teat!" Delilah finally lay long enough for the three pups to get going. We watched, exhausted, a few quiet minutes.

Which is when Dad walked up behind us, "How's it going?"

Nellie flashed him a glance. "Son of a bitch!"

"The pups look strong?"

Nellie didn't answer, so I did. "So far, they seem healthy. Delilah's pretty freaked out, though. Won't clean them."

"Ah well, it's her first time."

Nellie raised her palms, "I forgot you're the expert."

Suddenly, Dee hopped up, spilling the puppies as we rushed to grab them. Dee pawed and clawed the shredded blanket. Dad quizzed Nellie, "How long does this last?"

Nellie ignored him. We stared at Delilah wobbling and swaying on the threadbare blanket. Until she froze, her rear swelling with the puppy's weight growing from her. Nellie's hands reached, at the ready, right behind, until the puppy shot out, sliding promptly into her firm towel massage. It was a black and white boy, most like Bull's Eye. "I like him!" Dad exclaimed.

"We're working on Delilah's liking them."

Dad nodded.

Dee threw herself down, spent. Nellie palpated her for more puppies, pressing up and down Dee's ribs, waist, then groin, "Pretty smooth," she said. "We'll wait, but she may be done." We worked the puppies back onto her teats to nurse.

Dad frowned, "Four's a small litter."

"Your profits too low?"

"I read, like eight is more normal."

I blurted, "Not from underage dams."

Nellie clipped, "You're lucky they weren't oversized and impossible to deliver."

"You women get so dramatic about birth." He shook his head.

Nellie's jaw dropped open. "Miserable jerk."

"I'm just saying she's meant for this. Biological, you know. They don't get help out in the woods or swamps or whatever. Right? Come on. This is great. Look at them go."

I felt an overwhelming sense of exhaustion. The puppies, blind and deaf, squeaked as they pummeled valiantly for milk. They crawled onto each other in their milk-seeking fervor. If one got pushed off a teat, it sucked on another's ears or paws, floundering, persistent. I felt oversized, like King Kong. "Dad, we're pretty beat."

"Yeah."

"What would you have done without him?" Nellie snapped. "You had to work. *This* is work. It's life, too. A struggle for *life*. Tell me you aren't worried about how Delilah is rejecting these pups."

"I'm not worried yet. See?" Dad pointed to the nursing pups. "They're eating. She's just worn out. "

Nellie leapt up. Delilah ears flattened, but she remained down, eyes groggy. "Are you going to hold her down every time they need to nurse? If she does not start responding on her own, in two days they could starve. How can you not think things through?"

"Is this common? Look, tell me what we have to do." He flattened his palms against his ears. "Come on, I thought you'd be happy."

Nellie stood wide-eyed, unmoving, and then she began to cry, really cry. She plopped onto a chair and sobbed into her hands. This was the scene that repeated itself inevitably. I struggled to breathe. Dad rolled his eyes at me. As if we found this equally tiresome. I yelled, "She's right! You weren't here. They could *all* be dead!"

Nellie wept, "Aren't you a fine father?"

"And you're *nothing*!" He exhaled heavily, as if he'd actually surprised himself. Then he rubbed his forehead, "Come on, what's done is done. How can I help?"

Nellie glared, lifting herself. "I gave you a gift, Russ. I was so stupid, thinking you were somebody with a real plan. You're a nobody in a big hurry."

"Yadda, yadda, yadda."

I stuck my face into his, "Don't *talk* to her that way."

"I'm not talking." He grimaced. "To you."

Nellie grabbed her purse and jacket, "Dirk, check on the puppies at least once every hour, for the next few days. And Dee. Feed her double. She needs her strength." She was gone.

Dad declared, "I didn't get a chance!"

The quiet grew like a bad smell. The puppies fell asleep, lying in a clump. I rubbed Delilah who lay back warily. I gathered up the crumpled wet mounds of newspapers. I refreshed her closet with clean papers. With the tip of my finger, I reassured myself that all the puppies' tiny hearts beat. When Dee finally fell asleep, I crashed onto my bed. My throat burned. Delilah had had her puppies, four perfect, helpless, fractions of life.

Delilah refused to feed, clean or guide those puppies, except sporadically. Dad phoned Dr. Lance, and took off. He returned with a box full of cans and vitamins for the lactating bitch, and special puppy serums and animal nursers for at-risk pups. I set the alarm twice nightly, when I stumbled to the closet, splayed her white belly and clamped the puppies onto her teats. Dad helped me hold her down again at dawn. Mornings and afternoons, they nursed, cradled in my arms, from tiny store-bought syringes filled with simulated bitch's milk. We took turns rubbing the puppies' abdomens to get them to piss and poo. Dad said, "I read, most important, they gotta stay warm." I kept adding towels.

I skipped school. Mesmerized, preoccupied. I sat hours watching the pups navigating, sorting themselves from one another. But the calls started coming, school notices of absenteeism, then the threat of a home visit from a social worker. Even Mr. Koreman rang me up, "You can't drop out, not you. You have a future, Dirk."

The puppies didn't interest him. "We're talking about your *life*," he said. I wanted to matter.

Dad grouched, "This is our country's damn problem. We're supposed to be the land of the free, oh sure. Only if Government can control when it pleases. This is *our* small business, but clearly they won't let it be. Where's Dirk? Where Dirk? This country cripples entrepreneurs. Shit. They don't own you. Still, I don't want these people nosing around, understand? Go back to school. Come home at lunch to feed the pups."

Nellie, too, called when Dad wasn't home and urged me: "You've got a brain, honey. Use it or lose it, isn't that what you kids say? Plus, it's the law."

Dad nailed a plank across the open closet, so the pups were held in safely. When I came home, I cleaned up the piss and tiny shits that caked the papers. I changed the thrift store sheets and towels, loaded them into the wash. The pups congregated in piles, untroubled by a butt in the face or a paw pressing an ear. Late in the evening, Dad and I sat on the floor and studied them, "Amazing we come into the world so weak, huh?"

I nodded, "Seems cruel. The odds stacked badly."

"Rich or poor we're all born weak. What's cruel is being poor. Weaklings, the rich ones, most times, rule the world. Get things all screwed up for the rest of us. You got to fight to hard to get out from under them. Can't give up."

I waited two weeks before allowing Bull's Eye near, though Delilah was not the least bit protective. I'd found a used baby gate in the alley to block him off. Their smell sifting through the house kept him troubled. Finally, I let him near the closet, hand firm on his collar, and he tapped each pup with his black nose, sniffing. All at once, he stepped into the closet. I bent down, still holding him. He stretched out, and ardently started licking one pup. He tilted her sideways. He folded up her small malleable body, to clean her top and bottom. Delilah wandered off seeking a more solitary spot. Bull's Eye next cleaned the boy he'd most clearly reproduced. The little guy squeaked, crumpling his forehead. I'd read how dogs occasionally adopted other puppies, but that it was particularly rare for males. How like Bull's Eye to do the unexpected, taking over. The other two blind puppies, sensing his large warmth, eagerly edged over. Bull's Eye firmly washed them, working their digestive systems into action, something I'd been trying to simulate by rubbing their bellies with rags. A dog besides the dam usually represented a threat. Bull's Eye didn't seem to know this. And Delilah couldn't have cared. Our dogs got the rules topsy-turvy. Who learned anything normal in this house? I watched the pups push into Bull's Eye's belly, looking for teats, while Bull's Eye relished their massage. What a comic lot. Bull's Eye couldn't nurse them, but his presence could socialize them. Which might save their temperaments. He could prevent Dad from failing them. Maybe Dad didn't deserve that. But the puppies did.

What I thought a lot about that year of high school was how Dad had become a through-line to my losses. Delilah was a dismal disaster as a dam. Nellie had left us. So much for what Dad knew about women. He'd blown our chances; things around him turned sour. I couldn't see forgetting or forgiving his damage or the opportunities he'd lost. Not when they circumscribed my life.

Dad wrote an ad for some newsletters and the *Sun-Times*: "For sale. Puppy pit bulls, champion weight-pulling stock. Healthy as hell. $500."

"They haven't opened their eyes yet," I pointed out the obvious. "They're not even ready for temperament tests." Rusty, Maggie, Caramel, and Poncho.

Dad glanced up, "You plan ahead. School doesn't teach that?" He looked disappointed, "Can't you see I'm working for *us*?"

"But I don't want anything."

"Easy to say at your age. What do you know about life's responsibilities? Trust me."

The only pup Delilah had anything to do with was Poncho; she occasionally licked him clean, maybe because he was born smallest, this white dollop with a black mantle and black ear. Bull's Eye hung on, playing model dad, separating the puppies when they nipped each other too hard, pulling them away from the edge of the closet before they might fall into the hall's dangers. They slept curled against him.

At five weeks, Dad harnessed each puppy to a tricycle tire and watched. Maggie froze at first, then cautiously teased the weight forward, careful not to let it sideswipe her. Rusty and Caramel panicked, refusing to budge. Poncho took off, ears flapping, teaching that tire to follow. The next day, Dad called buyers who'd responded to the ad. A tattooed guy with curly hair, mud-black eyes and a sunburned face, came over, picked Rusty up by the scruff of the neck and shook him hard. Rusty scrambled berserk in mid-air. The guy said, "I like feisty." I argued with Dad in the kitchen, "You don't know this man. What's his training experience? He can't take a pup until it's eight weeks old."

"For all the good Delilah's doing them? Rusty'll get a better shot anywhere. They're eating solids. We're selling the dogs, Dirk." By nightfall, Rusty and Caramel were gone.

"We should have asked for references."

"References? People get their cousins or neighbors to vouch for them. A pack of lies. You can never really know inside a person, Dirk. In life, you gamble." Dad pointed at the green bills fanned out on the table, smiling. "We did good. You want to keep them all. I know. But we can't."

Sweet Caramel had been shy, but Maggie was a ball of fire, her dark brindled bundle slipping into the kitchen cabinets where she had a great time knocking the pots around. She climbed down the basement steps when the all others stared in fear. She'd been the first to crawl, the first to delve into bowls of food. Poncho following close behind.

Dad said, "Maggie's a natural leader. She and Bull's Eye'd make strong-willed piebald pups."

"She needs two years." I jammed two fingers at his face. "Two."

He shook his head, "Can you not compute how I'm trying to build us a life? A kennel name? A reputation? We started side by side; you crazy excited; you and me, we trained hard. Now you got your head in the clouds, so self-important. I don't get it. I just made $1,000, and you sulk. What do you want from me?"

He frowned puzzled, sincere in his way. But we weren't going to break through with a heart to heart, our souls lighting with hope. We didn't do that; it didn't happen. Our gulf continued to widen.

Dad wouldn't sell Poncho. "I only need a bitch. But I got a good feeling about him. Instinct."

"He's worth more than money?"

"Given the choice, yeah."

At least that relief.

A couple of months later, Poncho and Maggie had doubled in both size and daring. These days, the more determined Dad became about the future, the more I wanted to get out from under him. I'd learned that even when we won, we could also lose; and when the dogs paid a price, any price, I wanted to die. I felt entitled to piss Dad off by ignoring his orders, but it was harder to stay away from the dogs. Training, for me, was no longer about winning pulls or breeding or any of that. It was about the way the dogs became fully alert and alive, as you brought them to new skills they felt in their bones. They struggled, then you worked harder, and together, you grew capable and confident. Progress assured. I practiced their start-offs, increased their weights, treats doled out for each additional weight and distance. Only Delilah remained aloof. After she did her stint, she wanted to be kenneled right away. Isolated, head curled into her chest. Most times, when the puppies approached, she bared her teeth, and they zoomed back to Bull's Eye. Plenty ridiculous.

Poncho stuck his head in a paper bag and ran around the house, exhilarated, banging into walls. I wished Nellie could see. Maggie, the water nymph, leapt into Bull's Eye's water bowl, dousing the kitchen floor, again and again. And theirs was a slow reign of terror when it came to housebreaking. Which is what prompted Dad to section off a select rectangle of the yard. He poured a thick base of gravel and surrounded it with a chain-link fence with a gate. "From now on, put those two in here until they piss and shit. No walk, no coming in the house, rain or shine, *until*."

Maggie was stubborn as all get-out. From the minute she encountered that gravel pit it was like a switch clicked on; she would never ever do her business there. Poncho squatted his little white butt, did the deed, and got out. Maggie sat there. And sat, and sat.

It was January, fifteen below, and I'd waited half an hour for Maggie to take a crap. "Fine then. Stay!" I was frozen and left her, taking the others for their walk. In the brisk air, the dogs exhaled white ribbons. Blood rushed to my cheeks and ears; I rubbed and clapped my tingling hands, still clutching the leashes. No one else traipsed about the frigid sidewalks.

We quickly got back to the yard, I unleashed Bull's Eye and Dee, my fingers stiff as rubber hoses. Bull's Eye rushed to the enclosure. Poncho began barking and barking, a young terrified sound. Maggie dangled from the top of the chain-links. "Maggie!" Trembling, all thumbs, I struggled to unhook her, my chest heaving, as I clasped her limp stocky brown body. Had she envisioned clearing the top of the four feet of chain-link? Instead, the tiny link in her collar had hooked onto one of the wire points topping the chain link, and hung her there. What were the odds? A deep gash slit her throat, revealing the strain with which she must have fought her capture. Blood seeped through my fingers, dripping onto my coat: "Maggie! Maggie!"

It was all I could do not to vomit on her. Then, through my thumb, I felt a faint heart beat. I ran. I wrapped her in a towel. I concocted a cloth papoose out of the bottom of my backpack, carefully lowering her in. I grabbed my bike. I pedaled as hard as I could through the slush and snow, the twenty blocks to Dr. Lance's office. I ran in, yelling, "Help! Emergency! She's still alive!" Dr. Lance quickly put on his gloves to examine the small bloody bundle. He shook his head sadly, "Son, she's probably fractured her neck. She's critical," he said. "You'd better call your Dad."

Dad yelled into the phone, "You left a puppy alone. Now this!"

He spoke to Dr. Lance. When he hung up, he turned to me, "She's in great pain. It's best to put her down." Maggie's eyes opened; she made a gurgling sound.

I pointed at her, "Look! We don't know. She could pull through. She's a fighter. Let me call my Dad back."

"She's struggling hard. I can see that. But it doesn't look hopeful."

I couldn't budge Dad. "The cost of surgery, meds, hospitalization. And her, maybe become a vegetable. Are you crazy? And she's suffering. Act like a man. Give me the vet."

Dr. Lance elaborated, took my side, over the phone, "She might still be a fine house-pet. I've seen my share of three-legged or blind or deaf dogs, and the people who love them. Your son's very upset for her." A long silence followed. "No, she doesn't have to go elsewhere. I understand."

He hung up, "Her body's not moving, her neck is almost surely broken. My guess is she's paralyzed. X-rays cost, as does extensive surgery, and for what purpose? She won't recover her full mental capabilities. She lost oxygen, Dirk. Your Dad doesn't want her living in pain."

I gritted my teeth. Then I was shouting, "This is wrong! He's wrong! What if X-rays show we're wrong?"

"Dirk, this is a horrible decision to have to make. But she's smarting bad. And he's got legal authority. He'll make this same choice at another vet's. He was pretty clear about that. We're saving her from a lot of agony. I'm so sorry." Dr. Lance was doing his job, and I hated him. He asked quietly, "Do you want to be present when she goes down?"

Helpless, on the table, her sad brown eyes pulled me to her. She had plain bad luck. I had left her. And we were her lot in life. I rubbed her small blood-sticky ears, her tiny brindled body; I ran my finger down her nose. She gurgled.

"Yes, then?" Dr. Lance asked. I nodded. Tears poured down my nose. My feet froze to the floor, my hands burned as I tried to cuddle her. I stuck my face into hers, murmuring, "Pretty Maggie. Fiery little Maggie." She tried to stick out her tongue to lick me. Dr. Lance penetrated her with the syringe. Her eyes fixed on me, and stayed. And stayed. I choked. "It's over." Dr. Lance patted my back. "Her pain is over. She's in a better place, Dirk. Stay as long as you like."

I cried like a baby. I couldn't stop. Only an hour later could I unfold myself to ride home.

I couldn't open the refrigerator, couldn't set the table, couldn't get out of my desk chair, my head in my hands. When Dad came home, he grabbed a mess of leftovers, and called me to the kitchen. "I'm sorry. Hell of an afternoon. Try to remember, you win some, you lose some."

"You didn't give her a chance."

"We can't run a rehabilitation center." He paused, "She got herself in trouble. God knows what it would've been next. Let her go."

"You didn't give her a chance."

"You been to veterinary school?"

"She was alive. You killed her. That's the truth." I couldn't eat. I couldn't sit near him another second.

Dad reached for some cold meatballs, "Who left her alone? Brilliant move. Don't put it on *me*. Face a problem and move on. Haven't you learned that by now? Know what this cost me?"

"I couldn't care less."

Dad slammed his hand on the table. "Don't you ever say that. I've given my whole life to you. Don't you dare forget!"

I bolted for my room, yelling, "You killed Maggie."

I could still feel Maggie's bundle, slack-limbed, matted with blood. I *had* left her. A new paralysis ran the house, a debilitating limbo. Poncho sniffed under the couch and about the yard for Maggie, turning to me perplexed. He stole her old pink towel, and dragged it around. Every day, Bull's Eye navigated the house, pushing open all the closet doors, searching. I lay in bed for hours, sick with disgust, skipping school. I couldn't read. I couldn't move, the feel of Maggie numbing my mind. Why had this happened? Dad opened my door, "Hey! The dogs are going to get fat, and lazy. Get a grip. Something bad happens, you just fall apart?" Screw him.

Then Nellie called. I focused on the musical timber of her voice; "I'm sorry I stayed away. I thought I'd never decompress. Your Dad infuriates! Tell me what I've missed."

A welling rose in me, choking. I pressed my throat. I coughed. Then, all at once, I was sobbing like a pre-schooler, stammering, "Sorry, sorry."

"Dirk, tell me," she said. "Just tell me."

I blew my nose, "Poncho's the only puppy left."

"But your Dad wanted bitches."

"Maggie died." Nellie might hate me, but there was no other way but to tell. I tried to settle down and speak.

"She got sick?" Nellie hesitated. I told the whole story, raw. Nellie responded with a cold calm. "Your Dad has never understood temperament. He lives by the noise in his head; it's all he hears, no *listening* to the dogs. Maggie wasn't one to stay still in any place. A person has to understand these things."

"I didn't."

"You don't think you're to blame?"

"I left her."

"Listen to me; she wasn't supposed to be able to jump that high. You had three other dogs to care for. It was bitter cold and you had to keep moving. I've got to see you; we must talk. I'm not tossing the boy out with the bath water."

Michael complained I was the school's Biggest Hermit. Said he'd seen me, headphones on like I was digging the floor, shuffling through the halls, "You going for the strong silent type?"

"Yeah, it's working real well, can't you tell?"

"People'll start to talk, man."

"Look, just because I'm not out there waving pom-poms or chugging beer bongs doesn't mean I'm not getting my high school experience."

"It doesn't?"

"Hey, more than one way to skin a cat."

"What the hell are you talking about? You kill me. Call me up, dude."

Maybe, I should've hung out, loafed more with classmates. At home, I was edgy and miserable. Still, those times I lingered around some vague gathering, I worried about the dogs. Groups hung out on school grounds, spilling their time, not doing or saying much in particular. Smoking. Lying on the grass. Laughing. Without Michael, my wit fell flat. So I preferred to keep to myself. Except I was anxious about the big gap: girls. Yes, they interested me. I wasn't missing that gene. I noticed low-rise jeans with two dimples cresting above a thong or a pleated yellow mini-skirt floating over Jackie Arroyo's bronze thighs. Thank God for the mind's control. I filed these images like a Rolodex in my brain. Between classes, I collected new views, my headphones on to deflect where my attention was going.

When he saw me, Michael started in, "Where you been? Like for two weeks?"

I felt my face redden. "Hey, Mr. Social Worker, I'm not in your caseload."

"I'm just ragging you." He rubbed his palms. "Listen, there's a swim meet Thursday at Von." Michael had joined the team to stay in shape over winter. "I could use the support. Some school spirit."

"Hah, yeah, it's my dream to be your personal cheerleader."

God, I would've hated coursing through the water as the center of attention. Michael didn't relent, "You gonna wimp out on me?"

"You gonna win?" I high-fived him. "You better."

The old pool was in a tight space, narrowly surrounded by green tiles; the air, heated and moist, thick like a sauna. The heavy chlorine burned my nostrils. I removed my jacket. I liked the turquoise water with its sharp parallel navy-blue lane markers, dotted by ropes of buoys. A mathematical space; orderly, linear, divisible. I saw Seth High fans on the few squeezed-in spectator benches. I sat alone at the far end, first plugging in my headphones. Until the swim meet started.

Distances and names were being announced. Surrounding me, different voices swelled. Some grew familiar, as I followed threads of conversations. The Seth girls' swim team had come to lend support, chatting: "He looks so fine in a Speedo."

"Yumm…"

"It's Steve's turn, the one hundred meter fly. Yell!"

They liked abs, arms; they liked butts. When Michael's turn came, one girl cried, "Look at him!"

"God, he's gorgeous."

"Mhmm. Bet he knows it, too."

"Nah, he's such a sweetie."

"Really?"

"Uh, huh… Here he goes!"

Michael dove into the one hundred meter free-style, his arms churning, a working windmill. There was a button he clicked on. He simplified getting from point A to point B. It just wasn't as easy to do as he suggested. Michael had learned to focus intently at an early age, and, ever since, he'd kept re-fueling his drive. I was shouting, as he approached the finish line first, "Go! Go! Go!"

"You know him?" an olive-skinned brunette asked.

"Since second grade. Born athlete."

"Are you, too?" I was suddenly self-conscious. Her hair was all dark ringlets falling around her shoulders. Her eyes were long-lashed and brown. "You kind of antisocial?"

Her friends glanced over. I half-grinned, guessing I looked idiotic. "Aren't any of you shy?" Her girls smiled.

"Sure," a trim Asian girl tilted her head, swishing her hair. Michael was right. A guy had to get out now and again. See what the world offered.

Michael swam two more relays. We yelled our heads off, our voices staggering into the humid air. Parents here and there shared the hours of moisture. Michael's dad, shirtsleeves rolled up, waved at me. He'd come straight from work. Curly-haired Tina asked, "Why don't you join the swim team?"

"I spend a lot of time training dogs. Plus, I'm no Michael."

Her eyes were warm and attentive, "I had a white poodle when I was little."

"Mine are pit bulls. I could show you how I train them, over at my house, sometime." I could hardly believe myself.

Tina reacted, "For fights?"

"What? No! I'd never do that."

She shrugged, "People say pit bulls should be banned."

"Yeah, we also interned Japanese-Americans during World War II."

"Just saying." She looked at the pool. The ref blew a whistle.

"They're actually great dogs."

Tossing her curls, she said, "Let's watch."

I'd blown it.

The 400-meter race was on, the swimmers rolling back and forth hypnotically, and I felt horribly stuck. I put my headphones on, *Rolling Stones* blasting, my mind enclosed. I shouldn't have told Tina about the dogs. I'd pushed her away ... *jumping jack flash, it's a gas, gas, gas...*

Then Michael was in position for the 200-meter freestyle. He fixed his swim cap, snapping his goggles taut, arms pointed back, knees bent, toes edged over. Bang! The starting shot.

His body was a machine. But a guy from Von High, one lane over, was slamming half a body-length ahead. Whether Michael won or not interested me less than the way he pursued that water. But I jumped up and yelled, "Come on! You can *do* it! *Do* it!" Watching him – king of energy, champion of nerve – was exhilarating. And I did understand; a person was either hard-wired to this or not. It was true for other species, too. With Bull's Eye, desire overcame hundreds of awful pounds challenging his pull. Ambition was an ingredient in the blood, biological. There were others, like me, who studied the design of ambition, saw patterns, computed weight ratios. We liked to manage and manipulate numbers. Trace their opportunities. I had graphed the dogs, trying to design ideal balances between aerobic workouts and strength training; calculating percentages of food consumption to energy expenditure; measuring the elastic conversion of proteins to stamina. This much arranging was, I guessed, the smallest possible turn-on for a girl. Yet it was what I did. Even if the boy/girl dance demanded more. This Tina of the ringlets didn't know anything about my dogs, certainly not what I needed her to if I meant to interest her.

When the meet ended, I shuffled foot to foot, while the Seth crowd discussed their next meet date. Once the group organism got rolling, individuals became expendable, conversations interrupted, lost, started, mid-sentence, about noise, not talk. Michael exited from the locker room with three other guys, their faces fresh and ruddy, hair damp-combed. Everyone joked loudly. Michael turned to me, "Man, I could eat a horse. Come out with us." He thumped my shoulder, "I felt you watching. Brought me good luck."

"Can't. Gotta walk the dogs."

He spoke into my ear, "They've got you whipped, man."

"And you're a whore to the team. Great race, though. Great final push in the 200. Glad you won. Catch you later, man." A couple of people waved, and I nodded back, my headphones clicked on. If I could turn my head into a live concert, why shift and shuffle, wondering what to say next? I liked my world as a great musical score. I liked deleting unwanted scenes, bye-bye poodle Tina. ...*gimme, gimme, my very own girl...* I climbed onto the Kimball bus headed to Peterson. Took the next bus up to Ridge.

When I got home, the dogs' kennels quivered as they jumped and pawed in enthusiasm. "Hey you! Hang on!" I grabbed three leashes, took off my headphones, and ushered them into a walk under the blue-purple sky. The trees lifted pitch black against it, a scramble of limbs not yet budding, shiny from the wear of winter. Bull's Eye, with his big black patch of eye like a laser, pierced forward purposefully. Delilah walked by my side, ladylike and removed. And Poncho zoomed right then left then right, shimmying his small plump white butt in the brisk air, until I needed to correct him. How absurd for people to deny the breed's handsomeness. Square regal heads, trim muscular builds, intelligent brown eyes, such alert confidence. I watched the threesome; sire, dam and puppy – quite the family as long as you didn't ask for the whole story. Still, I loved this hour, just before nightfall. Winding down time. Most people settled inside for supper or TV. With the streets quiet, less to worry about, fewer people scared of dogs, no skateboarders or veering bicyclists. The air was full of lively smells the dogs deciphered, noses twitching like agents on reconnaissance.

Michael was wrong about one thing: dependence didn't *per se* make you a slave. If people thought *that* they'd never have kids. The dogs were my wards, and I was stronger because of them. This was leadership. Knowingly taking on dependents, wanting to protect, needing that because it enlarged you and your capacity to live in the world. I'd been alone, just Dad for family, Dad who demanded self-sufficiency above all. It wasn't dependence that worried me; it was the lack of it. Maybe everyone else was striking out for independence, but I wanted the opposite, though I was close to clueless as to how to start a relationship with any creature but a dog.

Which is maybe why, in Calculus, I could be counted on to be indefatigable. My teacher, Mr. Davario – Mr. Koreman had put me onto him – threaded complex numbers, going link after link. Studying was the art of dependence, a mad focus on the material, a mystery to untangle – a knowing I could rely on. Submitting myself, I connected. Focusing, equation by function by variable, I unveiled wall-sized conceptions, and found my understanding magnified ten-fold. If I was obedient to what Calculus demanded of me, it was for this chance to feel the powerful results, and know I was at one with their victory. In math, the battle of signifiers was always fair. This kind of involvement I understood a lot better than the erratic behavior of my classmates. Or Dad's pitilessness.

Lately, Dad and I avoided each other, in an unsatisfactory truce. "Where do you think you're going?" he harassed.

"My business."

"When did you start taking me for granted? Suddenly, I'm chopped liver?"

I didn't reply. The dogs grew; they did extraordinary things. Bull's Eye and Delilah could have towed a car. But the more Dad asked of me, the less I knew why I consented. We were less and less on the same page. His orders and requirements stale, perfunctory. It was the dogs' eagerness: *Come on, come on, toss us a Frisbee*, I jumped to.

Mr. Davario offered me work as a tutor, at $15 an hour, helping students on Mondays after school, "You're good, you're calm and you care. You have a real gift." He smiled, pushing up his black glasses.

"Thanks." Bashful, acting like an idiot, I tried to come up with a good question. "Any particular textbook you prefer I use?"

"They'll bring whatever's causing them trouble. You'll figure it out, or come talk to me." He paused, rubbing his forehead. "Dirk, look around you. Too many kids here are going nowhere. You're smart. College is the answer, Dirk, the way out of life as a treadmill. Believe me."

I did. Increasingly.

Sometimes, I saw Tina, books in the crook of her arm. She smiled and tilted her head, swaying her ringlets. I felt like a moron. One day, at the vending machine in the cafeteria, I didn't see her standing behind me until she said, "How are your dogs?" My face flushed, burning: "Tina, hey, what's up?" I was at least a foot taller than her. I should be protective. I didn't want to be a jackass.

"Nothing much," she waited, her brown eyes intent.

"Well, yeah, the dogs, when it's warm, that's when the weight-pulls start up again." She rolled a long curl around her index finger. I stammered, "And you?"

"I just came from Chemistry. I hate Chemistry," she said. "Well not *all* chemistry." Her eyebrows arched into cute little parentheses, her finger still giddy, twirling, "Some chemistry is good."

My tongue stuck to the roof of my mouth, my hands hung like bowling balls.

"Hey, d'you think, like you said, you'd show me your dog training?"

For a second, I felt her sitting on my bed. But who did I think I was? "Uh...sure."

She giggled. "Well, when?"

Okay, about 100 pistons were shooting around my head. "I'll call you." I walked off. Like an idiot. Had she just come onto me? Was I totally delusional? In eighth grade, I'd managed to hook up with a girl or two at a party, fondling in the dark, wordless. That was my limited experience, which Michael liked to point out was pitiful. Now I'd maybe lead Tina into my house, plain as it was. And I'd have to talk. Show her my life, which was me. Someone other than Michael would see it. Like opening a window. Ridding all the stale air.

I didn't know when she actually expected me to call. Or if I was really supposed to wait to run into her. Which didn't happen. Days passed. Maybe she didn't notice. But if she did? A week later, I phoned.

"It's me with the dogs."

"I thought you forgot."

"Do you want to see them?"

"Oh yes."

"Wednesday? After school? Umm, we could meet at the main door."

"Cool. All right then."

I had to remind myself to breathe.

Wednesday, the house was scrubbed spotless. I'd washed the dogs, too. I bought Cherry Coke I hid under my bed so as not to alert Dad. I still hadn't casually bumped into Tina, practicing small talk. But, after an endless day of classes, there she was Wednesday at the main exit, in a tight red sweater, her jeans glued to her curves. Her hair played like streamers down her back. I hoped I looked okay. Maybe she was more interested in dogs. I could hear Michael: *You're frickin' clueless. They look at you and you walk away. What the hell, man?* "We take a bus up Clark," I pointed her east.

"Sure." How could anyone in the bus keep his eyes off her? Her red sweater radiated, man. She chatted, "We live in an apartment so my mom won't get a dog. I mean, she'd have to walk it. She already works long hours."

"My Dad docs, too. But he has me." I shrugged, pushing my bangs back.

"He's lucky," she winked. I tried not to trip over my own two feet. I stared out the bus window. "Do you have a big family?" I shook my head. "I have two older sisters, one works at a bank, the other I'm counting the days until she leaves for college."

I pointed to the doors. "Next stop." Though the day was overcast, the high clouds moved quickly. At moments the sun shot free, illuminating the side of a building or a row of trees. It was chilly enough that we hustled the six blocks to my house. I wanted to say something witty and ended up saying nothing.

Tina put her backpack on the kitchen table. I handed her a Cherry Coke with ice. I pointed to the kennels in the yard, the eager barking. Dad would've yelled at the noise, and made them wait. I warned Tina, "They'll be overexcited. We don't have a very sociable house. Strangers are a big deal to them."

"They won't bite?"

"No, no, no, nothing like that." I opened their kennels. They loped out, thrilled. Licking, wiggling at, and smelling Tina. Poncho practically jumped into her arms. "Want to see what they can do?"

"Yeah." Poncho wouldn't stop licking her. "This one's young! Hey cutie pie."

I pulled out the training wagon, loaded it up with cement blocks. Two car tires were hooked to drag behind. "This is five hundred pounds," I said. I lined up Bull's Eye. He sat at alert, ready. I harnessed him to the wagon, ran to the demarcation line we'd taped down, and whistled. He reached me in eight seconds. I ruffled his neck, "Good boy!"

"Wow," Tina said. "He makes it look easy."

"Want to see more?"

"Even the puppy?" I showed her how we got Poncho ready, tugging a big stone in a child's wooden wagon. Tina clapped her hands as he, too, crossed the line.

"Want to see Delilah?"

"Nah, I get it. So there are competitions for this?"

I explained. Then, because she crossed her arms tightly against the chill, I brought her inside, without the dogs. She sat in the kitchen, real as day. The dogs pushed their faces against the glass door, my allies in astonishment.

"I've never heard of weight pulls. You live just with your Dad?"

"Yep. My mom walked out."

"That's awful."

"You want to see my room?" I blurted.

"What's *in* there?" She plunged her fingers through her velvet hair. It fell like long folds in a curtain. I led her to my room, with its twin bed and blue bedspread, my narrow wood desk, and books piled in stacks along the wall. "You don't have posters of dogs all over."

"Real ones are enough."

"Wow. You like reading!" She sat on my bed.

Just as I had imagined. I was breathing kind of goofy and hoped she didn't notice. If I didn't sit next to her, I'd be the biggest idiot on earth. So I sat down and my leg touched hers. "How's Chemistry?"

She laughed like light spoons clinking. "It's a total mistake they put me in that class. It's Chinese. But I don't care."

"Are you comfortable?"

Tina watched me without blinking, didn't answer. I followed the light motions of her breathing. I felt the rise and fall of her full breasts, as she exhaled, inhaled, exhaled, inhaled. I moved my hand slowly, over her warm faintly damp hand. She didn't pull away. It took about ten minutes but I finally traced a finger up her arm to the skin of her neck, her smooth olive-ness. Her curls slid under my hand. Then my finger traced her cheek. I pressed nearer, and then I was kissing her full soft, soft lips, slippery and wet. I smelled the wool of her red sweater. Then the fruity shampoo of her hair as it tumbled around her face and mine. I pulled away and looked at her. She touched my jaw. And I kissed her again, tilting her down onto my bed, one hand sliding under her sweater. I went erect. But she stopped me, saying, "Slow down, slow now." Every pore in my body was wildly awake. I hardly knew what to do. I concentrated hard on pausing, "You're beautiful," I said. "Your hair makes me crazy."

"Your blue eyes," she said. "They're so intense." She pressed her palm flat against my chest, "You must play sports. I can feel it."

"The dogs keep me in shape." She put her fingernail to my lips and pulled me closer. I didn't want to talk, anyway.

Eventually, she spoke, "You're funny. I never met anyone crazy about dogs like you."

"Do you like someone different?"

She traced her nails through my hair, and nodded. Her ease suggested mine wasn't her first fondle. If she wanted to guide me, I was all hers. The blue of early evening filtered through my window. She was here, right now, as long as possible. "When do you need to go home?"

"Soon. Homework," she said. "You'll call me?"

I whispered into her ear. "Of course. I'll walk you to the bus."

I held her slender chilled fingers as we walked down the street. I felt electrified. She kept looking at me, as if intent on sharing an important thought, but she didn't say anything. "You are so beautiful," I said, knowing I should do more than repeat myself, but my words were jammed.

I called her the next day. My mind had gone on delete, blanking everything but her. Not letting her slip away. "How come one day I run into you, then weeks and weeks go by and you wouldn't even know we're in the same high school?"

"Chance, I guess," she giggled.

"Where were you today?"

"Classes. Same old."

"What were you wearing?"

"What? Okay, okay, a black skirt and shirt, but the shirt has yellow lace trim."

"I wish I'd seen you. I know you looked good."

"You're making me feel weird."

"Meet me later so I can apologize."

"Tomorrow. After school, I hang with my friends in the park behind Seth."

"Come home with me, again."

"My sister went nuts when she heard I went to your house alone. I had to make her swear not to tell Mom. I'm not putting myself out there like that every time. That's loco."

"Can I see you at the main door, instead, for two minutes?"

"Dirk, my friends are fun."

"Please."

I got there early, wanted her to sense my devotion. She walked toward me in a white shirt so tight her nipples reached forward like searchlights. I pleaded, "Come on, Tina, come, come, come with me."

"You're such the loner. That's not good. Every time you hear something messed up on the news it's about somebody who was by himself too long."

"You think I'm dangerous?" I grinned, liking the idea.

"Come meet my friends."

"Tina, I suck at groups."

"But you'll be with me," she pulled my hand, dragging me down the path to the park. I tried to kiss her, "Hey! I don't like that public stuff, people hanging out their business."

"But you just said you won't be alone with me."

"Not today," she smiled. "You're not in some big hurry, are you?"

"Okay, make me crazy." Her waist was warm and smooth. "I'm counting on your coming over soon. We'll go for a walk. You don't have to come inside my house."

"Meet my friends."

"Another time. Later."

But I avoided her crew like the plague. Hanging out, for what? They'd just take me away from her, her joking with the girls, me trying to think of idiot stuff to say to the jocks. Tina fell onto my blue bedspread a couple more times. She kept my hands from going under her clothes, making me wild outlining her round butt, her full breasts, the cascade of curls dangling down her back. I bought her Cookie Dough Hagen-Daaz. I took her to movies. I ordered us take-out Chinese food, especially egg rolls, her favorites. A few weeks passed. I felt alive, newborn.

Then she said I wasn't holding up my end of the bargain. "You want me to drop off the face of the earth with you? Look, I've got swim practices. I like my teammates, my friends. I like people. It's not unusual, Dirk."

The thought of hanging out with stuck-up girls chattering in clumps made my skin crawl. Me, standing with them, cemented like a lamp post. I didn't, couldn't, budge. We went on like this for three more weeks.

"I can't do this," Tina decided. "Sorry and all, but it's ridiculous. I'm not locking myself away."

We were outside, on the school grounds. "Come on, don't say that." I grabbed her arm, pleading.

She yanked herself away. She went off, "Touch me again and I'll scream. You don't own me! Pervert. Screw your dogs."

"Hey!" I shoved my face close, "Don't you understand —?" She stared back panicked. What was I doing? I stepped back. "I'm sorry, I didn't mean -- Can't we talk? I need-- "

Tina started screaming, "Get away! I hope I never see you again!" She swiveled around, hurried away, shrinking smaller and smaller. I didn't move. I didn't even recognize myself.

When Michael heard this from someone on the swim team, he was all over me. "She's gone and told her home-girls who are like grand central news, that you won't talk to anyone, that you kidnapped her into your bedroom. Like some total psychopath. Says you're weird about dogs. This is *high school*, Dirk; people talk, people hang. What planet are you on?"

"I don't want to hang with her stupid friends."

"Look, Tina's a bitch. Screw her. But, man, you're going to end up all alone. Your isolation, it's like a sickness. Gets worse every year."

"It's a heavy training period for the dogs."

"I don't get you. Is this for your Dad or for you? What, he'll beat you if you don't? It's gotten absurd."

"Tina said that."

"She's right."

But I wasn't going to integrate into some new social group, and become a crowd regular. And I wasn't going to abandon the dogs. Bull's Eye was seven years old; he shouldn't even have been pulling anymore except that he wanted to. Maybe this *wasn't* about weight pulls. How much *did* I love the dogs? Did I lose *her* over the dogs? Or because I scared her? I didn't see the purpose much in most people, only a very few. Something might definitely be the matter with me.

I was pissed. And ached so bad. Demoted like a stupid kid-size cup at a counter of prized sundaes. I'd gotten a crush on a girl who needed her friends more than me. I was replaceable, disposable, dismissible. Alone.

Life was no Fibonacci series with numbers advancing unwavering in a perfect sequence. In life, you could add and add and add and come up with nothing. Michael said I made things complicated, "Fifty percent of the population is women, bro. Just move on."

"I don't want to be glued to *anyone's* group of friends."

"You got to get *out* of your *own* head." Michael tapped his finger to his temple.

I'd been having supper face-to-face with my Lone Star Dad since I could remember. One-on-one I understood. But, say – in classrooms – it frustrated me that the needs of the whole ruled. A group meant every individual had to progress at the same rate of sludge. Was it truly for the greater good? But, but, if you stayed solo, it wasn't better.

Fool, I'd estranged Tina. After pinning my hopes on her. So, if a person shone like a talisman for you, you joined her group? Moved slowly, slowly around her like you were stuck in molasses. Nights, I twisted and tossed, clueless and loveless.

Michael played the calm pragmatist, but mainly he tucked stuff under his belt better than I did. He forgot and forgave readily. He wasn't uncaring, or he wouldn't have bothered with me. He endured, that was for sure. Even when he gave me crummy advice, I couldn't be aggravated.

At the end of my junior year, Mr. Koreman and Mr. Davario offered me a physics and math summer tutoring position, at a $20 hourly rate. I'd be able to put money aside. College loomed; I sure as hell needed major financial aid. Though, I'd aced the SATs. No way on earth I was staying at home, commuting locally. Still, tutoring meant being away more and more from Bull's Eye, Poncho and Delilah.

When I tutored, my brain traveled on the smooth asphalt of numerical relations, white lines pointing to the clear horizon. On that same road, those I tutored swerved and hit hurdles. I slowed them down, "Or you won't think straight. Clear your head. Then focus." But they didn't want to lose themselves in computations, sensed no magic in falling upon numbers. They opened the *Algebra I* textbook to a mass rebellion of tiny black aliens; they grew tense and tired. Would have given their right arms to never see me, or Algebra, again. I'd used to lose myself whole afternoons tallying figures. Uncoiling equations, little seemed better, at least at school. Math taught me how much more there is to a kid than meets the eye. However messy his hair or stupid his clothes, inside he might be decoding square roots, anticipating new highways. But each person has doors firmly shut that are openings into light for others. You can't shove a person through a door and count him happy. I hoped my guidance might prop their doors open a little.

Nellie phoned dependably. One afternoon she said, "Hon, I miss seeing you. Can't I fix you a proper dinner? Take the El downtown to Columbia College, near my office. From there, I'll drive us to my place in Evergreen Park. You'll meet my girls." Her beloved dogs.

"Easy." I was curious. Her home; what would it look like?

"You still got a good appetite?"

"More than ever." Weird, but except for Michael's house, I never went out for dinner. Maybe because of the dogs. Or was it Dad, resisting the cost, or any crowd, another imposition of limitations. "Should I bring anything?"

"News about the dogs. Okay? Next Saturday, at five o'clock." She paused, "Don't tell your dad."

"Right." Nellie was probably a microcosmic blip in his memory with his fine capacity for erasure. Bull's Eye, Poncho, and Delilah circled me impatiently, eager to walk. "Off we go!"

Maybe Nellie could enlighten me about Tina.

Dad went and bought a second treadmill to work Bull's Eye and Poncho's endurance, while simultaneously strengthening Delilah with the springpole, claiming, "Efficiency's the name of the game. If you look at the broad picture. Know what I mean?" I wasn't one hundred percent sure, but he seemed to gradually understand I was going my own way. He had to plan how to care for them. Their coats gleamed from a new protein-intense diet, and their muscles rippled. Their jaw lines grew more pronounced after Dad raised the height and weight of the springpole. Only Delilah got crabby at times, lowering her brindled head and refusing tasks. Dad extemporized, "Bitch to the core."

Someone should've smacked him.

One Saturday, Dad returned from a long run with the dogs in the Forest Preserve, red-faced, his short hair wild. I asked, "When's the next pull?"

"Haven't decided. Might as well buff them up, though. The more muscular Bull's Eye gets, the more he's called to stud. I can always use the money. I been getting more in shape myself. My shoulders, my thighs, ache, all for the good." Even dressed for work in a shirt, apron, and trousers you could see the lines of definition of his fit body. He extracted a jar of instant coffee from the kitchen cabinet, boiled water in the microwave. "With you being Mr. Scholastic and such, I decided to take over more."

"Thanks Dad." I'd thought he didn't observe me, hadn't a clue. I felt strangely moved.

"Yeah."

"I'm still here, though." I'd been glad he'd given up the Happy Mart deliveries.

"Do you think about all I've done for you? Paying for dogs, the equipment. Vet. Your food. Your clothes."

"*I* buy my clothes." I'd been ten when he first handed me forty bucks and directed me onto the bus to Sears. That was that. He should have been impressed year after year I wasn't naked.

"Real taste you got, too."

"Like you got a clue." I walked out of the kitchen. Bull's Eye followed me, nails clicking on the wood floor in a dependable refrain.

Dad was close behind: "You can't take a damn joke, Dirk. You're at that age now where everyone else seems useless to you. But you should understand what I've wanted to do for you. I've been a good dad. I'm not stopping your pursuits."

It burned me up that when Dad chose to invest himself more, he turned it into a challenge. Like now I owed him even more. Where was *my* thanks? Jesus! Yet his insistence on being acknowledged was somehow edgy and pitiful, like he was suddenly alone, and I had done that to him.

Saturday's late afternoon light shot orange through the El windows, the downtown skyscrapers gleaming tall. I didn't aspire to walk the Mag Mile, flaunting shopping bags but, still, I had tightened the noose around my explorations, hardly ever coming downtown. These landscaped avenues, shiny sites and entrances, all kinds of scenes I'd never succumbed to, so caught in my habits with school and the dogs. As the buildings sped by, layers of steel, limestone, brick, copper, glass, I thought about architects. Someone graphed out the structural framework, the interdependence of materials. A fat equation and a result. A good profession.

Scattered passengers looked exhausted, exiting from the city's wear and tear. A grizzled black guy stared dully past me. We headed underground while the conductor sing-songed, "How many for WASHINGTONNN? JACKKKSSSON coming up my friends! HAARRISSSON?" My stop. I climbed up to the hiss of tires on hot asphalt. The evening was falling, going deep blue. Hotel and theater marquees flashed yellow, red and green enticements. Yellow and white cabs delivered people north and south. Nellie's red Mustang convertible waited by the curb with the hood down, the engine purring. I breathed in deeply.

She gesticulated, "Get in, get in!" And yanked me immediately into her warm hug. "Promise me you're hungry."

"Absolutely!"

She laughed, "Ah, I can teach you something! If your sweetie cooks you a meal, she's hoping you'll eat it all. She's feeding you her love, okay?" I nodded, grinning. "My God, you're tall, and fine looking. Yikes. *Has* anyone been making you special treats?"

"I just got dumped."

"That won't do! Believe me, anyone who leaves you has no smarts. A girl treats you bad now, she'll regret it someday; you just aren't there to know, see? High school relationships are nothing. Who was in love with Humphrey Bogart in high school?"

"Yeah, he was a real stud."

Nellie cuffed my arm, "Style, my boy. Backbone. The dark eyes."

"You think something's the matter with me?"

"Of course not!"

We pulled up to a redbrick ranch in the manicured neighborhood of Evergreen Park. "Its best feature is the yard," Nellie said. "The girls have a large area to run around and make mischief in. And they do." The lights shone inside, her whole place golden-colored. All at once, her dogs were greeting me enthusiastically. "Remember? Penny, Sandy, Betty and Millicent. Silly as ever. Tell those flirts to stay down." They were sleek, pictures of health and friendly exuberance. Happy dogs, well-loved. "Let's sit in the living room a sec. You like Otis?" I looked blank. She turned on her stereo and a deep grainy voice filtered through the room...*young girls they do get wearied.* "He died young in a plane crash. What a voice."

I listened.

"He makes you feel alive. All the Motown stuff does. Can't live without it." She sang along, "*Tryyy- ahh- little tenderneeess...*" If it mattered to Nellie, it mattered to me. I was suddenly aware that, unless we were in the basement working out, music just didn't run through our house.

Nellie pointed to the dining room, already set for dinner. "Let's eat." She lifted up a juicy T-bone steak. Then served us buttery carrots and string beans with flecks of onion. She winked, "German chocolate cake for dessert." I rubbed my belly. She urged, "Dirk, bring me up to date."

I found myself explaining Dad's new training regimen. When I described Delilah, Nellie shook her head, "He soured her. What a waste of a good dog. Truth is he'll *never* get what could really stun him because he won't *listen* to the dogs. He misses half the relationship, your Dad." She frowned, "Yet he's training them more. I suppose that's good; you know. The more you work with them, the more you find yourself connected, involved, which'll do him good, if you go away. You've got college. I was worried he wouldn't realize how much you've done over the years, the hours it takes. But if he tries to tell you Bull's Eye got ripped in a barbed wire fence, or Delilah ran into a wall, call me right away."

"What are you saying?"

"You know the bad uses the breed can be put to."

"Fighting? No, no. He's not that deranged. What would he do without his trophies?"

She studied me for the longest minute. "And our Poncho? My Penny's bloodline."

"He figures his way into or out of anything. That chump learned how to open the refrigerator." Nellie laughed in her pretty, musical way. She wore small gold hoop earrings, and gold bangle bracelets. Her nails were painted a peach-color, and her skin glowed in the warm light. Nellie made a person feel good.

Nellie played Smokey Robinson, more Otis, then The Supremes. "Motown doesn't waste time," she said. "Aims right for the heart." She danced, with a dish of German chocolate cake in hand, swaying to "Love Child." The dogs watched her, lying in her way, contentedly splayed out on the big round pillows she'd provided which they dragged over to favorite spots. Bones and toys littered the floor. "What lazy snobs," Nellie laughed. "Silly dogs. Hey, I should get you to the El soon."

"Not yet."

"You still blue, thinking about that girl? I wish your heart was never going to break. Trust that you learn something every time. Look at me. What happened with your Dad. I'll never risk one of my dogs again in a relationship. I misread him. I was weak, wanting things to work out. That happens, too, blind hope. But without him I wouldn't have met you."

"You're never coming back, though. That sucks."

"Come here. The door's always open. Dirk, it's one of the finer mysteries of life that not all traits get inherited. You are not your dad. You're college material, with a heart of gold. Handsome to boot. Dirk, you're going to make your own way, a better way." Nellie had seated herself straight across from me on the couch, and her brown eyes bored into me. "Listen to me. Become your own man." I nodded.

I smiled at her blissfully sacked-out girls. "In my next life I'm coming back as one of your dogs."

"You won't mind being a girl?" She arched her eyebrows. "Come on, let's get you home."

At the Harrison El stop, she waved, "Call soon. Meantime, don't let your Dad get away with murder." I nodded. I jammed my hands into my pockets, headed to the underground tracks. Two other people waited on the muggy platform. I jiggled foot to foot, hoping the next train wouldn't be long.

I bought a couple of sets of Motown classics. I reeled in Nellie's joy when I cranked up Marvin's Gaye's "Ain't That Peculiar?" My own mood perked up. I got hooked on Otis' "Sitting On The Dock of The Bay." Like it sang to every fiber of my being, defiant, mixed up.

Dad's eyes narrowed, "Where'd you pick that up?" Nellie had probably played Motown for Dad. Probably he hardly remembered.

Up and down Seth's hallways, where the biggest crowd pleasers were complaint and cynicism, I had Motown blasting possibility into my head. I would get the hell out soon. Climb over the horizon. A person could get thrown off track by the crap surrounding him, but that wasn't going to be me.

Dad assumed a new work schedule; his seniority at Happy Mart allowed him to hire an assistant manager. He came home earlier, and took off every other weekend. I walked the dogs in the mornings. But evenings he left to exercise them at a new training center. Poncho's white chest rippled with strength, his black poncho – as his back bulked up – spread into a cloak. Bull's Eye looked like he'd gotten jaw implants. All three dogs had concave trim waistlines, their legs flexing sharp tendons. I thought them too thin, but Dad was on fire about weight limits. More and more, when they were with me, I let them sniff and meander and goof off. Delilah licked my hand in affection, melting me with this habit from her old happier self.

One afternoon, right as we passed a Rottie, Poncho and Bull's Eye lowered their heads and growled. I yanked their leashes, hissing into their faces, "No! Don't you dare!" I drove their ears to flatten back, eyes down to the ground. Dad wasn't looking after their temperaments like I always had.

I cornered Dad. He waved me off. "If the Rottie raised his hackles, they responded."

"We never allowed that!"

"Where we train, there's lots more dogs. Ours are doing great, just a little more self-protective. Don't tell me you've never seen 'em edgy? Never? Not once? Come on."

"Do right by the dogs."

"Don't you dare question me. You're not hanging around tending to me, or them, in our old age, right Mr. Free-as-a-bird? Watch you don't burst your private brain bubble."

Dad's perception was that college was for delicate people who needed a whole extra level of instructions. "Ain't no one can teach life." He rounded corners with no backward glance, no nostalgia. "And another thing; ever noticed how people with degrees talk hours about a damn comma, but can't fix their own sink faucet? Damn useless, *help me, help me*, like babies in diapers. Can't deny I trained you to take care of stuff. That's how you'll stand out."

What mattered to me most was that the dogs remain *ours*.

My senior year, between filling out cartloads of financial aid forms, and tutoring, the days flew. My first choice was the University of Illinois at Champaign-Urbana's Engineering program. I needed a scholarship. I memorized and reviewed and analyzed and re-interpreted repeatedly, taking AP Physics, AP Calculus, pinning my hopes on the grueling hours of study. Michael jabbed me from behind as I sat bent in concentration in the Seth library, "You're so damn smart. Yet you're such the fretful old lady."

"Hate to break it to you, but some of us work our brains not our brawn."

"Ouch." Three colleges had approached him with baseball scholarships. He leaned over, "Like your brains fried or over-easy?"

I shook my head. But I'd have been damn lonely if he hadn't assigned himself to be my personal pain in the ass. I was more alone than ever. I flipped test questions through my mind like index cards. Senior year zoomed by. Now and again, Michael dragged me to a movie or a concert. He'd insist he'd already paid; I'd piss him off if I wasted the ticket. So, occasionally I met girls. Michael found nothing extraordinary in this. He trusted that girls were part of how the planet worked. Sometimes, a girl leaned into me, chatting. I couldn't refuse her attention. I liked a girl's soft downy arms, or the glide of her fingertip on my shoulder. Under their elastic bras, their breasts lingered soft as ice-cream. Touching them, my prick flew up against my jeans. I took care of that later, when I was alone. But I didn't warm up to any girl. Tina had put me on alert. I didn't want to undergo interrogation. Why didn't I want to meet her friends? Why didn't I ever hang? Did I think I was better than other people? Besides, these strange girls came and went with the events. With no more need for me. I found this insulting and a relief. After being let off the hook, I moved awkwardly back to my studies.

April came. My life centered on the mailbox. Crowding with useless flyers, coupons, bills. On the first real warm day, the sensation of spring finally in the air, I stuck my hand into a thickly stuffed box. A hefty white envelope sported the return address of the University of Illinois at Champaign-Urbana. I carried it to the kitchen table, put it down, and stared. As if it might move. It was fat, nice and fat. I sliced it open. But I couldn't seem to put my hand in to pull the papers out. My eyes closed. I wanted to die right there, to refuse to be on the fence, played with. But I shook myself out of this. It was fat. My fingers plunged in:

...Congratulations! ... You have been accepted to the University of Illinois... We are pleased to welcome you...

It had happened! For *me.* Me. My smile stretched ear to ear. I was elastic! I had to remind myself to breathe. I read on:

Please review the financial aid package being offered...

Yes, without that, acceptance meant nothing. I lifted the yellow sheets, titled FINANCIAL AID:

Dirk Seward... in recognition of your outstanding academic record, and upon careful review of financial criteria, we are pleased to award you a full scholarship to attend University of Illinois at Champaign-Urbana...your quick reply is required... Yes! Yes! Yes! All the studying, the insane forms, they *had* added up. My eyes stung, a lump formed in my throat. I gripped the back of a kitchen chair, steadying my breathing. I blinked my eyes dry. I inhaled deeply, gratefully. Then I ran into my room and catapulted myself on the bed. I leapt up and ran outside, shouting to the dogs, "I did it!!! I did!!" They rushed over, jumping with me: *yes, yes, yes!* I grabbed Bull's Eye's front paws and danced. His tongue lolled like a drunk gangster's, "You and me boy, we made it!"

But this wasn't Dad's impression. "You're sure about this?"

"Look at the paperwork, Dad. It's real."

"Chicago's got a college every two blocks. Not much reason to go out of town is there?" He spoke more quietly than usual, and this made me listen, to fathom him, fencing off my disappointment.

"But you knew I was going away, you said so."

"I thought, yeah, you'd move to the dorms, perhaps. In the city. I've been upping the ante, working the dogs, to see what their maximum potential is. You and me barely started with Bull's Eye, amateurs. Poncho's in his prime; he's hardly been tapped. I never had much occasion; having you, plus working so much overtime. Now I do. But I might need your help."

I practically exploded out of my skin: "This is the biggest thing that's ever happened to me! My God, celebrate!"

"It's great and all, Dirk. Yes, really, congratulations! But it's self-centered. I thought you'd be growing out of that, by now. Anyway, they should've told you it's cheaper to live at home. You're lucky I'm strong and able, so you wouldn't have to do anything here but study. You and me, Batman and Robin."

"What?"

"Wait, Michael's going. Is that it?"

"Nope."

"Guess I made it easy for you to leave. You're not a chip off the old block. Ever think about other people, like, say, your own father?"

I don't know exactly what I felt. I spun, dizzy with rage and pity, bewilderment, betrayal, and disgust. Nellie always said I wasn't like him, yet I was his and he mine. Now we were traveling a million miles an hour in different directions so fast I couldn't even see. What had I or had I *not* done? Dad looked beaten, his hair thinning, two thick creases cut across his forehead. Ice trickled through my heart, being in my own skin hurt.

When I got to Seth, that following morning, Mr. Davario already knew. He slapped me on the back, "You're going to do great things, Dirk. You've been a steady gift to me. You've made my teaching real; you're rare. Now, promise me you'll write when you're there. No reason to lose touch." He reached his arm around my shoulder, his grip quick and friendly.

"I swear, Mr. Davario, I couldn't have done it without you."

"You're wrong about that." He laughed, "I know you."

More than ever, I recognized his importance.

Around me, in the halls, were all the people I'd never gotten to know. Their presence suddenly seemed benign, swarms of ants building anthills, fish darting side by side in a school. This fall, I'd leave Chicago, looking to the future. I could get through anything until then.

Then Dad went and put the dogs in a kennel.

Michael dragged me to graduation parties, "You only live once, man!" I was in such a fine mood I meandered through blaring basements for once at ease. Because I'd made it out. That multi-syllabic name: *University of Illinois at Champaign-Urbana* played day and night into my happy ears. They'd started sending paperwork – informational documents, legal forms, medical releases – lots to return. In a fit of joyful determination, I bought myself a graduation present, a dinged-up old green Ford Fiesta, to get me to Champaign. A means to travel with the dogs at some point. More bang for the buck overall than a cell phone, I thought. Dad had taken one look at my Fiesta parked outside the house: "You never heard of busses, Rockefeller?"

But the meager savings that had bought it were mine.

The house, now dogless, was a tomb. I clicked open the lock. No welcome. No eager barking from the yard. Only the hollowness of each room. No eyes watching my next move, keen to follow. Now and again Bull's Eye had been temporarily gone when Dad put him to stud. But it had been forever since I'd faced utter silence like this. Dad refused to give me the kennel address, "Think about it from their point of view. They're adjusting. You show up and confuse them." I scavenged through his drawers, closets, and pockets for a business card or a scrawled kennel number, and came up with nothing.

"You couldn't wait until I left?"

"The world revolves around you, does it?"

When I reached Nellie, she said: "Dogs shouldn't be kenneled permanently. Your Dad knows that. Maybe there's acreage, agility courses; some of these facilities have fantastic stuff. I mean, he's going there, training them, right?"

"Seems yeah."

"Look, when your dad's hurt, he goes on attack. You're calling your own shots. Let him get pissy. He'll move the dogs back after while."

Weeks passed. Dad went straight from work to the training center. I intended to tail him, but hadn't gotten to it, what with so much end of school year stuff. Graduation day came. Dad sat in a back row of the assembly hall where I couldn't see him. When it was over, he ambled up, bashful. "Hey, I was thinking I'm the one showed you the way to books. Free, from the library. Remember?"

"Yeah." We'd gone to learn about dogs. A million years ago. When he'd been my guide.

He whacked my back, surveying my graduation gear, "Nothing like seeing you in a dress."

That evening, I went over to Michael's big blast of a party. Summer surrounded us like a promise. Everyone had something new to tell. We'd all been living toward this, these changes, paths of our own making. Our optimism charged the air.

It was an early June evening, darkening slowly, a few days later. Planes flickered across the sky. I sat out on my porch being damn lazy, nursing a filched beer. Beginning tomorrow, between tutoring stints, I'd be delivering Dominos Pizza from 3-11 p.m. Everything I'd resented calmly interested me in light of my departure; our lopsided porch, the cracked cement sidewalks, the salty smell of Chicago when it got hot. I was debating when I'd get off my ass and follow Dad. Then Poncho stumbled up the sidewalk, lurching in the dark.

He stood out even in the dim streetlight. Half his head mauled through to its pink underside. He panted through his split lower lip, this triangle of skin dangling like a handkerchief.

His backside was sticky with blood. He had to have been hit by a car. I ran down, trying to figure out how to hold him without hurting him, "Poncho, boy, where you been?" In a panic, I lifted his wet body into the backseat of my Ford. Smearing the blood off my hands onto my jeans, I drove, ignoring stop signs, aware Dr. Lance would be closed this late, the closest potential help a place that suddenly flashed into my unclear mind, the Noah's Ark Animal Sanctuary I'd passed on the school bus for years, not even sure what it was.

I barged through their door, holding Poncho, blood seeping through my hands, my t-shirt. Poncho bled like a sprinkler system. Some women shouted, "Quick! Go to the back!" Poncho kept his swollen eyes firmly glued on me as I ran. The air clung like a sopping rag, Poncho's sixty pounds to my chest. All I could guess was that he'd gotten loose. He was so damn *lucky*. To have found his way all the way from the suburbs. Man!

A nearly bald woman was upon me in their emergency area, pulling Poncho out of my arms, laying him on a big towel on a metal table, touching him all over, while his eyes fixated on me. I snapped, "Slow down, please. Be gentle!"

This plucked lady bared her teeth at me. Then cooed at Poncho, "Poor baby, the Vet specialist isn't here." She shoved her finger in my face and hissed: "Are you proud of yourself?"

"What?"

"Gillian!" Another younger woman, Gillian, ran over. She too prodded Poncho, immediately lathering him in white antibiotic cream. Over which she plastered a checkerboard of gauze squares. Within seconds, the gauze was bloody through and through. Gillian harangued me, "What the hell is the matter with you guys?" She addressed her colleague; "Mindy, get the van, fill it with blankets. This dog needs hospitalization. Immediately." She flashed on me, "We've got him now."

I stuttered stupidly, "He fled the kennel. Poncho, big boy, hang in there." I leaned in to rub his head

"Don't touch him!" Gillian turned to Mindy, "Can Phoebe process the release form?"

Mindy nodded, "Wait."

I stood between a compact metal sink and a bulletin board layered with pictures of cheery adoptions. Poncho focused anxiously on me, his body stiffening like a log. I murmured: "Poncho, hey buddy, Poncho." My legs shook. I put my hands to my face, and felt them sticky with blood. When a dog's face unpeels, his blood pumps out of hundreds of spurting capillaries. Poncho did not even whimper in that pain. He stared quizzically, as if asking: *What happened, Dirk?* I was supposed to answer. A headache thundered into my skull.

Mindy and Gillian ran back in with blankets; "Hurry. He'll dehydrate."

"Are you ready for the paperwork?" A high school girl held out a towel for me. "Maybe you want to clean up, first?" Her brow furrowed, an act magnified in its concern, the first kindness after these crazed others. Her eyes were gray-green like a stream. Her finger indicated a bathroom door. "I'll wait here," she murmured.

I stumbled toward the restroom. I slumped onto the toilet seat. Trying to gather my wits. Tears of grief and frustration stung the back of my eyes. When I emerged with at least my hands and face clean, I asked, "What's your name?"

"I need *your* name and data for the release form."

"No, tell me."

She was slim with dark shiny hair pulled into a ponytail. Her skin white, flawless like the inside of a tea cup. She looked serious and slightly afraid. I quickly explained, "Those ladies misunderstood. I would never hurt Poncho. Ever." I replayed his head lolling on the table.

"But you do want him cared for?"

"Of course."

"You have to release him to us then."

I grabbed the triple-copy sheet, furiously signed *Russ Seward*. But I clutched the paperwork. "Tell me your name."

"Phoebe."

"You live in Chicago?"

"No, I fly in from Dallas where I'm mayor." She shook her head. "My mom and I volunteer here. The release forms?"

I thrust them at her. Images of Poncho jammed in my head. A wave of exhaustion rolled through me. I felt nauseous.

"Thank you for the towel, Phoebe." She nodded. "I'll phone tomorrow about Poncho."

The hot night rushed around my ears as I drove home, windows open. Blood stained the back seat like a grizzly murder scene. I showered a long time, scrubbing to remove every trace of fur and sweat and blood.

I sat out back out on the porch, staring at the floorboards' peeling gray paint, trying to get something back. Bull's Eye had practically raised Poncho. I'd held Poncho when he was a goofy-looking pup with his eyes shut, a black patch hanging over his back like a blanket, which is how I named him. Where was Bull's Eye that they hadn't escaped together? Bull's Eye after all, the alpha, the mainline, my lifeline. Or Delilah? The night hit me like a tidal wave. Dad was nowhere to be found. I went inside and crashed into a deep burdened sleep.

I woke to the smell of coffee. Dad slouched in his pajamas, looking haggard. I poured myself a cup. I told him about the night. He said, "Now they have him; he's gone."

I smacked my hand on the kitchen table, "What? No, he isn't. How the hell did he get loose?"

"Too clever for his own good."

"That's not an answer."

"You know how smart he is. How determined." Explaining nothing.

"What happened?"

Dad shrugged, "He wasn't with me. And, buddy, I don't answer to you."

"So *what* happened? Jesus! And what about Bull's Eye?"

"I don't frickin' know yet."

"You should!" I stormed to my room. My head exploding, I slammed one book, then another, against the wall. I kicked my chair, knocking it to the floor. I hurled my shoes at the door. My brain flashed a gigantic neon sign over Dad: KING ASSHOLE. Poncho's muzzle hanging loose like the flap of a purse probably required sixty stitches or more. That he had found me through the maze of Chicago's streets was more astonishing than I could account for. But Poncho stopped at nothing to get what he wanted. I wanted to punch my fist through the wall.

Flat on my bed, I reviewed the previous night. The ladies had been yelling at me while my whole body shook, handing over Poncho. At least that girl, Phoebe, hadn't joined them. Her curious eyes swam in my brain. It was important she know I'd never hurt Poncho. When it was time to get him back, when he healed, I must talk more to her.

Leaving for work, Dad slammed the door, "You're not getting him out of there, genius."

I ate a bowl of Wheat Chex, glaring at the yard we'd fenced in years ago together. Four years ago, Poncho had been a puppy wagging his silly rear end. Now he was battling to stay alive. From a hit-and-run. Followed by a scrape, maybe with some stray dog. Dad hadn't known he was loose.

I phoned Noah's Ark, but phone service was limited to evening hours, six to nine. When I pulled in the parking lot around sunset, seven or eight people ambled on the shabby front lawn, walking these shelter dogs. A skinny old guy in the waiting room in a t-shirt with the giant head of a groomed poodle asked whether I wanted to adopt a dog or a cat.

"Last night, someone named Phoebe did my paperwork. I need to speak with her."

"You'll have to catch her on a Tuesday or Wednesday night. But I can process any papers for you."

"Is a black and white pit bull here?"

"Nope. Lost your dog?"

I shook my head. "Do you get paid to work here?"

"Are you joking?"

"Sorry. Thanks anyway."

I drove home. Poncho could not have lost so much blood he wouldn't make it. Not if they'd stitched him up right, immediately. He had a survivor's soul. What if I hadn't had my car? Funny, I'd envisioned my summer as a series of pleasant drives through the cool of night. I called Dominos, to schedule Tuesdays and Wednesdays as my nights off. To visit Poncho. I'd get Poncho safely home soon. I'd describe to Phoebe everything he could do.

The following evening, I drove by the Ark but Poncho still wasn't out. At least, I'd scrubbed my Ford so it no longer looked like a crime scene. That night, when everyone was long gone, I scouted the building's perimeters. I couldn't see in anywhere. I stopped by a couple of evenings later, but they still had no knowledge of Poncho. I worried incessantly, maniacally. I slept badly, mangled visions of Poncho pulsating through every synapse.

I focused on Phoebe's next shift at Noah's Ark; she seemed rare now, in being clear-headed. I drove up Chase Street to Clark then Howard. I composed my thoughts, playing Otis. He soothed me. Motown did. Phoebe would bring me to Poncho. Otis keened, and the sky seemed to inhale his voice, the curve of blue becoming richer, my heart thinking possibility ... *young girls they do get wearied ... try-y-y a little tenderness...*

I pulled into Noah's Ark's parking lot.

Volunteers again walked dogs of all shapes, most straining against their leashes, wanting to meet and socialize, but the careful volunteers kept them apart. A frantic white Scottie jumped circles around a fluffy-haired woman. I entered the plain cinder block and brick building, stepping into the waiting area. A woman in scrubs, with a froth of brown curls, appeared briskly addressing me, "I'm Terry. Can I help you?"

I said, "I don't believe so. I'm looking for Phoebe."

"Why?"

"She processed some paperwork I need."

"What about?"

"Whoa, why is this an interrogation?" Their human holding pen?

All at once, Phoebe materialized. "Mom, they need you on this adoption call."

"Did you work with this man?"

Phoebe grew pink. Her mother scowled. "Mom, the phone?" Phoebe gestured.

"Okay, okay, they can't wait two minutes?" Terry left, shaking her head at the ceiling.

I spoke quickly, "Phoebe?"

"I think we're done."

"I need to see Poncho. I came to thank you for helping the other night. And to ask when he'll be ready to leave."

"You're kidding?" She toyed with the tip of her shoe. She had this translucent rosy-blue skin. Her lips were plump and shiny like gummy bears.

"Can we talk somewhere?"

"I can't." She sounded alarmed. "I won't." Then tense. "You bring a dog in that condition, and you think we'll hand him back? Don't think so."

"He was being boarded at a reputable kennel. No one knows yet how he got out. Or how he made it back home."

"Someone from this '*kennel*' needs to explain things." She pressed one hand into the other, tensely kneading her thoughts.

"How about someone here explains why this '*sanctuary*' is more like a jail." I suddenly wished I hadn't said that.

Her beautiful jade eyes turned hard. "I don't like being toyed around. Talk to someone else."

"I'm not playing!"

She pushed her hand up her cheek as if she could wipe away her high color: "Good-bye." And turned away. I sat down, on the waiting room bench, my hands dangling like dead rats.

Within an instant, Phoebe's mom was back, "Really, can't I help?"

"Oh, you will."

I exited in long angry strides. Who were these weirdo people with their antechambers and ownership claims? I fired up the ignition, glancing into the rearview mirror. Phoebe watched from the back entry. Maybe she hadn't meant to be so hard. I cut off the engine. She was gone.

I phoned Michael, "It's been this day — Catch you at McMinty's?"

McMinty's was our favorite place, a combination wood-paneled bar and family restaurant. Michael and I liked the booths and the large-screen TVs. My brain roared with confusion. Like I was that poor guy on trial in a Kafka novel I' d read in English class, accused with no explanation.

"Hey, man--" Michael whacked me on the back. He slung down across from me. "You sounded pissed."

"I've just come from the Twilight Zone." I told him the whole screwed-up story.

"You're going to college, man! Can't let cuckoo animal maniacs twist you up."

Dad's first response replayed in my head: "You idiot. Animal shelter people are fanatic like Jehovah's Witnesses."

I'd argued: "How do you know?"

The Cubs came on McMinty's big screen. Michael ordered cokes. "Jesus, will you look at Kyle Farnsworth? Does he think he's tossing Easter eggs?" Farnsworth was removed and Michael cheered, "Damn straight." He turned to me, "They think Sosa can guarantee it all. They're going to bring him down with the rest." The Cubs lost. "Someone should strangle Ed Lynch. The man can't build a team."

"They're saying Poncho's been fought."

"Bullshit. Animal activists are fanatics. But, man, you're leaving in two months; you can't look after Poncho. Or Bull's Eye and Delilah. Your dad dropped the ball. Maybe it's for the best?"

"Screw that."

Michael gave my arm a shove. He'd gotten a full athletic scholarship to UIC. "You're an A-hole for leaving town."

"It's a short drive. You damn well better visit."

The kennel people offered Dad some vagueness about an unexpected broken gate. I obsessed over Bull's Eye and Delilah's safety.

Dad philosophized, "If your shelter's decided Poncho's been fought, you could be Jesus Christ and couldn't change their minds. They got the moral advantage on you, Dirk. They'll never give that up. It sucks."

"You get him out then."

A sneer slithered up and over his face. "And have them call the cops on me because they're convinced he's been in the pit? You're outstanding college material."

"Send your deficient kennel guy."

Dad plowed his graying thinning hair back with his tense fingers. He grimaced through his new brown-rimmed glasses. "You move on, Dirk. You move *on*. You've always been one to stew forever. It's a sickness with you." He batted his hand, dismissing me.

Sunday, on my fourteenth pizza transaction, half an hour to go before eleven, I had a whole ten dollars in tips in my pocket, wondering what I'd been thinking when I took this job. People are so weird in the city, the way they barely open the door to you, like you're about to run in with an Uzi, like Dominos is a huge decoy establishment for terrorist raids. I was eager to finish the last crappy night's drop-off: four extra-large, thin-crust, pepperoni pizzas. At a big white stucco house, two guys opened the door, blasting music. Before handing over the pizzas, you require payment, but I was holding four pizzas, so I forked them over to pull out the bill. "Yeah, hang on a minute," the guy in a yellow t-shirt said, closing the door. He didn't return. I rang. Repeatedly. I pounded on the door. It was a blistering hot night, and they were screwing me over. But I wasn't going to leap through any ground floor window. This was Dominos' problem, their damn pizzas.

I dialed my manager, who started yelling. I shot back. "Hey. Call the cops!" *This is my world. These are the jerks I serve.* People with nothing better to do than these stunts. And then I knew, as a non sequitur I suppose, why a man might do anything for love. It was the only balance to this shit. Without it, you wallowed in crap. My seesaw needed to tip, lift me high up and away. I didn't want to go back to remembering Phoebe, but I did, because she thought I was scum, which I didn't like. When I got to Dominos, the cops were headed over to the jerks' house and the manager recommenced shouting. I imagined him sunk under water, his big bass mouth blowing bubbles.

The dogs had always stopped me from asking: Is this all there is? Is this freakin' *it*? With sixty days left until college, Poncho was recovering in a shelter, Bull's Eye and Delilah were lost to me, somewhere deep over the horizon. Though I pondered the who, what, where, when, and why, of this I had squat. All at once, I wondered: How had those busy volunteers at Noah's Ark gotten there? The next evening I phoned.

A woman on the other end of the line worked her script: "Volunteer shifts are from six to nine every evening. An evening of training and an evening of shadowing an experienced volunteer are required. If you sign up, you're expected to show. Are you aware abandoned dogs can be a handful?"

"Makes sense."

"If you volunteer, you'll end up liking animals a lot more than people."

"I already do."

"Can you train Wednesdays or Saturdays?"

I remembered the original hysterical women worked on a Saturday. "Wednesdays."

A few days later, I was there, in a side room, answering a yellow form about whether I'd ever put a pet to sleep, or witnessed animal cruelty. Why did I want to volunteer? How would I describe myself?

"We like to know our volunteers," Martha, my teacher, smiled.

Two middle-aged ladies scribbled next to me. We were shown a video on domestic animal behavior in captivity, including dog aggressiveness, the anti-social nature of feral cats, how to open cages to prevent an animal from escaping, the proper disinfecting procedures in between walking dogs, and the required steps to cleaning cement cages.

I didn't see Phoebe anywhere.

Michael thought this was a terrible idea. "You're going to get angry, dumb ass, and then?"

"How's baseball?" Training at UIC was supposedly rigorous.

"Stakes are still low. No games yet."

"You could be delivering pizzas."

"You alone came up with that sorry-ass job."

"I thought I'd be spending my *days* with the *dogs*."

Noah's Ark scheduled me to 'shadow' Terry, who didn't recognize me. She tossed her short brown curls authoritatively, "We wash our hands before we approach the dogs. Disease, here, can spread like wildfire. So we're zealots about hygiene. Sounds rigid until you see a kennel outbreak." Terry pointed to a couple of sinks, smiled, and we washed hands side by side. Her t-shirt said: ASK ME ABOUT MY RELIGION. She showed me the grid of hooks on the wall: "Leashes hang here. Dogs in clean cages get walked first as a reward. We'll take Captain."

We entered a green-tiled space with row upon row of cement block cages fronted by chain link doors into a shrill, frantic barking. The stench of feces and urine battled with the sharp effect of disinfectant being sprayed with a hose into the already emptied cages. Poncho was somewhere. Dogs threw themselves against their chain link doors as we passed, nails madly scratching the floors, snouts pushing hard against the metal hinges, barking and barking. Terry said, "Wardens are city employees, and don't care. They chat on the phone in their offices all day while the dogs go stir crazy. Finally, evenings, we volunteers show up."

Captain, a German shepherd, methodically sniffed my shoes and Terry's. He had smart honey-colored eyes, and a thick rust-colored coat. Terry noted, "He came in skinny but we're fattening him up." Outside he undertook a thorough olfactory investigation of the length of the fence. "Now he's got your scent; he could pick out your car. Super smart." She squinted, reciting: *"The wolf shall dwell with the lamb, the leopard shall lie down with the kid, the calf and the young lion and the fatling together, and a little child shall lead them.* Isaiah. 11: 6. Guess we got a ways to go!"

Despite all my dog functions, I'd never been in a shelter. "That, yes." We were at the far end of the lawn with Captain. When Phoebe exited with Poncho. My muscled boy tugged, but not too hard because Dad and I had taught him manners. Phoebe knelt and rubbed his ears, concentrating. Then she nuzzled his sewn-together mug in the crook of her arm. He studied her, licked her, his tail wagging happily. He lifted his paws in alternating steps, expressing his excitement, his typical busy self: *Let's go here, no, no, even better further on, can I meet that bitch? Wow, there's a good smell right at the base of this tree! Aren't there any sticks you can throw me?* My heart cracked, watching him. He epitomized that expression; dogged enthusiasm. Phoebe was attentive and gentle, not perfunctory. As a puppy, Poncho'd slept fitfully, running in his sleep. He'd become this survivor, my brave boy.

Terry spoke, "We don't let the dogs interact. To monitor aggression, and communicable illnesses; parvo, kennel-cough, parasites, worms." Captain diagnosed the building's ground-line.

Phoebe's chestnut hair gleamed like something watery in the sun. But her face froze spotting us. She wore shorts, an oversized blue T-shirt, and white cloth sneakers. Poncho lifted his nose, sensing something, before he found me. All at once, he went into full horsepower, dragging Phoebe.

Terry continued, "Once over-excited, a dog could bite a volunteer. For the rest of his life, he's unadoptable."

Poncho leapt up, mad to greet me, paws pressing my stomach. I clutched him, hugging hard and happy. Terry cried, "Lord have mercy! We'll have a dog fight on our hands!" She lurched the rather indifferent Captain away, shouting, "Phoebe?!"

"He just took off!" Phoebe yanked Poncho away.

I shouted, "He likes me! He likes me, that's all."

Her face now scarlet, Phoebe shouted, "Please get away! Sorry! Sorry!" She hauled Poncho off, though he dug in his heels, swiveling madly to locate me. Anger shot like mercury up my spine. Terry snapped, "That new dog could've provoked Captain!"

"He wasn't aggressive!"

"It takes one second!" She pursed her lips. "We're not risk-takers, here. You do understand that?" After thirty seconds of tense silence, glaring first at me, then at the horizon, she pointed glumly to a large canister. "We dispose the dog poop here."

I glanced back at Phoebe, who stared at me in disbelief. She knelt, her arm around Poncho, working on his agitated state, whispering in his ear. I churned inside; this girl had a tangled kindness. Poncho turned, eyes bored into me, wide, waiting, asking. I was riding a half-baked plan.

Terry handed me over to two women inside who introduced themselves through their volunteer histories. They showed me the location of water bowls, dog food, and disinfectant, while they recited tabloids of mistreatment; an arthritic poodle found huddled in a parking lot during a hailstorm; a Rottweiler whose chain link leash had grown embedded into her neck flesh; a spastic homeless mutt who had chased his tail daily until he vomited, again and again. Each dog put into the world without a plan to end up here. Scared, circling their cages desperately, tearing at their fur, paws raw from bizarre obsessed chewing. Some lingered by their doors in brown-eyed wonder, whining gently at anyone who passed by. Animal refugees in a holding camp; so many.

My first task was to fill the dogs' water bowls. I fitted a bowl through the metal slot that lifted for this purpose, when I saw Phoebe leading Poncho to his cage. I hurried over, just as she closed him in. A large tag had re-named him Manny. Phoebe hissed: "What are you doing here?"

"Come to see my dog." But I didn't want to antagonize her. "I can't sleep, I can't eat. This is undoing me."

Poncho barked as we locked him in, tilting his hurt head, as if to say to me: *Didn't I work hard enough, for you, always?*

I pressed on, "Can't we talk? You're the only person here who isn't retirement age."

Phoebe's hands balled into fists. Her voice shook: "This place is no joke!" She pointed to a placard affixed to the green tiled wall. "Read." In blue lettering it said:

> *The moral progress of a nation*
> *can be judged by how it treats its animals.*

Mohandas Ghandi

"But I agree."

"You're using us to pay your vet bill!" Her collarbone rose and fell, a tightly trapped little triangle.

"No, I'll pay anything to get him back."

Her voice rose, exasperated, "Why am *I* involved?" Her face scrunched up, "You're used to girls flattering you."

I choked, "I don't think so."

Her eyes lost their hardness, puzzled. "You're not lying to me?" When she let down her guard, her face had such a pretty grace.

"I haven't lied to you once."

Her eyes shifted quickly away. "We'd better feed the dogs."

There was upset-stomach dog food called I.D. for sick or really freaked-out dogs, which was most of them. Others were still young enough to need puppy food. The rest were fed dry and wet food in a range of proportions determined by size. Some devotedly licked the bowl clean. Others ate a bit, then turned the bowl upside down and played Chase-the-Kibbles. One small beagle mix wouldn't eat at all; he watched the arrival of water and food with mournful eyes.

Terry appeared, wagging her finger for me to follow. "Come to the office to sign the volunteer release form." I followed. "Dirk, you go to church?"

I lied, "Yes ma'am."

"Good, honey, good." Terry enthusiastically gripped my arm. I signed.

"Could you wash the dirty bowls?" Emptied metal bowls were stacked high near the large sink. I filled the sink with soapy water, plunged into the bubbles and started scrubbing.

Phoebe appeared with a dishtowel. I was curious: "You and your mom close?"

"When I came along, she was in her early forties, had given up hoping she'd conceive. Her life since has been looking after me. We pretty much do everything together. You have siblings?"

"Nope."

"Guess the dogs are my extended family."

"Funny how that happens." As Phoebe dried, rubbing in circles, a silver ID bracelet with the initials *WWJD* dipped over her wrist. "Did your boyfriend give you that?"

She raised her eyebrows. "*What Would Jesus Do?*"

"Oh."

Her eyes crinkled into sparkly amusement. "My *dad* bought it for me."

I wasn't making a great impression, but felt hopeful enough to ask. "Can we walk Poncho together?"

His rear wagged like crazy. My eyes stung, tearing, salty. He showed his best behavior, sitting and waiting patiently for Phoebe to open the cage door, then looking up for me to indicate when he should move. He honored the discipline we knew, our secret code. "Who decided I can't get him back?" I asked.

"You signed papers legally making him the shelter's."

"I signed my father's name."

"Look." Phoebe pointed to Poncho's neck. "These are bite marks." Poncho stared at me, as if to say: *See what wild old stories we make up around here.*

"But you see what you want to see." She stepped back as if I'd struck her. Poncho's ears pricked up, his legs stock-still, on alert. I plunged on. "Listen, when I was a kid, an old grandma opossum crawled into our yard. Our dog, Bull's Eye, was sleeping on the deck. Crazy. That opossum must have weighed over 100 pounds. We heard a noise like you wouldn't believe. It took Bull's Eye maybe five minutes to kill her. He was still bit through and through and all clawed up. Twenty stitches. And thank God his rabies shot held. He looked fought, just like Poncho now."

She quietly traced a line up and down her sleek arm, "It's uncomfortable being the only one who knows who you are."

"Look, he's my life. I don't have much else."

Her ears and cheeks went pink, "Oh, put him back."

I felt her locking me inside myself. Declaring innocence wasn't enough. I would have shouted if I had known what to shout.

When I reappeared to volunteer next Wednesday, people grabbed leashes, skirting past me, hurrying outside. I joined the action with a skinny pit named Goldie. She'd exploded out of her cage, half-strangling herself to get out. When she realized she was tied to me, she chomped enthusiastically on her leash, skittering, backing up like I was a huge tug toy. She was so ardent, in fact, she tipped herself over. I pulled her to order, shortening the leash to get her moving tightly beside me. She had no idea why. The world must seem wacky to her. Who were these absent owners who'd expected their pets to train themselves, as if dogs were born knowing how to navigate human territory? It was a kind of un-loving, this unwillingness to devote oneself to a dog's potential. What a life to saddle your dog with; directionless and spastic. If you taught the dog nothing, then the best it could do was to guess wildly. You grew the dog into a world without meaning. You demeaned it.

My temples dripped in this thick Chicago summer heat. I wiped my face with the bottom of my T-shirt. Then a finger poked me. I swung around. "You're back," Phoebe whispered, her lips rosy and moist, wisps of her hair loose in curlicues.

"Did you rat on me?"

"No."

"You would have had me wrong."

Goldie stepped disoriented on Phoebe's sneakers, rubbed herself against Phoebe. Phoebe tousled Goldie's head, rubbed her skinny flanks, "Poor homeless girl." Her connection to dogs warm and palpable. She busily tucked back loose hair, as she asked, "Can we start over?"

I almost fell on my face.

"I want to know you. Just, I can't stand lies."

I pressed my advantage, "Okay, yes."

"Okay. From now on."

During the perplexing interim days since I'd seen her, Phoebe'd raised waves in my fishbowl brain. She'd swum under my skin. I'd been furious with her, but her watery eyes had shifted back and forth, twisting me in a dance. Her eyelids were rimmed in a bruised lavender. Her body was wraith-like, like she'd slip away, vanish in a twist of smoke. Lying in bed, pressure built in my groin. I imagined her leaning back in my arms, her jade eyes tender, her skin smooth as silk. I felt my own size as a barrier. When I'd been angry with her, I'd somehow felt huge. If only my heft could feel like a bulwark, a source of solidity, safe. If safety would help her feel easy and free. Freedom what she seemed to hunger for. I wanted her to trust me. I whispered, "I swear to God I have not lied."

She nodded. "Do you think love for animals is genetic?" Her dragonfly green eyes blinked, and she shook her head: "*That* sounded stupid." Her unblemished skin was nearly opalescent.

"You'll help me with Poncho's paperwork?"

"You still want to use me."

"Is that what asking for help is?" I'd avoided needing others my whole life.

"Can be." She pulled on her cuticles; I saw the jagged edges. "My parents are Fundamentalists. The thinking is, it's okay for some people to get out there in the world, be lightning rods for evangelism and such. So I wasn't home-schooled. But you know Rapunzel, locked in a high tower. It's been like that."

"The girl with all the hair? You need Prince Charming." I laughed.

She looked flustered, "Yeah it's funny from the outside. But I'm crazy reactive now to anything that smells like a lie. I've been surrounded by them all my life, and I'm not taking any more."

Someone yelled for Phoebe from the front office.

I found Poncho waiting in his cage. He flung his belly up in utter abandon. I massaged his torso; then, gently, his thick stitched-up white and black head. *Just a little while more, buddy. Get well, okay?* His tail thumped. *Then it's you and me, got it?* As I was closing him back in, full of misgivings, Phoebe appeared with a water bowl. I lifted the slot. Her hand retreated. I slid my fingers over hers, as if by accident. Her arm jolted back, suddenly brushing my chest. My heart did a small flip. Did Phoebe like big-boned blond boys? "Water for the others – too?" she asked in a tiny voice.

My tongue stuck

Cage by cage, we moved in rhythm, pouring and delivering water. She spoke to each dog, "Rufus, silly guy, was the Kong full? Noodles, you finally getting nice and plump? Girlie, bat those big brown eyes when the adopters come." She offered herself to them sweetly. My leg grazed hers. I felt her warm light regular breath, calm and arousing. I knew about girls who did everything with their mothers: shopped, went to movies, got manicures and pedicures. But Phoebe spoke of a familiar solitude. She put a fingertip to my forearm, vivid as a flame: "Are you and your mom close?"

"She left when I was three. My father, Russ, and me."

Her hand jumped to her face, registering shock. "Oh, but why?" What an old sad story it was. I was suddenly awake to it again. "Can you tell me?"

"I never share this." I mean, it wasn't flattering. It was Dad's drama, the way he told it. Though it always killed me. But I inhaled deeply. Maybe this was what Phoebe needed to believe me. "Yeah, well, my Mom had an appointment for a perm at the hairdresser's, and she brought me along. That was it. It was summer and boiling hot with all the hair dryers. I ran around. I climbed all the chairs, I was three, you know. I started whining, I guess, and threw myself on the floor."

"Perms take a long time," Phoebe said.   Of course. A girl would know this. "And then?"

"Mom's perm was half done. Peg, the hairdresser – I've talked to Peg since– faced two chairs and folded a rectangle of blanket, with a little towel pillow. Mom lay me down, and rubbed my back, and I fell asleep on the jerry-rigged bed."

"Just a little boy."   Her voice went sweet and high as if she grasped this young me.

"Except when Mom's perm was done, she ran to the Post Office. She asked Peggy, 'Can he stay here? He looks so happy, dreaming.'   Peg agreed; 'Sure, the kid's knocked out.' Mom stared a long while at me which Peg thought odd. But Peg was also busy with three ladies waiting for cuts."

"You can't do that today, just leave your kid."

"For good reason. Turns out, Mom didn't mail anything out of town but herself."   Suddenly, I looked around the kennel to clear my head, to feel the flat cold cement, see the old green tiles.   What I couldn't figure describing to Phoebe was how clearly I remembered waking and sitting up. The chair hard. I didn't know anything yet. But I sat there so still, near tears yet not crying. I can send myself right back to that awful chair. As if I *knew* nothing would ever be the same. And crying was too late. "Dad got a frantic call from Peg around five that evening. I haven't seen Mom since. Guess that's a relief to her."

"You don't know that." Phoebe's brow furrowed; she studied me with intent sincerity.

"Pretty fair guess." I'd deposited my story in Phoebe's lap. Opened a window onto myself. There was an edge to that.

"She wasn't loyal," Phoebe murmured.   "That's a serious flaw."

"I've got to believe that, to not go crazy with self-hate."

"The good Lord brought you back, Dirk!" Terry burst in like a semi truck.   She clapped her hands, "We have so few male volunteers. It's critical for the dogs to socialize with men." She gave my arm a little friendly shove. "I can't remember who said this: *In the Beginning God created Man, but seeing him so feeble, He gave him a dog.* God wants our joy!"

I smiled politely. "I suppose yes."

I wondered if Bull's Eye's stud fees paid for the suburban kennel, because how else did Dad have the money to board them? Maybe then Bull's Eye never regretted this new place, its satisfying demands. But I missed him insanely, my big warm boy. I had to focus, though, follow one directive at a time; get Poncho out, then find Bull's Eye and Dee. Perhaps this is what I told myself because I still had no clue where the kennel was. Maybe I was as ready as anyone to deceive myself.

I talked to Michael about Phoebe. He said, "You're conflicted."

"Who isn't?"

"If she's a religious nut job, why have anything to do with her?"

"I think she's trapped."

"People trap themselves, dude. That's how that works." He downed a Coke.

"So we give up all responsibility toward others?"

"Man, she's a total stranger." He grimaced like I was a special needs case.

"I like her."

Michael raised his palms in surrender; "You are one odd Romeo."

I had to see Phoebe outside of the Ark.

Wednesday, Phoebe was nowhere to be seen. In the office, three beleaguered adoption consultants bent over messes of paperwork. I asked, "Where's Phoebe?" A tall woman named Sally, replied: "She's only coming Tuesdays from now on, right?" The others nodded.

I'd thought we were beginning to understand one another. We'd been frank, our meanings clear. I thought she'd started to trust me. What had I done? Lonely as hell, I exited into the yard with its devoted dog walkers. I couldn't stay. I wasn't here for this. Whatever I was doing wasn't making sense any more. At least, Phoebe had to explain her departure, clarify. I'd find where she lived. I saw Terry at the dryer, gathering clean towels. She'd drive home tonight. I'd be right behind her.

Two hours later, I was parked on a side street, windows open in the dark, wishing I had some water to drink, questioning my sanity. I watched the lot empty car by car. At long last, Terry exited, locking the back door. She bounced over to her white station wagon, scrolling down her windows. Her Christian talk station shouted into the night: *Is any one among you repentant? Ask and be saved!* Terry headed south down Ridge Avenue's shadowy canopy of elms, then east, then south again on Ashland. Her back window crammed full of stuffed animals. Her trunk sporting a metal fish outline with a cross for an eye, and a mess of bumper stickers:

DON'T LET THIS CAR FOOL YOU: MY REWARD IS IN HEAVEN

MY BOSS IS A JEWISH CARPENTER

GOD IS MY CO-PILOT

More turns and we reached the Edgewater neighborhood, slowing onto Greenview Avenue. She pulled into the driveway of a white stucco house with gray-blue trim, surrounded by a black wrought-iron fence. Signs hung in the front porch windows:

JESUS LOVES YOU!

HONK IF YOU LOVE JESUS!

At that moment, I noticed the orange parking ticket stuck to the right under my windshield wipers. I'd been so caught up watching for Terry I'd missed it. When had I parked illegally? I yanked it open, and a white folded piece of paper fell out. No ticket.

Dear Dirk—

Mom thinks we were talking too much. Dad wouldn't like that. It's her job to protect me. I'm sorry I won't be seeing you anymore. It's the worst. But I tried to say it. I hope you don't mind this note. Try not to worry too much about Poncho; he's healing well; he's got good medical attention.

Phoebe

She hadn't wanted to leave. I could've done 1,000 jumping jacks on the spot.

Brick apartment buildings, composed and staid, surrounded the few scattered single-family houses. Her house was tucked between two other stucco houses, its wide front porch like an open stolid face. Rapunzel's tower, but not that daunting. The bedrooms must be upstairs. The upper windows were all dark. Phoebe's head would be tilted on her pillow, dreaming of what? Dogs? Escape? A clear blue lake? Me? Knowing she was near felt intoxicating. She lay asleep in her nightgown, her creamy legs wrapped in sheets, her plump mouth soft and mint-flavored from toothpaste, her dark hair tickling her shoulders, her heart beating. I was ready to climb up.

Which would only terrify her. I walked back to the car, jittery, glad. Phoebe had written me, me! Driving in the dark, under the awning of trees waving in the cool beauty of this hot night, I cherished this opening onto good luck.

Phoebe had grown up cloistered between parents. I'd been left countless hours alone. What opposites.

I wondered what it felt like to grow up doted on, surrounded, each step shared and observed. I'd forgotten to ask her where she went to high school, was it large or small? Were other church members there? Allies or enemies? I wondered about Fundamentalists at the University of Illinois at Champaign. I'd never have noticed them before, now I'd be alert. Still, I'd hardly been pondering my future lately. I was way too distracted. The first thing I did was to switch my time at the Ark to Tuesdays. That much I could do.

Saturday, Dad had woken me up, shaking me hard. "I'll be gone this weekend to the kennel."

I struggled to get my bearings. I leaned on my elbow. "I'll come with."

"Don't mess with me."

"Bullshit." I jolted up. "Dad, give me the damn kennel address."

"Nope." He tossed his car keys up and down. "You don't get it, do you? I work there now. I'm paid to get competing dogs in shape. I'm that good. But it's no day care center; here comes my kid. Always told you I wanted to strike out on my own, freelance. Opportunities didn't line up for me like bowling pins.

But I was patient, and now's it's happened. Bull's Eye and Dee like it. Money's decent."

"You never said."

"Did you ask? You don't answer to me, of late, I see. I don't to you either. We're moving on. Don't figure you're the only one going forward. You young people think you're the only ones got goods. You're wrong."

I wasn't awake enough to be anything other than all turned around.

I drove to the Ark, heat pumping at my temples from the open window, playing The Supremes. Yeah, set me free. Pulsating love. Twisting love. Love, love, love. What did I know about it? One flop with Tina. I must call Nellie soon.

I entered Tuesday, distraught, meeting the usual frantic barking of dogs waiting for release. Terry's jaw dropped open like a moat. She pulled me aside like a prison warden, asked me to repeat my history, the successful weight pulls, the years of strict conditioning and obedience work. "Okay, because we're short on trainers." Her fingers gripped liked pincers, "But stop bothering Phoebe." She looked absent-mindedly down the hall: "Adam gave animals their proper name and place in God's kingdom, but the kingdom's a mess today. Look." She walked me to a cage. "Buster was left for dead this weekend." As Terry shook her head, her ringlets sprung in tired chorus.

The pit's eyes were shrunk from scarring. Bumps disfigured his brindled skull; his withered legs could barely hold his thickset body. "Damn, he's ugly—" I felt myself reaching a limit of tolerance or endurance. There would always be abused dogs, gruesome damage; shelters would forever be full. The refrain was sick and dependable, tearing at me, this witnessing, the awful sure inevitability, I muttered, "Dear God—"

Terry fell to her knees, clasping her hands in prayer: *Not the least of them shall be unloved in His eyes*! She vigorously patted the ground at her side. Down I went, hoping no one would round the corner. Terry prayed: "All merciful God. Not one of us shall fall without Your knowing it. *Matthew. 10:29.*" She tapped my leg: "Did it ever occur to you what the reverse spelling of d-o-g is?"

"Ah, well, yeah."

She bowed in deeper concentration, taking my hand. "God, Father of life, give us the courage to do the work You ask of us, heeding Proverbs as it guides us. Lead us in the face of inhumanity to: *Know the condition of our flocks.* Without You we return to dust. Glory halleluiah!" After a silence, she murmured, "I'm glad we did that, Dirk." We stood up. "Buster may be beyond help. Our behaviorist, Mrs. Jodie, will do a full evaluation Friday, but could you tentatively test him?"

"Sure."

Buster watched tensely, chest leaning forward, his weak legs stiff, tail down, pointed, not at ease. Gray scars zigzagged across his chest like wheel ruts. I tossed in a few treats and he nibbled greedily. Good, he had his wants. I slid open the cage door, expecting him to lunge. But he waited, stiffly. I coaxed him with a few more treats, for which he stepped cautiously closer. I closed the door and left, to encourage him to want me. After awhile I returned; he sat at attention. Treat by treat, he approached. This time he came near enough for me to slip on a choke collar. He didn't resist; Buster wasn't people aggressive. We limped out. Passing the other kennels, he growled, but that wasn't unusual. I tightened his collar in disapproval with a quick pop-and-release. He looked at me doubtfully through his scar-slitted eyes. But, a minute later, when I repeated this, something seemed to click. He promptly stopped moving, studying me firmly. "Nice focus, boy." I gave him a treat. We walked out into the sweltering heat and Buster discovered the ground fertile with delicious dogness. He burrowed his nose in concentration. Whatever Buster had been through, he hadn't given up the pleasure of being a dog smelling the earth. People could learn a lot from dogs. Dogs, with their intense desire to *be*. Pits, especially, so hopeful; was it this in them that men felt compelled to destroy? Buster remained capable of relishing a fine moment.

"Sit!" I lifted up a treat. Buster sat. He took the liver morsel with a soft mouth. Amazing. Before throwing him into the pit, someone had taught him manners.

Terry appeared, "How is he?"

Sweat dribbled down my cheek: "Smart, willing to be happy. Hard to believe."

"Ready for a cursory dog-aggression check?"

"Sure." I secured the choke collar high, right at his throat, prepared for a quick pull back. Which is when Poncho rounded the corner, sniffing. Buster's hackles shot up; he yanked forward, but I quick hauled him back. He growled and Poncho's ears and tail pricked up with recognition then confusion, as if to say: *Is this a new game? Why are you with him, not me?* He charged toward me, determined, as Sally yelled, "*This* one!" And grabbed his hind legs. Poncho's eyes begged; *Shouldn't I run to you?* His luck to get blamed saving the other guy.

"He remembers me!" I blurted. "From last time!" A single idea buzzed through my brain; I'd put Poncho at risk.

"Too many volunteers been here between now and then," Terry disagreed. "Sally, report this to Mrs. Jodie."

The air was thick, suffocating. Buster waited patiently. I brought him to his cage, burly body wagging. Slid him a large bone treat. I rapidly headed for Poncho. He nearly gave himself whiplash greeting me, which he wouldn't have done if he wasn't at his wits' end. I crawled into his cage again. His rear wagged like a hula dancer. He near-licked me to death, while I apologized a zillion times. Right then, I understood I must stop coming. I'd lost my focus. I was hurting, not helping, Poncho. Putting him at risk of their insane critical determinations. They were misjudging him already. I had to get him out, stash him in my car and drive off. Figure out the best moment when no one would see.

"Oh Dirk, you're here," Phoebe knelt down, smiling shyly. "I just heard." Her hair clipped up, her throat and neck shone smooth as polished marble. Poncho leapt over to greet her. "You big boy." She rubbed him. Then her hands pulled on my thighs, as she brought herself in. I couldn't think. Her legs glued to mine. "He's almost ready for adoption, isn't he?"

"I have to stop coming here, Phoebe." Though caged together, we made Poncho euphoric.

"Please don't go." Her throat flushed; she put her hand up as if to hide the color.

"White-out my father's name and the address. Remove suspicion. Invent someone else, you can make things right, clear the path for me – if you choose to."

"I hadn't thought of that. You'll stay, then?"

Her hair smelled sugary like watermelon. Her thin shoulders glowed with a delicate sheen of sweat. "You'll remove the name?" She nodded, her eyes clear green lights. I touched her hand, to define something between us. She wrapped her thumb around mine. All at once, I wanted to kiss her, but this cage felt public, awkward. Her fingers on mine were light as bubbles. "I read your note, Phoebe, and I added Tuesdays." She lifted my palm, kissed each fingertip. I couldn't breathe.

"Who are you, Mr. Dirk Seward?" As if I might be some unexpected special. I laughed. Poncho squeezed into us. Loose strands of Phoebe's long hair flew up in a current of air, as she asked, "Would you come to my church?"

"Whoa! That's your best offer?" No girl had proposed this before.

"What am I thinking?" She let go of my hand, looking away, resuming her usual preoccupied frown. "See, my life's, it's so hard to explain. How encompassing this religion is, but if you see it... this world ... you'd understand. Better than I could ever say." Phoebe shrugged. "I'd better go before Mom shows."

"This sneaking around.... Your mom's comfortable with me now."

"Because she thinks you're a volunteer."

"I *am* a volunteer! What do you call this?"

Her cheeks flushed, her eyelashes tensed like little claws; "You know."

After she climbed out, I wagged a pull-toy at Poncho, he clamped on, cheerfully shaking it for: *more, more, more.* I wasn't prioritizing. I must choose. I was dispersing myself; pale volunteer, meek lover boy, failed dog rescuer, mixing everything so it turned to a mess of garbage spun loose in a crazy wind. Poncho, Poncho, Poncho was supposed to be the focus. Yet I was hurting him. Stupid. My trying to be useful here cost Poncho. Because now they were going to put him through a battery of dog-aggression checks. I remembered school parents whose volunteerism was award-winning but whose kids were jerk balls. Those parents ignored their own. They were pretenders. Now that had become me. Who the hell would save Poncho, if I didn't? He licked me like a praline-and-cream ice cream cone. Then panted into my leg; *I'm yours! I'm yours!* Everything topsy-turvy.

Phoebe saw me from the office window. Volunteers took breaks in the office, chatting, snacking, taking adoption calls, letting the better socialized dogs roam free a little. She stared through the glass, focused and intense. I felt undressed, hesitant, aroused. I glanced around, no one near for a moment. An invisible corridor sprang up, an express lane of connection winging through the air, grasping my shoulders. But then someone was addressing her, jaw opening and closing like a puppet through the glass, wrapping her in this greeting, turning her away. I left.

Plans for springing Poncho synthesized as I walked over to Michael's. It had come to me in the middle of the night. Phoebe's life *was* complicated, always under surveillance. I hadn't been thinking when I'd asked her to change the records. I had to get Poncho without her. Not arouse complications with Terry. Phoebe twisted me up like a pretzel. I wanted that, myself inside out, upside down, but not to hurt her. The empty July sidewalks seethed in the clammy air.

Michael's house was like an elementary school kid's drawing: a square topped by a triangle. Its siding was tan, the trim brown, and a scraggly yew bush half-straddled one side of the four front steps. Michael and his older brother, Bill, had always shared the one long upstairs bedroom, with its limited headroom when you stepped away from the triangle peak's center. His brother was working a summer job away at college. The room looked like a recycling center. Dad would've gone ballistic had my room succumbed to such disorder. I'd integrated his belief in the meticulous dogmatic placement of things. I instinctively sponged surfaces, lined up my books, ordered my papers into alphabetical files. Order was a constant counterbalance to the mess of life. Which was why I dug all the loose ends that were Michael, how he confidently plopped on his bed with his shoes on, fished his shorts from a pile crumpling off a chair, and left ice cream bowls floating around the floor. You stayed loose with Michael. It was his gift.

He answered the door in boxers, "Look who showed for breakfast."

"Go ahead. Eat me."

"Scary, man."

"Jesus, it's a morgue in here." He had the air conditioner blasting. He shoved the door closed behind me with his foot. The hall spilled a vinegary stench. "Open a window; dude, it stinks."

"I'm sorry accommodations are not up to our usual standard. How might I be of service?" He poured himself coffee, did I want some? I didn't. We headed upstairs.

"You can adopt Poncho—"

"Backtrack— yow! This isn't about that religious chick?"

I sat on Bill's bed. "We'll give you a job. Dress you respectably. Use your fake ID; yeah, you look over 21. You like big dogs but not ones that shed. You want a male. Do NOT say pit bull. Total red flag. Your grandpa died, leaving you a house with a yard with plenty of room, perfect to share with a dog."

He mock-scrubbed his eyes: "Man, you make me cry."

"Exactly. You'll move them, such a nice young man, wanting a big dog, the hardest ones to place."

He stretched his foot, surveying his hairy leg. "Did I say yes? You're going too quickly, sport."

"Michael, the minute Poncho sees you, he'll go nuts. They'll think it's a perfect match." I felt urgent with inspiration. Michael was charming in his easy, unobtrusive way. I'd never known anyone to mistrust him.

"This your girlfriend's idea?"

"No."

"Well, it's a stupid idea."

"Look, it can't be me. I'm on their records—"

"You're going to college. And I can't keep him." He stood up, "You hungry?"

I shook my head: "Dad'll take him."

"After he did such a great job of looking after him."

Suddenly it seemed possible Michael might *not* do this for me. "I'm very serious."

"I know." He sat quiet a moment. "How'll I run this past Mom?"

"You'll deliver him straight to my house. Poncho won't be here."

Michael grinned, "How the hell did I pick you as a friend?"

"You'll do it?"

"Graduation gift." He high-fived me. "Pal-o-mine, so what's my script as Superman Dog Rescue?"

"Act a bit religious," I extemporized.

"I knew we'd get back to the girl."

"Don't even look at Phoebe. Don't talk to her."

"See, I know when it's about girls."

"You idiot, I'd do anything for my dogs."

"You would?"

So I went one last time to Noah's Ark to assess the adoption process. Prepare Michael. I casually entered the office, "What's involved in adopting?" Sally, Melissa and Tom looked up, surprised. "I'm trying to get the bigger picture. Like when Manny'll be available?"

Sally smiled. Was it Sally who'd delivered Phoebe's note to my windshield that time? "Love, he's not neutered yet. We can do that much; reduce the birthrate of unwanted dogs."

"You didn't know?" Michael retorted when I explained inside McMinty's. "Get out into the world, punk, clear your head. *All* shelters neuter."

"How did you know?"

"Boy Scouts. Trips to the Anti-Cruelty society."

"Yeah, my Dad was big into Boy Scouts. I remember all the fun we had, marshmallows and camping. Bonding." I swigged my root beer.

"Okay bro, you were deprived. My heart bleeds." Michael clutched his heart, faking an attack, but he knew the truth. He'd always stuck by me, skirting around Dad, my sinkhole of deprivation. He raised a toast, "To the deed that needs doing."

"Dad's going to be freakin' pissed."

"Douche bag."

The Cubs were on replay in dismal action against the Cardinals, down six to one. Michael shook his head, "Wish we were at Wrigley Field so we could scream."

Phoebe lashed my brain like a Portuguese man-of-war. Stinging me with her odd church life. Making me squirm. I couldn't figure how to add up the parts, an inconclusive equation, not a golden ratio. Our situation felt goofy; I wasn't even clear to myself.

Earlier, I had stepped outside with Phoebe smelling lightly of talcum powder and grape soda. "Hey," she wiped the back of her hand across her cheekbone, her leafy eyes bright with trust, "About church? This Sunday, can you?"

"Remind me, why?"

"Seeing where I've come from, you'll get me. Shine a light on skin that's hard to shed even as I try." She bit the inside of her lip. "Maybe you'll run."

"Give me a chance, Phoebe." Put me on this peculiar path.

"I don't want to convert you."

I was glad to be leaving Noah's Ark, where we transacted in two-dimensional sentences. I needed to tell her, though. "You have email?"

"Yes."

"Give me the address. Wait, what about your mom?"

"She's scared of computers! I'd like you writing to me."

"I will."

"For church, dress conservatively."

"Where you lead, I'll follow."

She shook her hands in the air in a negating motion. "See? That's blasphemous. Don't joke like that."

"Come on." I rolled my eyes.

"New Testament, Matthew, 4:19, recounting Jesus' words, *Follow me, and I will make you fishers of men.*" Her hands shoved into her front pockets, her eyes squinted, suddenly fighting tears.

I didn't want to be a shit. "I'm new to this."

"I've never invited anyone."

"I'm glad I'm the first," I said idiotically.

"I'm afraid I'll remember messing this up for the rest of my life."

"It's okay. But listen –"

"If it was up to me, this wouldn't be the life I had to show."

"Phoebe—" I looked hard at her. Time stopped. I felt hungry and tense and chained to something I didn't understand. These stringencies. I wanted to slide my fingers into her hair. Trace the freckles across her nose like flecks of gold on a treasure map. I could press my lips to hers, but any second a volunteer might turn the corner. I grasped her wrist cool as a popsicle. Her pliable fingers curled into mine. My breath broke free, her eyes holding me firm. Then I knew what it was in her expression I'd seen before. In the one photo I had of Mom, she leaned in the doorframe, so intent, looking at the camera as if it pulled her, was magic and hypnotizing. This quality in Mom's eyes was knowing and skittish, eager and afraid. It was a look I'd been trying to understand for as long as I could remember. I was still chasing it. Here, now, in Phoebe.

Luckily Dad was gone for the weekend. His suit on me on Sunday wouldn't have slipped unnoticed. I walked awkwardly, Dad's navy blue wool suit stifling, ridiculous to myself. Ready for the Lighthouse Church for Divine Intervention. Depending, unclear how, I'd try to meet up with Phoebe at the end of the service.

Its dome-arched interior was massive. The polished altar set up like a theater-in-the-round, surrounded by rapidly filling seats. I was literally melting in Dad's dumb suit. Jostling people increased around me. I found a spot. I hadn't imagined the sheer size of the congregation. All at once, people shot up like pneumatic air compressors, valiantly singing. They shut their eyes and swayed their arms over their heads like loose palm fronds. Enthusiasts. Next came a lengthy prayer, another belted hymn, a series of general announcements, and another prayer.

All at once the room hushed. The assistant pastors walked away, and Pastor John swept onto the stage in billowy white robes: paunchy, with abundant curly gray hair. He pointed – to the congregation, the sky, the ground, and the screen behind him projecting in foot-high letters: *Living Our God-Given Roles.*

"Friends," he pointed back to the congregation in a deep voice. "Let us read—" All around, people hurriedly opened their Bibles. "Paul's epistle to the Ephesians: *Wives submit yourselves to your own husbands, as you do to the Lord.* Chapter 5, verse 22. Now, now. Ever meet a Mother who prides herself, saying: 'I've taught my daughter: To Thine Ownself Be True. Respect yourself. You are not here to *submit*.'"

"Poor Mom, I say. 'With that kind of pride you will *never* understand, *never* approach, the godliness of our own Lord Jesus. Worse, neither will your daughter. Is that your wish?"

Voices cried, "No! Oh no!"

"*He* gave *His* life for us. Where was *His* self-preservation? Did *He* say, 'Sorry, too few are worthy of my self-sacrifice, my submission to the greater good.' Would *He* have ever said that???"

"Never!" reverberated throughout the room.

"No, no. *He* said I give my *Life* for you. But us? We cannot *submit!* I ask every woman here: On what grounds would you refuse to submit to the father of your children? The man who is your help-mate. Your provider. Without submission, without deep humility, yours is a flawed, a limited love. Far, far, far from Jesus' love."

Some parishioners sat firm as stones; others vigorously shook their heads and open palms in assent. Pastor John indicated the huge Bible on a lectern, "I put it to you: What *does* Paul *really* say? Read the next verse, number 23, my friends, and – now listen for God's word – *For the husband is the head of the wife, as Christ is the head of the church, his body.* Would you dissuade a husband from *emulating* Christ's path? From finding his greatest strength in the responsibility of *your* surrender? Paul wrote; *Husbands love your wives, just as Christ loved the church.*

"Chagrined husbands ask me; 'How can I lead? My wife is up all hours reading about women's rights. When I offer guidance, she calls me Authoritarian.' My beloved flock, this pastor lays down his head in despair.

"Do we Doubt or do we Believe? Who are we to question *His* word? What if I said, 'This Sunday, I'll sleep until noon. Be True To My Selfish Wish.' Would you not say, 'Pastor John, I trust you. I count on your dependability. You are betraying my trust.' Yes! Yes! You'd be right! We do not come to church to exert *our* rights and wills and *our* wants. We come to be reminded of *Him, Who* gave up everything for us. *Who* offered Himself to the Cross. *Who* predicted his betrayal, but *Who never* wavered in *His* Love.'

"In *giving* we receive, and in *submitting* we are made strong. Follow the way of human will, and you will find Sodom and Gomorrah. The human will *is* toward sin. Jesus said: *Blessed are the meek for they shall inherit the earth.* NOT: 'Blessed are the willful.' Which of you here has the *courage* to be led? To welcome a Light brighter than any other? To give the gift of complete submission to *His* will?"

Around me people jumped up. "I am! I am ready, my Lord Jesus! Praise Jesus!" Transfixed, alarmed, I wondered what about this pastor so many here trusted. Women rose, undulating, hands reaching out to him in supplication.

"Friends, I say fear becoming the one-and-only lonely. *Receive* the news that Christ sheltered us, suffered for us. He loved us more than *His Own Life.* Friends, believe the good news. Jesus Christ is risen. Amen."

"Amen! Amen!"

"Let us bow our heads in prayer...."

I'd never thought much about the Bible, but I didn't assess it was literal. Less a manual of operating instructions than a text for interpretation. Pastor John was part of this movement to treat the bible as God's Word, which I'd read about in articles at the doctor's office. Dad would never have set foot inside a church. Yet this was Dad's brand of authoritarianism; submit or get trounced. I couldn't trust that.

Various groups lingered around, chatting and hugging. I wiped my sweaty neck. I made a beeline for the men's room, headed for a quick piss and exit. And then Phoebe was at my side: "I hoped you'd stop here! It was the only thing I could think of to find you. I do get to go to the rest room on my own!" She laughed, her full lips pink and shiny. Her dress was pink with a pattern of coiled white daisies; her chocolate hair fell around her shoulders.

"Some church. Phoebe, man, that guy could preach for the Taliban."

"Or American Fundamentalists."

"You want your husband to be your general?"

"I'm trying to figure out what to do."

"About?"

"About getting away, finding my way, alone." Again, I felt her push-pull. Pristine, but she looked at me with intent.

"That's all anyone can do."

"A church moves with such power, sailing in big numbers; you feel huge."

"But it's a construct."

"I know."

"We're born alone. Separate. Friends can be leaning posts. But everyone has to face being alone."

"Hah! Not everyone accepts that. It can be too hard."

"So fall in love."

"What?" Her eyes opened into little round green ponds.

"It's a good distraction." I grinned, wondering what the hell had gotten into me.

"I'd say." She smiled so broadly that for the first time I noticed she had dimples. Her head thrown back in laughter unfurled her tender throat, her pliable pretty tendons.

"A good marriage isn't about being commanded." Like I knew. What a yarn.

"You believe in true love?"

"Haven't had much luck."

She tilted her head, "You always tease me."

"Really?" I reached for her. Just touching her arm, sparklers lit the air, ignited my skin. Startled, I pulled back, murmuring, "Bring me good luck." She turned cherry red, and warmly watched me.

At home, I extricated the note she'd nestled in my jacket pocket right as I was leaving. Folded into a small tight square, it read:

Remember: Phoebegrace@noahsark.com. Grace is my middle name. I'll look for your email. XoX. please write.

A chink in the wall, a lovely sight. My brain ran the refrain: *Phoebegrace, Phoebegrace, Phoebegrace.*

From: Dirk Seward <ponchosboy@aol.com>
To: Phoebe Turrett <Phoebegrace@noahsark.com>
Subject: Hey you
Dear Phoebe, I think you are so pretty. You'll know me as: ponchosboy@aol.com

The next day she wrote.
From: Phoebe Turrett <Phoebegrace@noahsark.com
To: Dirk Seward <ponchosboy@aol.com>
Subject: thoughts
Dear Dirk,

So now you know my world. Because our Christianity is all encompassing; you must live inside it at all times. You might think I'm playing games. Yet you go where you want at will. I am supposed to be God's, and my parents act as the border police. All my life I've been as safe as a prisoner, nowhere left alone. Once, this didn't bother me, but I no longer believe that God wants to be a jailer. But my doubt is so lonely. As a kid, I stared out my window, watching kids whooping and speeding on bikes, neighbors kibitzing, the mailman joking, not that they didn't sometimes speak to me, Mom's arm wrapped around my shoulder, sure to hear everything I heard. I still stare, from the car, and in free moments in class, watching people free to live. I'm determined to find out: is life better or just harder when you choose your own moves?

Last year, Mom had a vision she was needed by God's creatures. She prayed hard and convinced Daddy we needed to volunteer at Noah's Ark. Think I was meant to meet you?

Yours truly, me.

P.S. No I don't want to marry a general.

She was in a bind. So was I. But were we helping each other out of either mess?

From: Dirk Seward <ponchosboy@aol.com>
To: Phoebe Turrett <Phoebegrace@noahsark.com>
Subject: my idea

Phoebe, listen, I went to your church, but it was hard for me to understand. I see it as a crutch. I think spirituality is like as a spark waiting to be lit inside each person. Personal responsibility is what counts; that's how I measure godliness. If you follow orders, the pastor owns you. Who is he to claim another person's soul? It's wrong, horrible, really. It's very good you have doubts.

Poncho's boy.

I still hadn't shared how I was hurting Poncho by appearing at the Ark.

Again, she emailed:

From: Phoebe Turrett <Phoebegrace@noahsark.com>
To: Dirk Seward <ponchosboy@aol.com>
Subject: church doubt

I started to ask questions at Youth Ministry and I got into trouble because questions represent Satan's influence. My parents were alerted. I scared my mom. It hurt, to see her so unhinged. Now I keep my thoughts to myself. You're the first person I've told.

Phoebe

I wrote right back:
You go to church for your mom?

She answered:
One more year, then I graduate. After high school, being eighteen, not a minor, I can't be forced. See how sweet Mom is? She tries so hard to do good. She's given her whole life to me, my mom. That hurts. One more thing. This faith isn't about personal vision. We're born sinners, we're defective. Our visions aren't trustworthy. Listen here: "Trust in the Lord God with all your heart and lean not on human understanding; in all your ways submit to him and He will make your path straight." Proverbs 3:5-6. God will always know us better than we know ourselves, that's the idea. You can't follow your heart! "The heart is deceitful above all things and beyond cure. Who can understand it?" Jeremiah 17:9. According to Lighthouse you're making up false beliefs.

I was taking a leap of faith in her. Phoebe might as well have been in Finland, for how hard it was to see her. I wasn't returning to the Ark. I was hardly sure what I felt. Forever, I'd trusted three things: my dogs, Michael, school. And solitude. Adding up the hours of my life, I'd accumulated advanced expertise in isolation. A yearly full-time position. Like the onset of a virus, my aloneness occasionally felled me, but mostly I trusted it. Isolation's claws now started scratching in her name. Though I really had more important things to address.

From: Phoebe Turrett <Phoebegrace@noahsark.com
To: Dirk Seward <ponchosboy@aol.com>
Subject: thanks

Dirk- you give me such hope, you cannot imagine. I count the hours until your words appear. So you won't come to church again? I'll miss you. Please be patient. Little is more frightening than removing my believing glasses. Who am I to challenge God? Is my doubt insight or insanity? I'm opening my eyes. I want to be brave. So much is unclear.

Yours, xoxoxox, Phoebe

We wrote more, about different things.   Still, we skirted things. Impulsively, I wrote:

I wish I could kiss you, that's what. Again and again. How does that sound?

Poncho's boy. And yours.

That night, I tossed and turned. What a moron, pressing *send*, what a joke. A river of anxiety threatened to drown me. Until she replied:

Oh yes, yes, kiss me.

Which is why, that next Sunday, I crawled back to Lighthouse. I'd finally told her I couldn't return to Noah's Ark when it was cruel to Poncho. She'd been doubtful, anxious. I hoped to explain myself face-to-face. I nixed the business suit.

Once more, people circled each other, tooth-flashing welcomes. When a moment of dentistry fell on me, I felt like a goddamn Christmas present. I moved away, but when I thought I had escaped, the stranger in the next seat stood and opened his arms wide. I didn't want to hug, but he was all over me, me as helpless as a potato. Ridiculous.

Mercifully, the service began: "You are here today because God led you here." People nodded like bob-along dogs. "To find your way as His sons and daughters. Call *His* light into your body. Please join hands in prayer." My neighbor grabbed my hand, nearly giving me a heart attack. But I wouldn't resist feeling God. Sure, I'd take in God's light. I shut my eyes, imagining filling with brightness, catching God-energy. Nothing entered my dark and narrow soul.

Had Dad brought me as a kid, I would've been thrilled. Joining an extended family. Biological family wasn't a guarantee of happiness, when, instead, here, everyone tried so hard, willing to give a damn if you were happy or not.

I wondered if the congregation's benevolence was constant. In the entry hall, a huge display of brochures had offered guidance: *What Does God expect of Man? What Does God expect of Woman? Will the Holy Spirit Fill Me? How Can I Share My Faith?*

Bible Resources to Help You Grow. God Exists! Who Are the Chosen? Being the Vessel of Faith.

Once again, Pastor John rose, robed like an angel. "Friends, which of us has kept the innocence and wide-eyed wonder of a child? A child says: Water! Sun! Snow! Birds! All things are a miracle to a child. But we, their supposed teachers, in our great hurry, curse the elements. We resent the silver rain, chafe against the summer sun, grouse at the glistening snow. Do we stop in our tracks to listen to the sparrow's song? Do we relish the bright tulip pressing courageously from the moist earth? How sad we busy adults have become; very, very sad. The earth is God's creation. It unfolds for us. Complex and miraculous, vast and infinitesimal, seasonal and eternal, the sum of all God's wishes. Do we listen? What child is bored outdoors? The speeding wind, the green and yellow leaves, grass thick as a blanket— each is a cause for amazement. Yet we forgo that. Why? To claim our glumness? And minimize the miracle of life? Children need to be fed and clothed and guided. But we need *them* to remind us just how gorgeous a spontaneous faith is. It's ours for the asking any time, any day of the week."

People waved, "Amen! Amen!"

Well, yes, children found the smallest things delightful, but no child lived in unbridled joy and hope. I had used to lay on my bed so alone my skin hurt. My heart contracted, withdrawn like a prune. Where had my wonder been? What about all the millions of orphans, starving with distended bellies? This God might expect them to proclaim, "Stars shine through this torn tent! Not to worry, I'll eat the air! Oh, that hypodermic needle saved me!" As if happiness was proof of godliness. But how could a God think their suffering was some personal failure? No compassionate God could. Even Job didn't cause all his losses, and supposedly God recognized that. Twenty centuries after Christ, most people acted like scum, embittered, cutting each other off at every pass. These wonder stories lied. Callous.

I spied Phoebe sitting twenty rows from the altar. My heart bounced. In a midnight blue dress, her hands rounding her knees. She leaned toward a man who must be her father, Earl, mustached, with a stiff military posture. Terry beamed, staring at Pastor John in a reverie, hands clasped. I studied Phoebe's profile. She had a powerful attentiveness.

She didn't know I was here. Although, after, I waited outside the rest rooms awhile, she didn't show. Driving home, I thought about how Dad and I had lived without a God. Dad hated ceremonies. Never one for parties or holidays, he certainly wasn't milking our last weeks together. He didn't ask about health insurance or tuition. He'd said, "Colleges are over-rated. Your mom and me had nothing to do with them." But I'd figured out he was hurt I was leaving, and that touched me.

The morning after graduation, waiting at the kitchen table, his oversized mug of coffee steaming, he'd said, "Look," pointing to two packages wrapped in newspaper and twine.

I'd opened, first, a square tin with two prepaid gas cards inside. "For the road. Wasn't sure which'd be most convenient."

"Yeah. Thanks Dad." Then I unwrapped a portable yellow tool box set, "You'll be one of the few knows how to use them. Might come handy. I taught you some things, didn't I?"

A thwarted saltiness burned the corners of my eyes, "You did."

"Come on give us a hug. You haven't forgotten how those work, have you?"

"No sir." It felt like I was in someone else's movie.

I told Nellie about Phoebe. "I don't know what's happening to this country," she said. "Churches becoming indoctrination centers. Belief shouldn't be a challenge to free will. You're getting mixed up with a girl who proselytizes?" I tried to explain. "I wish you'd find a girl who wouldn't complicate your life so much," Nellie said. "You really like her?"

"I think she likes me, too."

Nellie grinned like I was a triple-layer chocolate cake: "So the trouble begins."

Back at home, I had messages in my Inbox.
    From: Michael Gregorio <mikeatbat@yahoo.com>
    To: Dirk Seward <ponchosboy@aol.com>

Subject: vanishing act
Asshole, where've you been?

Then one I didn't recognize:
    From: Sally Vine <sillysally@yahoo.com>
    To: Dirk Seward <ponchosboy@aol.com>
    Subject: new site
    Dirk -- Sally (from the shelter) is my friend. She put my note on your windshield that time. I visit her Saturdays. We met at Lighthouse, and she teaches me knitting and crochet. She thinks my parents are too constrictive. LOL! I'm on her computer. Sally says you're a good egg, it shows in how you treat dogs. She believes you didn't fight Poncho. I'm going to tell you something. You have strong shoulders. When you bend down, I imagine how you might fold your arms around a little kid, keeping her safe. Sally says love comes from heaven; it cannot be irreligious.
    XOXOX. Phoebe.

My strong shoulders? They hungered. I replied:
    From: Dirk Seward <ponchosboy@aol.com>
    To: Sally Vine <sillysally@yahoo.com>
    Subject: *for Phoebe, Confidential.*
    Phoebe -- Wow. I agree with Sally; if there's a God, he must be where love is. There's a Supremes song: "Love is in Our Hearts." Know it? Or: "How Sweet It Is?" Listen to the lyrics. Can I write you here now? Know what? My arms are meant to hold you. Write soon.
    I kiss you xxxxxxxxxx. Dirk

I'd go to the Ark one last time, just to see her. Give Poncho a quick check.
    From: Dirk Seward <ponchosboy@aol.com>
    To: Michael Gregorio <mikeatbat@yahoo.com>
    Subject: still here
    Hey, some of us have jobs with long hours, scuzball – meet me at McMinty's?

Monday, the air burned like a skillet, blanching the sky white. I was at the grill, searing a hamburger for myself before my Dominos shift. Dad came home. "Throw one on for me. I could eat a horse."

"How's Delilah?"

"Fine. Bull's Eye, too."

Hearing their names hurt. I flipped the hamburgers, tiny bubbles of fat sizzling, anger rising. I added buns to the grill face down. "Share any details?"

"Actually, I ate them. Dog meat's delicious."

My seething rage suddenly fired through my arm, exploded like lava, so that his hamburger pitched from my spatula smack into his chest, beef grease spewing, soaking into his shirt. Dad yelled, "I was a damn idiot to raise you." He tugged at his shirt, frantically patting himself with napkins. "Grill another one, you little turd."

"I don't *have* to do anything."

I woke up wanting to punch him. I still couldn't grasp why he'd hadn't consulted me before moving the dogs. Poncho was evidence enough that this *professional* move was a failure. This was why sons left home, refused their fathers.

The hours until Tuesday dragged. I started searching for references to love in the Bible on the Internet:

My beloved is to me a cluster of henna blossoms. Song of Songs.

And, even better, *Like a lily among thorns is my darling among the young women.*

Ecclesiastes, *Two are better than one...If they fall down they can help each other up.... If two lie down together they will keep warm... how can one keep warm alone?*

Biblical passion.

On Tuesday, when Sally saw me she said, "Manny passed his evaluation this week-end with flying colors. Friday he goes in for neutering. Monday he's ready for adoption."

My legs stiffened. Phoebe, my henna blossom, my lily, rounded the corner. I blurted, "I can have Poncho Monday!"

She reflected: "But you can't take him because you're going off to college."

"Are you telling me or asking?" She looked confused. I didn't know what to think. "Do you even get me?"

"Please. You're misunderstanding— "She wrung her hands, her knuckles sharpening grey-white. "It's just a question. I've been thinking, with your going, you can't take him. You trust us, by now, right? You can't bring him back to that kennel. Dirk, I cleared your name from the files. Now what's best for him?"

"Not treating him like a stray." I couldn't believe this was in question.

Suddenly Phoebe was gesturing no, no, no with her palms: "I'm a real idiot. I'm sorry."

I couldn't speak. I headed for Poncho. His happy white butt did the shimmy, the proverbial tail wagging the dog. I'd wanted to tell Phoebe about his skinny point of a tail when he was a puppy, his nose that gleamed like a black olive, how we'd put that first harness on and he'd been all go, go, go. Except I'd been struck dumb.

I met Michael late at McMinty's. He asked, "Preacher man, how's the love?"

"You have to adopt Poncho right away."

"I always wanted a big family." He smacked his hand on the table, grinning.

"Or I'll end up stealing him back out of someone's yard."

"Chill, dude, I told you I'd do it." The front door kept opening, spilling in more patrons, sucking out the air conditioning.

"Michael. On Monday, first day he's available. No later."

"You're a pain in the butt. Doggone crazy, man." I didn't bat an eyelid. Michael scowled. "Okay, I'll call tomorrow."

"Tell them you're coming Monday."

Sunday, I went over the plan. "Sport that winning smile. Request a big, shorthaired dog. Never say 'pit bull.' Don't say 'pit bull.'"

"You told me like twenty times."

"In the fifty yard dash, there's no leeway for error."

He rolled his eyes, "Bite me."

"Your grandfather died recently. You need a companion. The house, your yard, they're big and empty."

"You're killing me—" Michael clutched his throat in mock strangulation.

I impressed upon Michael the zeal with which the shelter sized up prospective adopters. Because volunteers saw how the dogs came in, they didn't easily let them out. But Michael's charm was contagious; who better to convince them? Poncho's picture would be stapled into the "Available for Adoption" book, placed in the waiting area.

I didn't tell Phoebe about Michael. She had mystified me. I felt a dull hard ache when I contemplated her attempt to waylay me, unsure if that was even the case. I'd email her when Poncho was safely with me. One step at a time. Lately, I wasn't even thinking about college, which was way weird, because the hope of it had kept me going the last four years. I still had forms to send in. I was obsessed with Poncho.

When I got home, the squeak of my shoes magnified the awful dogless silence. I thought about all the TV series, where crises get solved, pronto, with a cop and a sleuthing lawyer. Progress assured. Life was a different mess.

Monday afternoon, I cancelled Dominos, mock sick. To distract myself, I wiped down the kitchen counters, mopped the floor, Pledge-sprayed the furniture, playing Al Green. I dumped spaghetti into a pot of boiling water. Dad came home, plunking himself across the table. "Goddamn economy, shipping our jobs off to the Chinese. Since when are they our *friend*s? Working two cents an hour."

I hummed, tuning him out. "Average man today needs two jobs, just to pay the bills. No free time, no sitting around, feet up." I ladled tomato sauce onto his steaming spaghetti. "You got to be an entrepreneur; it's the only way. Think outside the box. You're lucky I'm in shape, and I got ideas. Most men my age are tired of life."

He swirled up a forkful of spaghetti. About now, Michael would be headed to the shelter.

After I did the dishes, I rearranged the assorted cans and boxes of food in the cabinet. Moved upcoming expirations forward, arranging similar sauces, sweet condiments on one side, sour on the other. Dad watched TV, downing a Bud. The night gaped like a huge cavernous mouth, casually, chewing the minutes. Listlessly, I flipped on my computer. It flashed an Instant Messaging box.

Ponchosboy: Who's there?

PhoebeGrace: Wow, u answered. Quick. I want to be the 1 to tell u. Some 1 is here, looking to adopt Manny.

Ponchosboy: Why r u there on a Mon?

PhoebeGrace: He's kinda slick. He wants a big dog. Manny's gone crazy for him, licking him like a steak. Tom thinks it's a match. But I'll fight it. Trust me.

Ponchosboy: Listen, Phoebe, hey! I've been stubborn. If Tom's in favor, he knows, right? He's done this 100s of times.

PhoebeGrace: But I know u. U'll think I betrayed u.

Ponchosboy: Wrong. Phoebe? Phoebe?

The screen gulped. No reply. I typed in her name, again, then again. Nothing.

I box-kicked my door. I charged out onto the porch, trying to see straight, half-blind with mortification.

Not until nine o'clock did Michael round the block in my Fiesta. I'd bitten my nails down to the flesh. Disgusted, I sat like a block of cement.

Michael climbed out. He folded his suited-up arms on the car roof. "That is one messed up place." I nodded glumly. "Trial by fire, man."

"Tomorrow—"

He came around curbside, "You owe me big." And there was Poncho, his butt wiggle-wagging before he shot, bullet-fast, into my arms, licking my ears, nose, scalp. Sixty plus pounds of healthy devotion. "Calm down, yeah buddy!" I laughed, rubbing Poncho's big old hard head, scratching his ears.

"Michael, how? How the hell?"

"You going to invite me in?"

"Mr. Wonderful's in there watching TV."

"He's not getting Poncho."

"Yeah, well, no argument. But come."

Poncho furiously sniffed the porch, retracing his old haunt. His tail swung like a crazy metronome. I opened the door, and He charged toward the noise of the TV: "Hey! Hey! Where? What the — "

Dad appeared, Poncho following devotedly, licking Dad's feet, then his knees. Michael proffered his hand, "Evening, Mr. Seward."

"My favorite athlete. What's up?" Dad stuck his hands in his jeans' pockets, which gave him the appearance of tilting back.

"Got your dog back for you."

"Suspiciously kind of you, Mikey."

"Dad, I asked him to."

"Now and again you come up with a good idea." He rubbed Poncho's head. "I'll re-settle him in training in the next couple of days."

The room seemed to swirl in a strong head wind. "I paid for his release, Dad. He's staying here." Poncho gave a brief happy bark.

"Wow. A seventy-five dollar adoption fee, Chief. Don't make me laugh."

"Kennel him when I'm gone."

Michael spoke, "That was no place for a dog, that shelter."

"Well, your friend delivered him there, not me. He seems to have forgotten I own the dogs." Dad threw back his shoulders, hands on his hips, a cowboy gunslinger, my Clint Eastwood.

"Actually, Mr. Seward, he's now legally my property."

"That paperwork's a sham. You're not of legal age."

Michael squared his shoulders, and took a step toward Dad: "What, you going to the shelter to verify that?"

Poncho's round brown eyes studied us, divided, seeking his next command. It always killed me, this trust. I couldn't speak. I'd understood in a flash that Poncho was not safe for having gotten home. The moment my back was turned, Dad could take him. Poncho's tongue lolled, he needed water. I got him a bowl. Dad dismissed us with a wave, clomping back to his TV.

Michael said. "You can't win with him."

"That's what he believes. Think this deserves a beer?"

"I'd say so. Then I gotta get out of this suit. I'm liquefying, man."

We sat on the porch, the beers cooling us slowly. I had to simmer down. Poncho sniffed the floor, the chairs, our shoes. After a bit, he sighed, and stretched at my feet. I rubbed his big white and black head. The world had a center to it with a dog. Michael reported, "They interrogated me like I was Jeffrey Dahmer. *Let's say he chews up your Nikes, what would you do? Have you ever hit an animal in anger? What makes you think you could love a dog? Do you plan to chain him outside? We may have to inspect your property, ensure it meets safety standards.* Twilight Zone, man."

"You don't see the screwed up people who dump the animals there in the first place. Then all the adopters who return the dogs after a couple of weeks. It really messes up the dogs."

"I saw your lover girl. Freaked me out. Challenged me: *A dog's a big commitment. What's your work schedule? Why don't you wait?* Took me awhile to realize it was her."

"She wasn't supposed to be there on a Monday."

"You're not supposed to hook up with a fanatic. She'll be knitting sweaters with puppies, have napkins printed: *Jesus Loves*

You." He made a barfing gesture. I whacked his arm. He laughed, "Remember, as kids, if *anyone* accused you of liking a girl you had to call him a slew of names, push him to the ground? You've so matured." Michael had stuck around, God knows, making me lucky. "Dude, promise me, you're not in love with that crazy chick."

Poncho's tail smacked the porch cheerfully "We just talk."

"Well, count me *out* of any more brilliant rescues." I flashed him my empty hands, no more demands. I watched Michael recede into the night, ambling home. My head and legs felt rubbery. I flopped on my bed and, just like once upon a wonderful time, Poncho rested his head on my stomach.

I listened to his rhythmic breath. My dog, this dog. Poncho's journey had come full circle to a good ending. I kneaded his pointed silky ears. I'd miss him in college. Maybe after the first semester, I should get an apartment, bring at least one of the dogs there. Yes, I'd do that. Now, August was mine. I'd work Poncho gently back into shape, rebuild his confidence. I'd find Bull's Eye and Delilah, I would. Tomorrow, I'd resign from Noah's Ark, making myself into one more proof in their eyes of how undependable a volunteer could be. Maybe Sally would help me reach Phoebe.

Poncho's face-licking woke me. I rubbed his belly, savoring his solid warmth. I stumbled into the kitchen. Sitting at the table, grasping his black coffee cup with his newspaper snapped open, Dad watched Poncho tag behind me: "So what is it exactly you want with him?" He surveyed Poncho, checking the brightness of his eyes, the muscle tone of his flanks. Suddenly he slammed his hand down. "What the hell; he's been neutered."

"They *do* that at animal shelters."

"He won't be game with no damn balls." He frowned in disgust. "You've ruined a perfectly good dog." Poncho lay down happily between us.

"Tell me a neutered dog never won anything."

"When the pressure's greatest, operated dogs fail you. Got no balls."

"Did you fight him?"

"I wish I had, don't I now? Fond fool that I was, I let him run around loose; that's how he slipped out. Gets to me he made it all the way back."

"I don't believe you."

"I can't do nothing about that."

I waited for him to give Poncho a serious rub down, or a tug of war on a pull-toy, a proper welcome. But Dad had that capacity to turn off which he considered his strength. He stretched his arms over his head: "Won't be home 'til real late tonight."

When I phoned Nellie, she said. "I don't know about your Dad. But you, I've been thinking, why do you have to live in the dorms? Off-campus, you can keep Poncho, which you'd love, sweetheart. Right?" She paused, "How's your girlfriend?"

"We have to find other ways to meet."

"Didn't convert to her church?"

"No freakin' way." My body hungered for the smoothness of her wrists, her straight lithe waist. My hands wanted to know the length of her spine, her slim secret hips. I ached for her to touch my rough boy skin with its squiggled hairs. I wanted her to not want to lose me. I'd written, explaining my relief at having Poncho, explaining Michael's role. She wrote back:

When I couldn't stop the adoption, I thought you'd never speak to me again. You thought you couldn't trust me, but you could. I cried myself to sleep.

I quickly typed:

I was trying to protect you, keep you out of it. I'm so sorry. Please tell me there's somewhere near your house or school where we can meet?

Still, I had yet to tail Dad. One of these evenings after his shift. My next project was, finally, to discover Bull's Eye and Dee's whereabouts. It took a few days before dad had 'training plans', but then I was driving in rush hour traffic, squinting into the blinding sunset, trying to keep an eye on Dad's blue Chevy from a few cars back, his *Bulls I* plate taunting –blink – before slipping away behind another car. Forty minutes later, we were headed into Schiller Park. Planes landing at O'Hare practically strafed the slow traffic, dropping large and fast, their engines deafening. Dad turned south along a stretch of Forest Preserve that marked the east edge of Schiller Park. He curved into one of the park entrances. Minivans dispersed little league players. Runners and bicyclists skittered by. Dad parked near the large stone Park District building, entered and, ten minutes later, exited with a bearded man. Both climbed into a white van with the insignia:

Schiller Park District
Safe Parks & Forests

The van entered a nearby neighborhood, row upon row of identical brick bungalows. At one dead end, it pulled up to the last bungalow, a house bordering an overgrown industrial lot. The yard, which had to be huge, given the extensive high brick wall, was otherwise invisible.

Dad slid into the side door to the detached garage, which quickly shut. This evening was a waste. I wrote down the address anyway, to feel mildly competent. Where were the dogs? I couldn't picture myself in college, not having properly said good-bye to Bull's Eye. I imagined being there, hanging, chatting, stretched out with Phoebe on a grassy lawn; that picture highlighted in every college brochure. Unreal. Tomorrow, I'd reach Phoebe; at least that.

Dad and the man suddenly emerged from the garage, carrying dog crates carelessly draped with large towels. These, they slipped into the back of the van. My palms sweated, sticking to the steering wheel uneasily.

They left, returning again to the staid Park Preserve building. A royal blue twilight silhouetted the unfettered branches of trees. Wardens appeared in various vans with megaphones announcing closing time, chasing out straggling bikers and cars. They locked the Preserve's gates. I retreated to a street a couple of blocks away, waiting a cautious half-hour in my car. Skirting the edge of the woods, I found a gap in the fencing and slipped through.

In the increasing dark, I approached the back of the building. Things appeared pitch black inside, except for a light bulb above a flight of basement steps, visible from a low window. All the other windows were boarded up, perhaps against rats or raccoons. I tested the back door: locked. A light flickered from deep in the woods. I moved quickly, ducking behind a dilapidated garden wall. Through some broken bricks, I saw a bit. Five men, two flashlights between them, approached, crouched and furtive, cursing as they stumbled. They headed purposefully toward the basement door holding a key. Smacking each other forward, and down the steps, they disappeared inside. The door locked behind them. Silence returned except for a proprietary owl announcing his whereabouts.

After about ten minutes, two pot-bellied men came out to smoke. One took a long piss, "Love the great outdoors."

The other: "Blazin' inferno in there."

They wore jeans and t-shirts and they laughed, turning back in, without clicking the lock. I waited a few minutes. I propelled myself toward the metal door. Which heaved open to the basement steps, followed by a low hallway. Boisterous voices blistered the air, "Douche, don't gripe. Tom calls the shots." The heat was intense for a basement, but no windows were open. It smelled like baking mold, a humid swamp. I moved inch by inch, praying no one else headed out this hallway, which ended veering in a ninety degree angle to another hall zipping deeper in. A bright light from a far room to the right lit up the opposite wall. I heard maybe ten or twelve voices, burly, excited.

Further down the hall, I would have a diagonal view into the bright space.

Sudden cheering: "Bitches!" I saw a narrow closet door and threw myself in, against the brooms, mops, and stacked chairs. "Molly!" one voice cried. "Ginger!" Another. Strippers?

I stepped out, restless and alarmed. I slipped to where I could see a broad triangle of the noisy room, one corner lined with a low wood wall like a mini corral. Everyone else invisible, my view angled. All at once, two pit bulls slammed against the wall. One brindled, one red. Jaws clamped on one another. But the red suddenly lost her hold, wild-eyed, seeking her bearings. I closed my eyes.

"Hold on, that's the shit. Go, go, go, Molly!" Molly's owner pressed her advantage.

But now Ginger was re-oriented: "Rip her in two!"

Men blurted, hissed: 'Yeah! Yeah! Hey! Yeah!"

Molly's canines punctured Ginger's throat, who swung wildly to shake her off. Flung her side-to-side, smashing her against the wall repeatedly, thudda, thudda, thudda, like a sack of sand. Blood sprayed through the air in an arc, sticking to the carpet, sliding down the wood, dripping off the dogs. I broke into a cold sweat. My back was glued to the hall. I remembered the bearded man, years ago, whose bellicose grey pit had enraged the crowd at the weight pull. He'd been shunned, thrown out. Dad had been urgent to put the scene behind us.

When Ginger slammed her roughly to the floor, brindled Molly still held firm. Even when she got flung so hard the crunch of breaking bones crackled through the air, and blood dripped through her teeth. "Stay on her, Molly!" Again and again, the slamming, the splintering bones as sharp as a tray of breaking glasses. My hands pressed to my ears.

All at once, Ginger let go, yelping just as blackened blood pulsated like a fire hydrant from her throat. She veered sideways, frantic to lick her unreachable wound. "Don't go cur on me!!"

Ginger lay down, blood still jetting an odd smell of liquid rust. The announcer shouted, "Ginger to scratch. Or Molly wins."

I should've known in my heart I'd never find Dad in the lap of luxury, no bucolic place in the suburbs with well-groomed dogs. But I'd wanted to think it was possible; he talked about progress, moving ahead. Our dogs deserved it. Yet it had never made sense, and I'd known that, and I'd let it slide.

A loud bell clanged abruptly. Now the bitches again slammed into the corner, a lump of Ginger's neck swinging loose like the flap of a purse. Sprinkling blood, spraying her hide. Molly's hocks shone wet. Her back left foot limp and dragging. She struggled valiantly to maintain her tripod balance. A rank odor penetrated like shooting flames. The bitches bit into each other, foaming pink. I began to shake. Uncontrollably. I backed out, stumbling. I reversed toward the door, clutching my stomach, trying to make it, but I buckled over, puke spewing onto the cement steps, my shirt, in mustard lumps on my Adidas.

Fouled and stinking, I straightened up outside, breathing raggedly. I slipped off my t-shirt and balled it up. I wiped my shoes with clumps of leaves. Jesus. The sky was black now, worried back and forth by late night planes.

Everything was in shades of darkest gray; the crouching trees, the path ahead, the building behind me. As if, folded into so much darkness, nothing much could be happening. The owl had gone quiet. I tripped. How could Dad? Where the hell were

Delilah and Bull's Eye? Phoebe hadn't believed Poncho's wounds were accidental. Her bolt of insight rushed through me, exposing my internal fault line. What willingness Phoebe had had to listen to my protests, maybe Poncho wasn't fought, but maybe he was. Maybe she'd wanted to scream: *Wake up you idiot!* All at once, I really missed her. I did not have her concern to spare. Suddenly, my whole life was different.

I'd bet that if I'd asked folks living in this area, "You got a dog fighting problem?" they'd frown in scorn. Sure, gangs, yeah, blacks on the south side, *they* had no conscience, *they* gambled on dogs. Sure, you could hardly cross a street in Englewood without seeing some punk kid with an over-muscled pit. But the south side, *that* was the projects where kids ripped their own playgrounds to shreds, and house after house had plywood for windows. *This* was the suburbs, white folk, family men with jobs and vacations, and barbeque grills –betting on which dog was the gamest killer.

I drove back to the dead end bungalow, trembling. I parked a few houses away, unsure what I expected. Dad had sure as hell gone into that basement. I wanted to cry. About an hour later, the white van reappeared, followed by Dad's Chevy. He helped the man carry four crates into the garage. This time, a brief clatter of barks disturbed the air, then silence. Worn to the bone, my soul in shreds, the evidence damning, I left quickly.

I thought of Poncho with increased agitation. And more about Bull's Eye and Delilah. Once again, I saw the night Poncho limped up to me, looking like he'd been hit by a truck. Dad would never hurt our dogs. Look at me, loyal until the end, blind-sided by stubbornness. When I reached home, Poncho ambled up, half-asleep but wagging his tail. I threw my arms around him. He enthusiastically sniffed my disgusting shoes.

What was I going to do? I stripped off my clothes, threw them into the washing machine. I soaked my Adidas. I took a long hot shower. I gave Poncho a bone. I didn't think I could sleep, but Poncho's raspy breathing soon lulled me. I sank like a stone in a well.

When I opened my eyes, daylight was flinging its radiant energy across the bed. Poncho paced the floor eager to be let outside. I wasn't leaving him alone at home; he was coming with

me everywhere. I shook myself awake. I made coffee. I'd phone
Nellie, then Phoebe. But, first, I called Michael. And was
apparently incoherent because Michael said, "Slow down, let me
get this straight. You think he's fighting dogs?"

"Yes."

"Your dogs?"

I paced. The percolator bubbled. "Well, where the hell else
are they?"

"My point exactly. Chill. You didn't see Delilah or Bull's
Eye. Their kennel's probably something totally different. Your
Dad, he never had friends, right? So of course when he finds a
pal it's some jerk-off. I'm not condoning. Just saying, keep the
issues clear."

"What happened to Poncho, then?" Poncho barked in the
yard.

"Who the hell knows?

"The dogs were soaked in blood."

"That's bad, man."

"I have to get into this guy's yard. You be the look-out."

"No more adventures. We agreed. Seriously."

"I'll do the breaking in."

"Dirk, we both got scholarships. Don't mess with that. Tone
down the break-in and accomplice crap, Vin Diesel. This isn't a
movie. Call the police."

"When they confiscate fighting dogs they can't rush fast
enough to euthanize them. First, I have to find Bull's Eye and
Delilah."

"Don't know, man." Our conversation went back and forth.
"I should get a prize for being your friend," Michael complained.

"You're my personal hero."

I'll bet he wanted to flip me the finger.

"I owe you, man."

"A thousand times over."

I worked three nights delivering Dominos with Poncho next
to me, going nuts over the constant smell of pizza. I plied him
with free bread-sticks. Dad had pushed up his glasses and
pointed his thumb at Poncho, "That your new date?"

"Sure, we're getting married."

I wanted to phone Nellie, I needed advice, but I kept thinking how this would hurt her, and knowing us had been a string of wounds. This, now worse, because this was unbelievable. Caring about people meant not throwing everything at them, letting them be at peace awhile until it was absolutely necessary. This was protecting those you loved. I needed her but she didn't need this. Let me last as long as possible.

Late evening, Dad watched pro-wrestling, feet up, in his boxers, at ease in his kingdom. "Come here, boy," Dad cajoled Poncho who scampered over. "Good boy. I'd never have robbed you of your jewels." Poncho licked and licked his hand.

To enter the garage, I needed Mr. Schiller Park in the park, and Dad working late at Happy Mart. I'd re-checked his house. Seems the guy had no wife, kids, roommates. His name was Bob Fitzgerald and he worked mostly night security at the Forest Preserve. I dialed 411 with his street address and his phone was listed. I'd call. If he answered, my investigation was postponed. As I once used to as a scared kid, I phoned Happy Mart for Dad's schedule, which he'd forget to share. "Yeah, next two weeks, Tuesday through Thursday, he closes at midnight."

I reached Michael. "This week then?"

He moaned, "It's stupid. You got gloves? Duct tape for the hostages? Pantyhose masks?"

"Hilarious. Don't forget your driver's license."

"So the cops know who they're arresting."

"Wednesday, around nine p.m."

"I don't believe you."

"You'll do it?"

"You get to me, A-hole."

Wednesday evening, Fitzgerald's line rang and rang.

Slouched in the passenger seat, Michael muttered: "You're not normal, Dirk, know that?"

"If this is the idiot Dad's left the dogs with, I have no choice. I have nightmares."

"Spare me." We passed Home Depot, Popeye's, Taco Bell, Mickey D's, then rashes of tacky strip malls half-full with dry cleaners and nail salons. The Midwest was flat. No panorama. Low planes again accompanied our drive to Schiller Park. "Don't these people complain about the noise?"

"Maybe they get used to it." I pointed out the Forest Preserve's entrance. "That's where."

"Your tax dollars hard at work." Michael drummed his fingers on the dash. "A regular Fresh Air Fund, urban dogs welcomed to the great outdoors."

I turned down Fitzgerald's street. "If anything gets weird, some old woman starts peering through her curtains, leave. Head home."

Michael oozed disdain. "You've watched too many derelict movies, dude. I'm not *bailing*. *Try* to be careful."

Fitzgerald's block was quiet in the fading light. I rang the doorbell; good, no answer. I stretched a blanket across the back seat, preparing for Bull's Eye and Dee. I stuffed a wrench and screwdriver in my pocket.

The air was boiling. I curved around behind the house, into the empty industrial lot where I could heave myself over unseen. Though it took three tries, I finally gained a foothold in the brick yard wall and vaulted over. I'd brought a baggie of chopped-up hot dogs expecting a guard dog. But, though thick chains were bolted to the ground, the yard was empty. Just all dug up. In the semi-darkness, I moved cautiously. This was no garden, though it was maybe an acre, huge for this area. The streetlight shone onto three treadmills, the narrower sort used for dogs. A thick tilted plastic awning hid them from any prying neighborly view. Hanging from a massive old locust tree were two spring poles. I nearly stumbled over the wagons filled with weights, harnesses draped loosely on top. Dad would be like a pig in shit here, surrounded by all this training equipment. It felt eerie, though, like an abandoned amusement park.

The garage had two doors, one to the driveway, one to the yard. Sweat greased my fingers, but I could turn the handle. Locked. I unscrewed the metal plate keeping it in place. Doorknob in hand, I entered into sudden barking. "Quiet! Right now!" They'd blow my cover. The smell of piss and shit flooded my nostrils. I flicked the flashlight on. Crates were stacked two high. One mama pit blinked at the light, two pups crushed and whimpering at her side. With no ventilation, the heat was suffocating.

Another bark. "Quiet!" I reprimanded, swinging my light to locate the culprit. And there he was; his face swollen and torn: Bull's Eye. My tongue grew like a football in my mouth. My fingers turned into clumsy sausages as I struggled to unlatch his crate. He lurched out, his tail half-wagging. I clasped his black and white head with its festering sores trying not to gag. I quickly offered him the hot dogs, but he looked away, unenthused. His left front leg looked pussy and infected. My head reeled. I made a weird involuntary sound, *Uuuh, Uuuuh, Uuuuh.* "Where's Delilah? Delilah?" I searched, cage to cage. The tired dam watched with her mournful eyes. Another pit oozed blood from where his ears had been. One tawny male's head was so swollen, his eyes had almost squeezed shut. No Delilah.

Trembling, I took photos, focusing the flashlight. Sweat ran off my forehead. My stomach reeled. I repeated, "Delilah? Delilah?" The two pups would not stop whimpering. Should I spring them? And the others? My mind jammed. I couldn't free a pack of dogs. I'd have a slaughter on my hands. Even the looniest humaniac at Noah's Ark knew that fought dogs turned dog-aggressive out of self-protection. I scattered the hot dogs into the crates. I urged Bull's Eye out, limping, stuck fast to my side.

Michael was waiting out back. I called over the wall, "It's a blitz. I dunno what – I can't think, man. I found Bull's Eye. He needs a vet."

Michael's low voice: "Can you lift him over?"

"He's bleeding, slippery." Bull's Eye had lost weight, but he was still thick, hard to flip over a wall. His legs flailed in my face, "Stay still! Stop it!" I stammered, "I'm trying!"

"Get moving, Dirk."

"There are others. But not Delilah."

Michael's wiggling fingertips were all I could see of him. "Get him over!"

I staggered in the heat, my arms shaking under Bull's Eye's bulk.

"Do it!" Straining every muscle I sprung Bull's Eye over. Michael exclaimed, "Good, we're good! Jesus! Poor boy! Remember me? I'll bring him to the car. Hurry up."

I scrambled over and high-tailed it to the car. I saw Bull's Eye's mangled head in the back window, roving back and forth, looking for me. I clambered in. Michael urged, "Let's scram."

"We have to wait. Fitzgerald might bring back Delilah." I rubbed the dried pus off Bull's Eye's face with a rag; the sores underneath looked infected.

"You've flipped your lid." Michael's voice rose in frustration. "Things get too complicated with you."

"I'm deep," I joked to feel less rattled. An elderly neighbor exited and returned. A man and his tipsy high-heeled date leaned on a door, laughing.

Michael scowled, drumming his fingers on the steering wheel. "Deep in shit. You've got enough of a problem on your hands right here."

Bull's Eye moaned, low and strangled. The heat was harsh, miserable, seeping like fire in my veins. Michael was right. "Yeah, go, go. Damn it." I stroked Bull's Eye, avoiding pressing on his putrid sores. Even the rush of relief had to tire him. But he hung on, his eyelids pulling shut, then flipping quickly open to find me. My old, old friend. "Oh, big boy." He would have followed Dad's orders, and found himself in the pit, Dad yelling, another dog circling him, baring his teeth before this enemy lunged to clamp on, Bull's Eye fighting for his life. These wounds weren't old. Under these, perhaps he carried the scars of other fights.

At two in the morning, traffic was sparse. The thick thrum of planes had died down. My limbs, my head, weighed like lead. Bull's Eye needed serious antibiotics, stitches, x-rays. But any vet, even Dr. Lance, was legally bound to report evidence of fighting. I couldn't risk that. I'd clean him myself, try to staunch infection. At this hour I couldn't phone Nellie. But morning wasn't far.

Now I'd tell her how Dad had betrayed everything, bartering our sweethearts just to measure their capacity for desperate struggle. Other people's madness wasn't enough to entertain him; he threw in our dogs. How could we have shared this home? He'd crossed into that mad space that defended killing as sport, a hard pleasure. He'd taken the dogs from under me. One deviant idea, someone's suggestive phone call, and everything decent in him had shattered.

Michael pulled up in front of his house, "Listen, let me stay over with you, help."

"No, man. I'll call tomorrow. Thanks a million." He waved dully. I took the wheel.

I wanted Dad to see me walking in Bull's Eye. I fumbled with the keys. Or I'd yank him awake. Bull's Eye hobbled to my room, where he'd always loved to sleep. Poncho bolted toward us, sniffing and licking Bull's Eye, before I could push him away. Bull's Eye stiffened, eying him with mistrust, but he didn't growl. I murmured. "Remember Poncho?" I urged Bull's Eye into the bathroom. Dad wasn't home. I grabbed towels and a pan of warm water. Slowly, slowly I wiped away what I could of the dried blood and crusted pus. He didn't whine or flinch. "Brave boy. There, there." Dirt had molded into some wounds. I lathered on Neosporin regardless. His left paw was swollen twice the normal size, his right leg slashed. I scrubbed his ears and nose, and wiped his caked eyes clean. I tried to cocoon him in bandages, but he pawed at the sheathing with such distress I left his head clear. As a kid, I'd occasionally dolled him up as a hobo or a clown, but he'd always struggled; the only thing he wouldn't let me do. Now I poured him fresh water and set out a raw hamburger, which he only licked, a bad sign. I lifted him up on my bed, "Sleepy time, my friend." Poncho pushed near, curious and eager. Bull's Eye seemed to remember something he hadn't known in months, and closed his eyes.

I couldn't undress. I sat immobile, agonizing. I saw the pits' half-dead eyes, flies crawling all over them. How easy it was to imprison a dog. How hard to explain. Those mortified brown eyes had stared, confounded. Hoping against hope for the nimble fingers that could open latches. What had Bull's Eye done except everything asked of him? His exhaustion flooded through me. He'd stared at me perplexed, worrying about his confusion because he always wanted to get things just right. I couldn't explain this. I hadn't even known where he'd gone. Nor where Delilah was. I was stupid. I gaped dumbly at the blank ceiling. My life seared wide, wide open. When I woke up I didn't know where I was.

I bolted straight up. Poncho and Bull's Eye anxiously reciprocated. Pots clanged in the kitchen. Here he was. I had no brilliant strategy. I wanted to hurt him. I coaxed Bull's Eye, "Come boy, come." He limped off the bed, eyes obediently on me, stopping obediently at my side, as I poured myself a jolt of coffee. Dad watched. The sun fell brightly through the sink window. Next, Poncho wandered out, too. Minutes passed.

Then: "This one arrived in the middle of the night, too?" Dad being Dad.

"Something like that." Bull's Eye did not greet him.

"You fought him."

"That's ridiculous. I love that old boy. He helped me keep some of the young ones in line. With just a growl, his unblinking glare. He got real good food, and ran free all over the place, evenings when the others were crated. But you know he was never a stand-back type. Last week, he got provoked. I had to drag him off this top young fighter, and Bull's Eye got pretty cut up. One of the pit-falls of the trade. Hah! Our medical guy was coming this week to clean him up."

"Was this guy going to tend to the others?"

"Listen to you. So that's what you were up to." Dad shook his head in an exaggerated sort of way. "That's trespassing. Fitzgerald won't be happy." He paused, suddenly glaring, and leaned in inches from my face, "Wait. Did you follow me?"

"You let Bull's Eye get infected. Look!" He looked like hell. "We've got to do something."

Dad relented, "Surprises me he got bad so fast. You know how he always healed; no dog had a better immune system." Then he picked something stuck between his teeth before he turned to me. "You never had two jobs, bucko. Your nose buried in books, you haven't lived the real world yet, where you run out of time and can't get to things. Yours is a privilege I never had. Don't you jaw on about my not having done enough for the dogs."

"You were supposed to be training them."

"That's right. And get paid."

"To kill them."

"Bozo, you train a dog because you want him to win. Always. You want him to win. Nothing else."

"But, at some point, he loses. A dog reaches his limit, he's done for."

"You surprise me. A record of wins can't be erased. Never. You win; that's on permanent record. You should know this. I train dogs to win. Win!"

"So where's Delilah?"

"Here we go."

"Where's is she?"

Dad studied his coffee cup as if it held great powers of interest, "She was a cur."

He might as well have sucker punched me, "What the hell does that mean?"

"A cur. Not game. Not your problem."

"The hell it isn't!"

"I would've sold her in a pinch but no one wanted to buy her."

I launched myself like an exploding grenade, kneeing him again and again, keeping him pressed into his chair. He grabbed my hair, smacked my head into the table. I rolled loose and leapt away. Both dogs went crazy, barking, dashing back and forth. I spewed, "Mother puss bucket! They trusted you. You're sick! Sick! I hate you so goddamn much. What did you do with Delilah?" I propelled myself onto him as he jumped out of his chair, shoving him to the wall. But he got me turned around and slammed my face into the kitchen counter. Half delirious, my nose running a stream of blood, I blurted, "Know why Mom left? She was way too smart for you—" Bull's Eye suddenly clamped onto Dad's pants, stumbling, while Poncho yowled, running back and forth, banging into things. Dad lost hold of me, and I turned and pushed him so hard I knocked him off balance onto the floor. I flung myself on top of him. I couldn't believe all this, us, Dad yelling, looking up at me, "What the hell do you want?"

"Where is Delilah?"

"Idiot, she's dead. Remember how she'd bare her teeth at the pups? Something was wrong with her from the start. Got so she growled at me. I thought I saw a fight in her, so stubborn and pissy. A game bitch visited from out of state. There was pressure, high stakes. No reason not to try something once, I got lots of encouragement, people rooting for me. She's gone, okay? I was sure she'd win. Instead, I lost out. I'm not doing that again. I put a lot of money into her. Now I owe people."

My adrenaline pumped like high-speed baseballs in a batting cage. I had trouble seeing clearly. My hands clamped around Dad's throat, a tightening ring of blazing fire, clenching harder than I'd ever thought possible. His knees buckled up under me. I straddled him, squeezing tighter. His face turned red then purple. Poncho barked maniacally. Bull's Eye staggered, and suddenly dropped to the floor. And then I was crying, sobbing like a baby, while I shook Dad's throat again and again, his hands clawing at mine. I could not let go. Me, the guy who believed he was going somewhere. Oh God. Dad was spitting, hacking, scratching my arms, going purple. I let go. His hands rushed to his throat as he rolled on his side, coughing, fighting to breathe. When he could stand up, he stumbled around, before coming back to punch me. I fell heavily. Sprawled on the warm linoleum, cheeks soaked, stinging with tears, shaking, blood snaking from my nose to the floor, Poncho licked the blood. Dad frothing and spitting. Bull's Eye skirted the wall. Dad screamed hoarsely, "You no good son, piece of shit, you. Get out of here! Get out!"

I pressed my palm to my nose, trying to staunch the bleeding, tottered over to the sink, splashing cold water on my ailing face. I grabbed ice from the fridge, and bundled it into a compress. Jesus, I hurt. The dogs watched, disoriented. Trapped by the human world. Locks, crates, gates, cages, fighting pens. They lived on hope, blind hope. I had to pack my books, dogs, computer, and leave. Find an SRO. Hide out until it was time, soon, for university. Dad wanted me out. Mom had done it without his asking. Simply erased the past, the misery and mistakes. She hadn't looked back. But fleeing the scene left debris. Others had to go through the muck, there was always muck others cleaned up. Then I understood something.

Leaving Dad wasn't good enough. Allowing what I'd discovered to stay as it was. It was cowardice, if all I did was save my skin and psyche; it was small, this self-serving. Look at Mom; she'd left nothing behind, not a lesson or a trinket, not the smallest part of herself. Had she had so little to spare? Something would have been much better.

Ice pack shoved against my nose, I blundered into my bedroom, Poncho and Bull's Eye close behind. Dad had left an hour later for work, shouting, "We're not done!"

Time had erased our happy history with the dogs. No, time wasn't the culprit. It was a person who changed.

Bull's Eye's face swelled absurdly. His left paw turned big as a cauliflower. Again, I cleaned out the pus, which had to hurt, but he watched expressionless. The dense humidity stuck like glue, making thinking hard. How I wished for air conditioning. My nose throbbed like a siren now that the bleeding had stopped. I needed help. I called Nellie. No answer. I rang every half hour, growing desperate. At noon, Nellie answered. I blabbered, "There's a fighting ring in Schiller Park. I got Bull's Eye out; he's real bad."

"Christ! And Delilah?"

I hesitated, "Dad said she turned cur."

A sob lurched from Nellie's end. "I did this to her, oh! That poor baby. Hon, I can't bear it." She was crying, blowing her nose.

"Please Nellie, help me. I'm scared – the infection – "

I could hear Nellie click into gear, Nellie who understood these dogs like no one's business. She turned firm, and ordered, "Pits are tough. Non-stop talk to him. He has to hear your confidence. He'll respond to that. Don't let him out of your sight in case he seizures. I'll try to wrangle some meds. Dirk, the animal shelter, they've got medications, supplies. They'll help."

"Yes, right." Knowing I'd never bring Bull's Eye there.

"Are the dogs safe with you?"

"What more could Dad do to them?"

"Give Bull's Eye courage."

"Okay."

He lay in a lump, sunk in deep sleep. Poncho sniffed him. I was afraid Bull's Eye would fall into a coma. Impulsively, finally, I wrote Phoebe.

> From: Dirk Seward <ponchosboy@aol.com>
> To: Sally Vine <sillysally@yahoo.com>
> Subject: hello
>
> *Phoebe, the last few days have flown by. Poncho's settled in. He's well. But something more, much worse, has just happened. I found another of our dogs, Bull's Eye, injured. You always suspected. I'm an idiot beyond description. Stubbornness blinded me. Right now, now, it's an emergency, no time to reflect or recriminate. I'm so afraid of losing Bull's Eye. Can you get antibiotics, through the Ark? I can't bring him there, start that all over. But he's hurt so bad. I could meet you anywhere. The minute you tell me. Could you?*

The reply flew back:

> From: Sally Vine <sillysally@yahoo.com>
> To: Dirk Seward <ponchosboy@aol.com>
> Subject: good bye
>
> *Dirk, I'm deleting your message. You are not what I thought. Snake in the grass. Phoebe is a special kid, don't you get it? Phoebe sobbed when Manny was adopted, sobbed for you. Terry was hysterical with worry, she doesn't really know about you two. We had to convince her it was just the female thing. But it is always the male thing. Then, last week, you just cut out of the shelter. Don't you ever bother that sweet child again. I'll delete your messages. And whatever awful thing you are doing with these dogs, you sicko, you deserve hell.*
>
> *Sally*

Phoebe was crying? No, no, we'd gone over things. Bull's Eye labored over each breath, gurgling and rasping, not at peace in sleep. I searched the Internet: *dogs + infection + fever + head trauma.* Warm compresses, constant supervision, recommended urgent medical attention. Time wasn't on our side. I had to risk going to Dr. Lance. Bull's Eye's facial swelling had climbed around one eye and shut it tight. I wrapped him in a blanket, and lifted him, straining to lay him gently in the back seat. The car blazed like an oven. It would be a long ten-minute drive. "Hold on, boy. We're getting there." Bull's Eye had saved me as a child. Look what he got for it.

I didn't have a cell phone to reach Nellie. There wasn't a pay phone in sight. I carried Bull's Eye up the two steps in, unresisting as a sack of stones hanging over my forearms. The vet technician leapt up from the front desk, "Quick, in room two, here. Heck."

Dr. Lance appeared immediately, "Dirk, what happened?"

"Doc, if Bull's Eye dies I don't know what I'll do."

"He needs fluids right away." The technician hurried off, and brought a syringe. Dr. Lance pinched a fold of skin from Bull's Eye neck, slipped in the needle. "Next, the wide gauze." The technician handed him thick squares. "The infection's set in. His leg's broken." Dr. Lance scraped and layered. He drained fluid from Bull's Eye's skull, pressing with a slow circular massage down to his jaw. The absorbent sheet grew yellow with pus and ooze. I winced. He injected antibiotics. "What happened, Dirk?"

I'd been at war with myself. What to say? I expected to confide in him. But only if I felt sure he'd give me back Bull's Eye. I became afraid of what I didn't know that could follow, how control could be wrested from me, again my dog handled and tested by others with their missions, obsessions, ways of justice. That wouldn't do. On what basis would I trust others knew best? So I lied. "He's been missing over a week. We put up signs everywhere, called all the local shelters. Then last night he comes stumbling out of the dark, up the porch steps, like this. We think someone fought him."

"Looks like it. This city's a terrible mess, piss poor law enforcement. Disgusting."

"Fights going down in basements, I think." My temples were wet, my hands heavy.

"The miracle is that he escaped. Had the will to get to you. That's some fierce devotion, Dirk." The technician caressed his ugly head; Bull's Eye'd feel her concern. Dr. Lance said, "Let's force down a little water." He squeezed a dropperful into his mouth. "He needs a hospital. I'll call and prep them."

"Please! Don't. He'll fight harder for Dad and me. He's been taken away once by crooks. Again, it'd break him. I'll be with him 24/7. I'll call daily."

"I've got to report this, though. Got to make these criminal activities public. Your dad can help? Bull's Eye is very serious."

"Dad's real upset." Sugarcoating was the only way.

"Bull's Eye needs strong sedatives. Uninterrupted rest. I'll splint his leg. He's shown he needs you. You cannot leave him alone."

"I was seven when Dad found Bull's Eye. I'm not leaving him."

"All right. But I'm photographing him today for my report." When Bull's Eye's head lolled back, knocked out, Dr. Lance slipped alcohol-saturated gauze between each swollen toe of his left paw. Then they wheeled him away. And I waited. An hour later, Bull's Eye's leg looked like a baseball bat, with layer upon layer of adhesive thickly circling and secured to a splint. "He won't get that off." Dr. Lance muttered, "This boy needs a long rest now." I nodded. "He may not blink an eye for 24 hours. The longer he stays still, the more his energy can go into healing.

"—I'll be glued to him. I'll phone tomorrow."

"Good rescue work, Dirk. I'm sorry this happened."

I was a man overboard, clinging hard to a raft. I carried Bull's Eye out, dead by all appearances.

Two messages blinked on the answering machine at home. Nellie: "Where are you? I'm out of my mind with worry. I've got bandages, and oral antibiotics. Hurry. Call." Then Phoebe: "When I deleted your information from Poncho's paperwork, I copied down your phone number. And you haven't written. I miss you. Remember I'm like Rapunzel, who believes somehow she can escape."

Dad hadn't wanted an answering machine, saying, "If a person can't reach me when I'm here, why would I want him to reach me when I'm gone?" But I wanted to be reached. I re-played Phoebe's message. Her voice swirled into my room.

I called Nellie. "Finally!" she exclaimed. "I'm on my way."

I rang Phoebe, but the home answering machine clicked on. I couldn't leave a message. The silence saddened me, crumpling my expectation. I'd never felt more aware of the obstacles between people. I lay down next to Bull's Eye, clutching my disappointment.

I woke to the repeated pulsing of the doorbell; impatient adamant rings. Nellie looked frantic. I hugged her: "Sorry, I fell asleep."

"I thought you'd had to rush him to emergency, that he wasn't making it."

"He's knocked out. Dr. Lance said to let him rest." She knelt, her hands roaming up and down the bulk of Bull's Eye, judging his condition.

"I thought you refused to go to him." I shrugged. "Dirk, can you get me a drink of water?" We sat in my room, staring at Bull's Eye, while she sipped, brow furrowed. "What are you going to do?"

"I need help."

"That I get. Be a little more specific." She patted my knee.

"Dad has to pay." I hadn't expected to state this so clearly, but when I spoke it felt right.

"Oh, sweetheart, that makes perfect sense, but you're starting college in a month. Your entire life lies ahead. Don't waste time on your father. He'll suck you down a drain. You saved the dogs. Your job now is to save Bull's Eye. A pit does everything with his whole heart. *Tell him to heal.* If you want to move out, I can definitely help."

"Nellie, he *has* to be made responsible." It was so clear, even as saying it hurt. Which pain I didn't understand. I did not feel merciful toward Dad. Insane. But there had been afternoons, many afternoons, spent at his side, no need to speak, as we trained the dogs, proud together. And our dogs had transformed, showing off jaw-dropping talents. It was the everything, such abundance of work and connection, the daily journey into our shared love for the dogs. Deformed by Dad's special twisted disease, senseless, progressive, consuming. You couldn't forgive a person for getting sick with greed. The slap of change startled.

"Dirk, free yourself."

"No." Sitting in my blue bedroom, my old solitude thickened like callused skin. Dad had taught me never to trust handouts. Think for yourself, he said.

"I'll report him to the authorities. You've earned your exit, your right to steer clear. The dogs depend on you now."

The front door was being loudly unlocked. We froze, eyeing each other in alarm. I shrugged, "Who cares?"

Dad entered, lowering a crate to the floor. He rolled his eyes at Nellie, "So this is the problem?"

"Go to hell, Dad." The bruises on his throat gave me small satisfaction.

"Hello Russ," Nellie countered. "I've just seen Bull's Eye."

"Nellie's kind of old for you, Dirk - used, I might add."

I took a step toward him. Muffled barking pulsed from the covered crate. "Fitzgerald, gave me these. Not that he cares about Bull's Eye. It's the principle. Because you stole, I owe him." He lifted the covering. The two filthy pups I'd seen in the garage pricked up their ears seeing people and light. "I'm jump-starting them young."

"It's illegal to fight-train. I can call the police."

"Go do that, Dirk. You got time to waste. Courts don't give a damn about me exercising puppies. Jesus! This city's got bigger fish to fry." He shook his head, "My luck to get a bleeding heart for a son."

Nellie's eyes were saucers. Her face was red, and not just from the heat. She asked, "Are you going to wash those puppies?"

"Would you like to?"

"Yes." Her voice gone cool as ice.

She must want to get them out of his hands, study their condition. Were their bones intact? Did they have fleas? I said, "We can soak them in the bathtub. I'll get towels."

Dad grinned, watching Nellie open the crate, "You like dogs more than men, don't you?"

My fingers curled into fists, but Nellie grabbed my arm. "Let's do this together." She wasn't just talking about the puppies, this I understood.

The next morning, the scrappy puppies yipped and yapped at our feet, one male, one female, maybe five months old. Their tails wagged, they pierced my forearm with love bites. They weren't housebroken. Any pup was going to be more or less of a challenge. These had a clock ticking on their lives. "Your darling got them spic and span." Dad picked a Corn Flake from between his teeth. "Now they need training."

"Before winding up dead."

"You're thick-headed, which blinds you. Seems I can't change that."

"Right."

"I'm telling the you the truth. You don't want to hear. I don't fight dogs. I strength-train them. A dog decides if it's going to fight or not." Dad spoke calm as a windless day, as if his info was reasonable, and I was the loose cannon.

I snapped, "Christ, Dad, you don't train dogs; you put them on suicide missions."

Dad grinned unpleasantly, "See, this is where education fails. You got all this vocabulary and you forget that words are created to get more precise with telling the truth. Ever watch boxing? Notice a fight is a real hard competition? When a dog wants to give up, he gives up. Loses the competition. That's not suicide."

"Plenty of owners burn their losing dogs alive."

Dad's good-looking face furrowed like I was a stinking turd: "Who controls them? People choose their own perdition. Those crazies, they're exceptions. I wouldn't abide by them. I train winners. Period."

I gripped the table's edge. Dad paused, working something in his head. "Guys like me, chances don't come along regular, I told you this. Understand? You *know* this country's corrupt, the rich stealing from the poor and then some. Wages that've always been scraping the barrel. Then, an offer comes along. I'm going to get paid to do what I'm good at. Hell." He glanced up as if judging the overhead lamp, "I never saw a space ship beaming me up the American Dream; won't happen for you, either. I wasn't sure at first, but now I've seen a fighting pit, I know they're wired for it. I'm building my reputation."

"It's sick."

He spooned up the last soggy flakes, dumped the bowl in the sink. "You can never pay me back for all the years, all that time, I gave you. Now you're running away like a bunny rabbit. So go."

The dogs had become a means, not the end. What a gut-wrenching yank of gravitation. Dad leaned forward, his wrists pressed stiff onto the table in right angles, "You trust this economy to lift you? You and your degree? This so-called democracy is full of crooks bleeding the country straight into their private accounts. Buck the system, slip under the radar; those're the only real smarts. My joints, my damn back, are arthritic from lugging boxes and hiking into the damn freezer all day. You don't want what I'm earning now? Don't worry, it's mine."

"Don't train the pups."

Dad whacked his hand on the kitchen table. "Before you get high and mighty, think! Anybody else would." Like he knew deep thinkers. "Those pups have nothing ahead of them but playing fodder for bigger dogs I can tell you, unless they start training. Once they respond to commands, know how to find their potential, then they get a relationship going with someone." Dad stared out the back door at our yard with a newfound fascination. "Know what I don't understand?"

"What?"

"You want college so bad. Got big ideas for yourself. Want to stand out. Don't you think a dog knows the difference between just being and being fully alive? Life's rotten, a crying shame. But some creatures will always risk everything to prove their own gold metal value. Why would you ever stop this?"

"We wired dogs to work for us. To seek themselves reflected in our eyes. They count on that; you're telling them to die."

He paced in front of the refrigerator, gesticulating like a traffic cop. One puppy yanked at my shoelaces. "No one forced Mohammed Ali to be the greatest fighter in the world. So now he's got the shakes. You think he regrets his career? No way. No pain, no gain, truest thing ever said. Let me repeat: you cannot force a dog to fight. You want the world easy and sweet, everything on cushions. It isn't. There's the real awakening, Dirk. Can't deny nature by playing King Fucking Moral." He looked repulsed by the room, our words, the hour ticking on the clock.

He wasn't stopping. "Courts don't care about Evil Dog Fighters. There's maybe a fine to get your dogs back. It's why people do it, stupid. Chicago has the highest murder rate in the country. Dogs are no police priority. Face reality, college boy."

He walked out. A regular hard-working guy, headed for Happy Mart. What a dumb world, people judged by appearances when the real ugliness reared inside a person's skull.

But Dad wasn't gambling on me.

Bull's Eye didn't move for forty-eight hours. I felt sure I was losing him, though I remembered Dr. Lance's words; *Rest is most important.* On the third morning, he lifted his head, his eyes cautious but clear. His facial swelling had been retracting; he almost looked like my boy. Poor guy, born unlucky. Slowly, slowly, he limped into the yard to do his business. He sniffed the air, the ground, getting his bearings. I kept the two puppies away. It was enough that Poncho licked him like a pork chop.

Nellie telephoned, "How are the pups?"

"Heart-breaking."

"Listen, I've got calls in to the Humane Society, the ASPCA and an advocacy group called. D.O.G.S., Dog Owners Get Smart." Her voice was urgent and warm.

"Bull's Eye is moving."

"You gave him hope."

"I don't know." I didn't like Nellie's faith in these rescue organizations. My cautious heart doubted. I feared their agendas, the specific blindness of each organization, their devotion to a chosen vision. One group euthanized all pit bulls. Another only sheltered pits. Another required employees to be vegans. Another accepted that dog meat was dinner in certain cultures. This, the fate of humankind, to navigate with one driven determination or another, at the exclusion of others.

Evenings, Dad strapped on weighted collars to bulk up the puppies' necks during treadmill work. I joined him in the basement, "Their bones aren't fully formed. You'll stress their joints and ruin them."

"Their goddamn bones are fine; they've got energy to spare."

In the daytime, I removed them from their crates to play with each other, knowing that socializing limits aggressive tendencies. I almost rushed them to Noah's Ark. But once Dad knew, he'd make a point of replacing them with new pits that he'd lock up somewhere harder to trace.

Just a few days felt like years. Even if I'd wanted to bolt, Bull's Eye was healing; he needed comfort, stability. In between a reduced schedule of pizza deliveries, I sat around the house: miserable, bitter, researching as much about Chicago's dog fighting as I could on the Internet. The bloody fight, the injured dogs, the cheering spectators revisited me day and night. If there was a way to stop this, it required staying here. Learn and see.

Nellie phoned up, excited. "The ASPCA will send an animal cruelty investigator to take the pups. But they want you to step out of the way."

"No, no, no." Case after case of animal abuse ended with a slap on the hand, just as Dad had said. My research confirmed this. Search warrants ended up rescinded by judges, minute technicalities stalled case proceedings, eyewitness recanted, or officers missed their court dates, and without their testimony, cases were tossed. "The issue's dog fighting, Nellie. The rest will distract. Please."

Slumped into my chair, I wrote Phoebe, once more:
From: Dirk Seward <ponchosboy@aol.com>
To: Phoebe Turrett <Phoebegrace@noahsark.com>
Subject: lately
*Phoebe, I wrote but Sally deleted my communication, I phoned, you
don't know. I still want so much to talk, somewhere, sometime, with
you, just you. But you have to tell me how, Phoebe. I hope.*
Dirk

Michael rang me, "Dude, let's go to the beach. Catch some
sunburns."

"I'm in no mood." Nothing sounded more alien to my locked-
in position.

"You have what, three, four, weeks left? Come on."

"Another day."

"This is eating you alive. Dude, what are you proving?"

"Dunno, that the world is upside down?"

"You're a bummer, man."

It was later that evening, Dad still at work, when Michael
phoned, shouting, "Turn on the TV, CBS news! Hurry!" Men
were being led out of a two-story house in handcuffs, police cars
blasting sirens. One shot revealed pits with different degrees of
damage being loaded into crates in vans. Some terrified, others
growling, pushed by metal prods. The recap, maybe three to
four minutes long, described dog fighting in Chicago. Presented
a cop on a mission – Sgt. Bruce Wheeler, head of the Police
Animal Abuse Prevention Team. Gave his precinct number.

"So they arrested all the fighters?"

"Pretty serious," Michael explained, "They found corollary
evidence of gambling, drugs, weapons."

I searched the Internet: sure enough, Sgt. Bruce Wheeler,
Precinct 14. Articles in *The Chicago Tribune* and *Sun-Times*,
described various raids, quoting him: "There are 25 police
districts in Chicago, twenty-two of them have dog fighting.
Parents take their kids to these fights. Spoke to a fourth grade
class on the west side. I asked: who's seen a dog fight? Nearly
every single kid raised a hand. This is our future? The most
common psychological profile of a serial killer is that, first, he
abuses animals."

The next morning, I was searching more articles when the phone rang like a trumpet. I nearly jumped out of my chair. Nellie was breathing hard, "Dirk! Did you see the news? We can get Fitzgerald on a Class Four Felony. One-to-three years in jail. He'll lose his job. It's big stuff."

"I read the police must catch perpetrators *at* a dog fight, fighting their *own* dogs. To clinch it. "

"If your Dad's *at* a fight, he'll get arrested. That'd wake him up. Shake his confidence. Truthfully, I wouldn't mind seeing Russ handcuffed in an orange suit. But at least we can scare him. Most important, he won't be allowed to keep dogs. A misdemeanor on his record, and no dogs. I'll bet you can live with that." She paused. "I'm still at work. More later?"

She was right; this wouldn't destroy him. But it might twist him all up.

Course and campus catalogues continued to arrive from the University of Illinois at Champaign-Urbana. Orientation started in three weeks. But I'd been shoving everything into a cardboard box. College had started to seem an act of negligence. Bailing out, giving up. I'd waited so long for this chance, this freedom. Now the dream slipped and slid like an oily road: no longer the only right way. Though I doubled over, thinking of what I was giving up, just about all I wanted.

From: Dirk Seward <ponchosboy@aol.com>
To: Phoebe Turrett <Phoebegrace@noahsark.com>
Subject: madness

Phoebe, where are you? I need to see you. More than you imagine. I understand your life is circumscribed. With God in it. I'm not good at this, you know, talking about God. Phoebe everything lies ahead, that's all I know. Tell me when I can see you. Soon, please.

me

I contacted Sergeant Wheeler. Or tried to for three days in a row. No response. I finally yelled into his voice mail, "I've got a dog fight location. You don't call me back today, I'm going to CBS to break this. And the ASPCA."

He rang me back. "Wheeler, here. We get lot of calls, sorry. Only three of us on staff. We're inundated. Tell me what you got."

"It's my Dad." I gripped the receiver. My thumb hurt.

"You should be calling Social Services for family trouble, son."

"I'm talking about dogs. Fighting dogs."

"I need evidence. To do anything."

"You'd prosecute, right?"

"We catch them in a dog fight, we go for a Class Four Felony. Would you be the John Doe?" He had a worn voice.

"What?"

"Someone who provides eyewitness evidence but doesn't have to self-identify. Or give testimony in court, any of that. You write down the info and sign: John Doe."

John Doe. "Yes. Yes."

"About the ASPCA, they mean well, they're devoted people; if you let them in on a fight, they'll rescue the animals. But not being a proper police raid, they won't have search warrants or legal jurisdiction. Means you can't prove culpability in court."

By now I grasped the picture, its easy unraveling. "Understood."

"Get me hard evidence, son; names, addresses. I don't mean to be discouraging, but we got to have something solid to pursue."

"All right."

An email cropped up from Phoebe.

Don't think I don't miss you. How slow time feels when you don't care about much. The days have been endless. I can skip knitting next Saturday to see you; I'll ply Sally. Would that work? It was sweeter when you were in my life.

Phoebe

Though I was relieved, my head was splitting. The sun slid in bright afternoon stripes through the narrow blinds, striating the wall, but I felt darker than a coalmine, the black of suffocation. For years, I'd owed nothing to anyone but Dad. I'd become accustomed to Spartan-ness. I lay down next to Bull's

Eye who raised his head like a weary philosopher. He *was* an old dog now, twelve or thirteen. "But you didn't die, you old codger," I whispered. Tears slipped down the side of my face, wetting the pillow. "You wouldn't give those assholes your life. They didn't deserve you." I started sobbing. I couldn't squelch the hard racking sobs, that were for Bull's Eye, and Poncho, and Dee, who'd been wronged, and for myself, no longer an arrow targeted for college, free and deserving. For having instead to wait and wait for the police I didn't trust, no longer self-sufficient, no longer clear to myself or anyone else. Just a freakin' mess. Bull's Eye licked me dutifully, while Poncho paced back and forth, waiting to be included. I wept for all I might yet not do, failing my own ends. Poncho lifted his head over the lip of my bed, resting it on my leg, waiting to be allowed up. I stretched my arms around Bull's Eye's thick chest. I could feel his heart beating in my palm. It beat strong and hard for such a thick old dog, telling me, *heyimstillhere, heyimstillhere, heyimstillhere.*

I woke in the dark, Dad's pale face hovering over me like a freakish papier-mâché. "Well, if it isn't Sleeping Beauty. Where's dinner?"

I mumbled, "What time is it?"

"Past eight. You cook anything?"

I shook my head, jolting awake.

"Screw it, I'll do it." Dad strode out.

My eyes adjusted to the dark, pieces of my room shaping into familiar gray belongings. I'd gotten my answer just before I fell asleep. I now woke up to the clarity I'd been desperate for, for days. I had to nix my sullen, pissed-off Boy Scout morality. It wasn't taking me anywhere. I stumbled out of the room. "Sorry. I'm beat."

He was frying eggs. "Never heard of an alarm clock, chump?"

I rinsed my hands. "So, at what age can the pups be fought?" Dad wheeled around like I'd pointed a gun.

He scowled, "Over a year old, two is better. Can't be puppy-goofy. Focus makes the difference."

"Same as weight pulls then, right?"

Dad studied me shrewdly, "Are you on drugs?"

"I slept them off. What about bitches, are they as game as the males?"

"Bitch to bitch, sure. Like in sports, you don't mix women's teams with men's." He sized me up, "You writing entries for Encyclopedia Britannica?"

"I want to understand." I rubbed my forehead to display modest concentration.

Dad poured salt on his eggs. He stabbed the eggs with his fork tines like they might jump up and run away. "Yeah, well you've got a lot to learn."

"I know."

He squinted. "Sucker."

Nellie hated my staying at home. "You stick around trouble too long, you forget the alternatives. At least, visit me for a decent meal." The El whipped downtown, trees and rooftops zipping by, buildings fading into purple-gray. Dark flagpoles and lights slashed the evening's brilliant blue. Peach-red light streaked the tops of a few skyscrapers. It was August; sunlight stretched late.

Outside the Harrison stop, she waited in her shiny red Mustang. It announced the saucy mettle at her core. She waved, "Get on in!" Otis belted. And I was right with him, on his dock, looking around, doubting that anything would ever change. God, it warmed my heart. Just that I could not, absolutely not, remain the same. Suddenly, Nellie and I joined in, crazy, out of tune. We laughed. I loved her.

Nellie served us pork chops in onions, seared cauliflower, thin-sliced beets, and thickly sliced cheese garlic bread. I ate ravenously. Her four girls crawled closer and closer: *That plate coming down?*

"No manners. Pouring on the guilt." Nellie smiled, put her hand on my arm, "Keep your focus. Don't get waylaid."

"It's just that—" I put down my silverware. "I can't go to Champaign."

"Oh yes you can."

I lifted my plate. The dogs' ears perked up. "May I?" Four noses zoomed to my side.

"Yeah, yeah." Nellie studied me unhappily. "Is it Phoebe?" she repeated flatly. "That girl." She tapped the table. "Come on, Dirk, spill the beans."

"More than a girl."

"A girl you've got a crush on."

I hadn't thought about Phoebe exactly in these terms, not out loud. It sounded strange, but it felt almost right. "Yeah, I think, maybe." I confessed, "But it's not that simple."

"Ha!" Nellie threw her head back and let out her big warm laugh. "It never is. Tell me."

"She's not unbalanced, like some animal people who think dogs should run the country, or no one's good enough to adopt them. She blushes easily. When she does I get this feeling like fireworks up my neck. I get weird and can't speak. We haven't had much real time together. She distracts me. She's tried to help me. Her eyes are gray-green. Dogs take to her like glue."

"Why should she affect Champaign?" The dogs sighed, and repositioned themselves, arranging for a good nap.

"Not her. It's Dad. I can't run away. Like I never learned loyalty from the dogs. The shame'll fester like an infection. Dogs at the shelter are people's failures. People fail a lot. I have a chance at getting evidence for the police. But not if I head off to Champaign."

"I'll take over. I've got contacts. Good ones." But she didn't have my position, an open view. Dad's blood, living under the same shaky roof.

"Don't worry. After things settle, I'll enroll, maybe in a community college."

"Slow down. You're going to Champaign, Dirk. Do you think they give scholarships away easily? They want you. Just postpone."

"How?"

She paused. "Call Champaign, say... your dad's ill... a time-sensitive condition. You're an only child, and have to delay for a semester, one semester. That enough? Put the authorities onto Russ. Start fresh in Champaign in January, far from this crap." Nellie watched me intently, processing, "Your plate's full, really full."

"But if I trust others, even you, Nellie, more than myself, I'll feel trivialized. Self-infantilized. Trust me, please."

"Dear God, I hope I'm right to agree."

Postponing the scholarship had never seemed a possibility. I felt a rush of hope. I'd still make Mr. Davario proud. Nellie walked into the kitchen. She removed a magnet off the fridge. She handed it over, "For you."

Why not go out on a limb?
That's where all the fruit is.
Mark Twain.

I laughed, "You slay me."

"That better be a compliment."

"Nothing but."

Maybe we'd turn this mess of wrongs on its head, spin a victory from dirt.

Late in this derailing summer, I burned with agitation.

I'd reached the Admissions department at University at Champaign-Urbana. Had a long talk with a solicitous counselor; "January," she said, "is not so far away. The life of the mind includes knowing how to care for those we love." But she warned that scholarship funds couldn't be kept dangling indefinitely. I reassured her the need was time-limited. She wished me well. I hung up, expecting the receiver to recant: *What you just heard is a joke. You really expected things to work out? Hah! Hah! Hah!* But the phone remained peaceful in its cradle. When my deferment documents arrived, I signed, relieved and amazed.

I'd studied various histories of the big guns in the dog-fighting world, men who staked thousands on their dogs. When they got caught, because there had been police raids and arrests, even negative press, they always – call it an ironclad guarantee – paid and walked. Defense lawyers claimed *unlawful defamation of character*, an *invalidated arrest*, accusations of *hearsay*. The big guns sauntered back to their *sport*, amused by this country's pansy ass laws. In Illinois, two men were currently in jail for dog fighting. Two. The irony of it dripped with someone's fat. Dogs battered in crates, dead in basements, blood streaked across carpeted pits, added up to nothing but *supposition*, nothing to hold up in a court of law. The public might make a bad example out of a famous athlete, but far from the limelight, hundreds of smaller fish scrabbled undeterred, this was the bigger truth, the one no one cared to wake up to. Besides, before you knew it, the athlete was back getting paid millions for a new national team, like he'd been in a game of musical chairs. The one likely inescapable scenario, the only potentially and maybe ironclad case, was getting caught by the police with a valid search warrant, in the premises where a dog fight involving the perpetrator's dogs, was actually in process. A confluence of variables, generally too much to ask the law to hope for.

I decided to risk irritating Dad, not exactly foreign territory. A few evenings later, Dad arrived home harried from work, grabbing slices of cheese, some sticks of beef jerky, "I'm out tonight. Feed the pups, will you?"

"Training? Like me to come?"

"Are you out of your mind?"

"I'd like to come. Or you going to a fight?"

His jaw dropped, "You hallucinating?"

"I thought about what you said. How I don't know a game pit." I stared at him, and he stared back. I tried to sound unhurried. "It sounds crazy to me. But I'd like to see. If you're right."

He tapped his forehead with his index finger, "Damn straight I am. Shit. What makes you think I'd let *you* tag along?"

"I'm your son—"

"That's no recommendation to Fitz." He cuffed the back of my head, hard, testing me.

I got up, headed to the basement, "Whatever. Sorry I asked."

He snorted, "There's plenty you don't get about me."

"I know."

I concentrated on Fitzgerald's garage. The first pics had turned out gray and fuzzy, no kind of evidence. This time, I'd turn on all the lights, go slow. I had a new special camera, narrow as a magic marker, with excellent resolution. Driving, I played Smokey's *Tears of a Clown*, trying to clear the mess in my head, thinking about how a person covered up. His syncopation propelled me.

I'd be an urban studies student exploring the city's industrial wasteland, and vault over the back wall, but this time, I carried a hefty Ziploc bag with fresh ground sirloin, because I predicted a guard dog.

My technique had improved; I jumped over smoothly. And, in fact, a sturdy red-nosed blue pit bared his canines, his healthy red gums, growling long and low as he shot over. I greeted Bad Boy with cheer and forced calm. Tossing a bloody clump of meat between us. Eyes firm on me, Bad Boy interrupted himself to eat. I moved sideways toward the garage. What I thought was: Bad Boy's here because other dogs are here, too.

I carefully sprung the locked side door open and a triangle of daylight pierced the interior. Dogs blinked and barked. I shut myself in, gagging from the reek. I flicked on the overhead. This time, I counted seven dogs. Another young bitch with full teats had one eye sewn shut, and a left stifle bandaged. A swollen black and white spotted head hoisted up. Others lay zombie-like. One brindle's yellow eyes were glazed over like congealed wax. A muscular black pit raised his hackles, watching through furious eyes. Two other trim and well-built red males snarled across crates egging each other on. A couple of young dogs whimpered. I snapped shot after shot.

Bad Boy yowled, his nails scraping the wood door before he threw his body against it, abbreviating my reflections. When I opened the door, Big Boy snapped his teeth, testy with impatience. I tossed a fistful of sirloin high over his head: "Catch!" He got it, hurtled back. I played the meat toss refrain, clump by clump narrowing the gap to my exit. At the wall, I pitched the last of it hard and far, still in the plastic sandwich bag so Bad Boy would have to probe his prize while I jumped over. Not spoiling his guard dog was just one of Fitz's mistakes.

Phoebe flew in and out of my mind, knotting up my thoughts. I was going to meet her in a coffee shop, the situation absurd in its normalcy. As we sat, our table, our coffee cups appeared to me in exaggerated definition. Phoebe murmured, "Tell me what's been happening. You know I can keep a secret."

So I did, explaining, "I'm in touch with the police. It can't get messy, public. Funny thing, how people get well intentioned, all righteous, storm over agitating to save the dogs, and end up killing the legal evidence. Check the books, prosecutions are incredibly rare. The minute a whiff of a whistle-blower's apparent, these guys clean up everything. Easy. The case becomes a pain in the butt, not an incarceration. The surest thing is that it'll blow over."

"You've gotten closer to this than anyone gets." Her eyes swam across my face, a brush of cool water.

"I'm counting on my wits. Doesn't feel too impressive."

"You've got more than wits, Dirk. For one, me rooting on the sidelines." She flashed me a sweetly unafraid smile. This was the Phoebe I hadn't met before, this girl palpable in the world.

"I need that."

"All yours. Cross my heart, hope to die." She drew a quick "x" wrinkling the shirt pocket over her heart.

"Sally's forgiven me?"

"That was my fault. Yeah."

I covered her hand, so light in mine, like a toy. "Some day I'm going to kiss you someplace like this, people bustling about their own things. All I'll think about is our kiss. If you let me."

"I'll let you."

"Then I have to see you again."

"Oh, you do." Her eyes opened wide, eager and playful, before she slipped away, hurrying down the hot street in her light yellow dress. When I'd let go of her hand, she'd raised it, fingers crossed, playing up her Girl Scout promise. She lightly bit her shiny lower lip, and winked.

Later that evening, I walked Poncho under a few bleary stars. I medicated Bull's Eye's wounds. His cuts were scabbing cleanly, improving. But he'd been hurt in some place I couldn't get to. He studied the world from dulled eyes, not my joker pal eager to get a laugh. Emptied, a shell of himself.

Nellie repeated herself like a scratched CD: "Don't you see your dad will have won if you ruin your life?"

Her worry, her kind fretting, seemed funny like banter on a sitcom. "Nellie," I repeated myself too, "If there's any way to, we have to get Fitzgerald on a felony. Dad paying *some* price."

"Think about your future."

"Whatever happens here stays with me the rest of my life."

"Dirk, aren't you just getting information to hand over to the police? Don't you dare get too deep into all this."

"I'm just getting information to hand over to the police." Being worried over, well, I hadn't prepared for that much care.

Part of my photographic record also had to be the Forest Preserve site. After parking my car near a smattering of families cheering for their Little Leaguers, I jogged back to the building. So many nice families prancing about, barbequing or biking, unhurried in the summer heat. While I snapped my pictures and drew a map.

Then, as if Providence had generous ears, Dad caught a bad summer flu. Couldn't leave his bedroom, heavy-headed with high fever. Sweating, vomiting, swearing deliriously in his sleep. His face red as a ripe peach, Dad gleamed, replenishing his sweat, throwing the covers off, then huddling under them like a mole, yelling at me for water. I brought him broth, a pitcher of ice water, then more broth. He lay trapped in his own skin, so fitting. Strangely dependent in my hands.

Finally, he stumbled into the kitchen, hacked loudly into the sink, and, scowling through his fevered haze, and said, "I can't drive. You drive me. I don't see why you can't bring a book and wait in the car."

"For?"

"Me."

"Jesus, Dad. Where? What? When?"

"What am I going to call Bob, say I have a cold?"

"Okay."

Dad's fever heated around him. He dripped and swore and blew his nose, "Think I caught tuberculosis. Unbelievable this shit."

I fed the dogs. Dressed in a loose navy shirt; the camera hung inside, ready. I'd repeatedly practiced positioning the small lens to peek through a slit between buttons.

Dad looked at my shirt, "This ain't no party."

"I like this shirt."

"Don't be a faggot."

"Should I change?"

"I'm the fashion police? I don't got time for this shit." He exploded into a coughing fit.

I drove, taciturn, Dad barking directions. "There's a lot about me you've never appreciated or understood."

An icy snake of sweat trickled down my back, jolting me in the gut. "This is your chance to show me. Should be you who shows me."

"Is your damned job to get on my nerves? This isn't an invitation. Brought a book?"

My heart pounded like a flat tire hitting the rim. I told myself: *Slow, slow down.* I wanted to wake up and dismiss this nightmare. And wanted to grab it. With a handkerchief pressed to his nose, Dad eyed me up and down, "Know how strange you are?" I shrugged. "You don't know who the hell you are, and you don't know what you want, that's your problem."

He shook his head. Out of the city, we parked on a neighborhood side street. I tapped my foot on the floorboard like a metronome. I plunged in, thinking to butter him up, "Look, to me it sounds messed up. But you say. I don't know. Plus I thought – "

He raised a contemptuous eyebrow.

"—I brought money. If you tell me the dog to bet on..."

He shook his head. He ran his fingers through his thinning hair, showing off the biceps of which he was so proud. While I counted the seconds, he frowned, "So you got money?" He was crossing the divide. He rolled his sickened bleary eyes, "Anyway, you aren't allowed." He got out, hoofed it.

When, at the distant end of the sidewalk, he'd shrunk into a white thimble, he slipped under the Preserve's inefficient fence, hurrying down the faintly moonlit path.

I realized, sitting there like a lump, that my investigative journey might be long and dull. I opened Hemingway's collection of Nick Adams' stories, but the lines jumped around, every word a cricket on the loose. I stretched back, hope against hope something brilliant would come to me. Sneaking up on Dad would lose me the real advantage I craved; open access, the straight view.

Dad was banging on my tinny door, "Hey. Come on. You narcoleptic." He honked into his handkerchief, spat on the ground "Now or never, doofus, " he shouted in my ear. I almost knocked him over, flinging open the door.

"Zip your lip. No college boy crap. Can't talk moral shit around these guys, bleeding-heart dog-lover crap."

We high-tailed it to the park district building. Dad curled his fist and rapped out "happy birthday" as the metal door opened onto a fleshy face with a fat unibrow. "Hey Joe. My boy: Dirk. Fitz approved him."

The corpulent guy opened his meaty hand, "Thirty each." He tilted his head back, pointing us down the basement steps to the hall. Talk thickened the dank air. Jangling issued from metal chairs, keys, belt chains, and beer cans tossed into aluminum bins.

Now that I could see the entire space, it was clear this had once been a rec room. With pool tables, or maybe easels set up for a still life painting class. The stark raw wood enclosure, about fifteen feet square, three feet tall, dominated the room. The Pit. Braced to the floor with reinforced plywood. Carpeted to stop the dogs from skidding. The pile was threadbare toward the center; former scrubbed-down bloodstains remained visible. Dad pointed to a blue line drawn across the middle, "Scratch line." The folding chairs were arranged two deep all around. Men talked and gesticulated, slugging down beer and whiskey sold out of coolers.

Sweat oozed through the windowless room. A black-haired man in a white button down shirt and jeans, the stakeholder, energetically waved his arms: "Tonight's match, Midnight favored over Red Warrior, three to one. Taking all bets— Taking all bets— "

"Should I—?"

"Wait!" Dad snapped.

Anne Calcagno

Suddenly, voices flared. The dogs, separated only by a blanket stretched like a makeshift curtain, were ushered down the hall. An officious-looking man followed. "The Referee monitors now," Dad elaborated. "The washing. Owners can't wash their own dog." Owners washed their opponent's dog, sponging hard to ensure the pit's sleek coat hadn't been doused with poison, hot-pepper sauce, or a liquid sedative. "Good dogs've been ruined by one mouthful of foul play." He pointed out where the corner men stood, a couple of steps behind each corner, ensuring no hands but the owner's were laid on that dog after washing. "Trust isn't big here," Dad laughed, then coughed.

Thirty-five or forty people crowded the basement. One teenager draped his arm over a younger brother. Men postured, wads of money bulging from their pockets like talismans. Bets continually being handed to the stakeholder, who regularly interrupted to announce, "Bob Fitzgerald's 'Midnight,' three-time winner. Against Karl Riordan's new boy 'Red Warrior,' one time winner, come back and looking real good. Three to one odds, Midnight's favored. Forty-five pound limit; both dogs weighed and confirmed. Starting in three minutes."

I pressed, "Aren't you betting?"

"Shut up. I'm thinking." Watching him, disbelief and sadness mixed. I folded my arms at chest level, ready to pretend to fidget with a button when I clicked. When everyone focused on the fight, I'd begin.

One man never budged from the room's only exit, surveying the crowd. His legs spread in a firm V, as he tucked his fingers into a holster that swayed below his gut, carrying a black revolver. Dad grunted "hi" to two passing men. He was sweating from the flu, because he wasn't usually a big sweater. Three floor fans whirred lamely. He combed his fingers through his hair, jaws clenched. I snapped a shot of him, his muscles tense as bungee cords.

Now the dogs were being guided to their respective corners. Each faced away, head pressed to the back wall. Neither officially alert to the other, yet. Bob Fitzgerald touched his brow with his index finger. Dad shot up, extricating bills, reaching the stakeholder in long strides, handing him wads of twenties. I clicked.

"That was my signal."

Holster Man shut the door. Most everyone sat down. The silence turned bulky, expectant, faces in profile glowing from the overhead fluorescent lights. Eyes on the pit. "No one's allowed to leave during a fight. Could be a rat." Fitzgerald straddled Midnight, the angry black pit who'd raised his hackles in the garage.

The referee challenged, "Both corners ready?" At a nod from both owners, he proceeded, "Face your dogs." Whereupon, the dogs went rigid. The Ref shouted: "Five! Four! Three! Let Go!"

The dogs charged hard and fast, head to head, teeth bared, back legs shifting for position. Midnight's canines suddenly pinioned Warrior's neck. Warrior flipped Midnight like a big stuffed toy. Blood splotched the air. Midnight hung. No barking, no growling. Chilling silence. Bob and Karl, forbidden from touching their dogs, cajoled them, circling. My ears pounded, my insides churned. I got up to lean against a wall. The smell of the dogs' blood tasted like a mouthful of pennies, salty, acrid, rising, burning through my nose hairs, bleeding out my ears. My stomach threatened to turn inside out. The crowd sat riveted, mute but for rare exhortations. Blood dripped from Midnight's jowls. I clicked picture after picture.

It was maybe fifteen minutes later when Warrior unhinged Midnight's clasp, smashing Midnight against the wood enclosure, burrowing his teeth into Midnight's right front leg. Midnight bounced off the wall, lost his balance, crashed on his side. Warrior bit hard into his ribs, while Midnight kicked and scratched. Warrior clung. Blood doused them both. Men cheered, moaned. I looked away, my lungs thick as a mound of gravel. Fury snapped the camera shutter, *click, click*, grabbing these fervid faces. The crunch of bone crackled through my scalp. Midnight lunged up and caught Warrior's nose; blood shot from his nose. The crowd inhaled. Warrior pummeled Midnight. Driven to fight. Wasn't it driven to *live*?

"Midnight's a hard punisher," Dad rubbed his hands. "Good match, nice and close." Dad whispered, "I been training his brother, Speedo. Came up with new exercises to build up traction in the hind legs, so he can keep a hold for real long. I could patent this, it's a whole system: weights on the treadmill, isolating the legs. Tell you, I got more ideas." I hoped Sgt. Wheeler would claim that discovery. "Excellent wrestler," Dad muttered. "Curious to see what he'll do in the pit."

All at once, Warrior abandoned his battle stance, stumbled off. "Turn!" The Ref cried, "Men, handle your dogs when free of holds."

The dogs were returned to their respective corners. The Ref handed the owners sponges from his well-guarded bucket of water, doused to wipe down the spit, lather, blood. The crowd engaged in a quick flurry of arm and leg stretching. At 25 seconds into the third minute, the Ref called, "Get ready!" The count down, "Five! Four! Three! Let Go!" Warrior had to cross the line first to prove he still had fight. He charged Midnight. They circled each other, wily, alert, Warrior's black nose glistening, a dangling lump. Fifty-five minutes of fight had passed. Midnight lunged, clasped Warrior's ear; Warrior responded by dragging Midnight, clenching, along the wall, striating fresh blood. Then Warrior flagged, and again, let go of Midnight. His eyes suddenly heavy-lidded, unfocused. Midnight stood on top of him, jaw buried in his neck, pressing his advantage.

Warrior looked away, maybe hoping for a better place, another place.

Again, the dogs were separated, sponged down. But Warrior would not budge. Midnight stumbled into the pit alone, with a firm look in his swollen eyes. A cheer went up. "Midnight wins! Gentlemen collect your bets." The room grew voices, quarrelsome and jovial. Dad said, "You ever seen the likes of that?"

I shook my head.

"I made two benjamins on my six hundred. Sitting here. Tell me someone was forcing those dogs to fight."

"Nah, I can't." I felt filthy.

"That's what I hate about people judging what they've never seen. Like they know what they don't."

When had this kind of reasoning gotten a hold on him? What had carried him this far past compassion? What mattered was getting my camera out intact.

"Fitzgerald allowed you here. You got to thank him, especially after your stunt with Bull's Eye." Down the hall, the dogs were being treated, lying on old school tables. Karl was sewing Warrior's nose back on. Warrior's chest, gaping with a hole large as a fist, was stuffed with an antiseptic rag. Both dog had white streaked into their coats, just having been greased with meds, local antibiotics. Half of Midnight's face had already swelled thick as a baseball mitt. "Lost two teeth," Fitz said. I wanted to crack his skull.

At the end of a harsh coughing fit, Dad spoke, "Dirk's been speechless all night."

I stuttered. "Congratulations. Midnight's, wow, real impressive."

"He's tough, he'll make it. You the one broke in?" His eyebrows lifted as if reacting to repellent.

"I grew up with Bull's Eye." I shoved my hands in my pockets.

"You're lucky he's old. Or you would've had hell to pay. I usually don't take stock of nobody, but your dad's quite a trainer; got the real instinct for these dogs." Dad dropped his glance to the floor, pretending modesty, though he didn't squelch a small, sly smile. "Your dad spoke up for you real convincing. I thought maybe if you saw a fight, you'd get the honest view. Notice *we* had to stop Midnight?" I nodded. "No more playing Rescue Squad, hear?"

"Yessir."

"I keep a gun. And don't hesitate to use it on assholes. Bull's Eye was your dad's. You're lucky, kid. I wouldn't be near so understanding." He snorted. "Anyway, now you're here. You know what gameness is. There ain't nothing like it in any other breed. That's the damn truth."

Dad looked like he wanted to nominate Fitzgerald for senator. Astonishing what made him tick. The same blood, shared genes, didn't guarantee a person anything. We had become foreign to one another.

For about fifteen minutes, though, clarity loomed, perfect, shining. I had ironclad evidence dogs were being fought.

I couldn't wait to tell Phoebe. First, I'd develop the film. Yet it struck me like a bolt of lightning that I was not dropping off my critical evidence at a Walgreen's or Osco. In the hands of some model citizen lab technician, a supervisor could be alerted. Who might confiscate my ammunition. I called Sgt. Wheeler.

"Can you get to Henry Horner Housing? My precinct's here." On the south side, the projects. "We've got lab facilities. Never deal in pretty images. We could start on your John Doe statement, too. I'll have the forms ready."

"I'm heading over."

Before leaving for work, Dad had grunted, "Red Warrior died. Seizure. Hard to see it coming, not much you can do. Midnight's fine."

I couldn't think what to say.

Poncho jumped into the Fiesta. He was another record, relevant evidence. "You're a damn miracle," I told him. He wagged his tail, happy to be traveling. We headed into the late morning heat, noise, grit, and backed-up cars edging tensely downtown. Poncho's head stuck out the window, making sure he could see and be seen properly. South, on the Dan Ryan, the congestion finally lightened.

When we reached the Horner parking lot, Poncho leapt out to relish the fresh challenge to his senses; new asphalt, different garbage, changed cars, buildings. The police station occupied the ground floor of one of the brick buildings. Sgt. Wheeler came out from behind the counter, "Brought your own protection, huh?" He rubbed Poncho. "And the film?"

I patted my pocket. His desk was stacked with a mess of papers and files. We sat face to face. I started, "I'll wait while the film's being processed. Eager to see what we've got."

"The film goes to a central lab."

"Oh, I'll go there."

He coughed a wheezy, mirthless laugh. "Dick, it's not a public service. It's for officers working their cases. You have to go through me." Wheeler was maybe five foot ten, his legs and arms wiry, sprouting like toothpicks from his potbelly. He leaned forward. He rubbed his nose. He spoke slowly as if to aid my imperiled IQ. "Has it occurred to you that if these go back home your dad could find them? Then what? Here, they're safe."

"The name's Dirk."

"The film's no longer yours. Nothing personal." Not personal? His eyes were squinty blue, his lips thin sardines. He tap-tapped his fingers on the desk. "Don't screw up. It's a case for the police."

"It's *my* Dad. I'm keeping my ear to the ground for the next fight so you can arrest the assholes, right? We're working together."

"Strictly speaking, you attended an illegal dogfight, didn't alert any authorities. Let me do my job."

I couldn't believe this. "Like you've done so far?" Hearing my anger, Poncho bolted up from where he'd been lying mildly awake. "You think I *want* to do this?"

Wheeler jumped up surprisingly fast, nearly tripping over Poncho, in my face, "Whoa! Dirk, all things in good time. In two days, I'll show you all the prints. No one else will touch them, promise. Thing is, your taking risks right and left, it's not smart. I'm talking the need for caution. Work with me, kid. Don't be no vigilante"

"I'm here, aren't I?"

"These guys don't screw around. You touch their livelihood, you could be dead."

"I'm just as dead serious."

"Those – " Wheeler pointed to my pocket, " are real."

I felt frozen. Poncho studied me. I handed Wheeler the film. He nodded, reached over and shook my hand. "Now we're on the same team."

I gave Poncho's leash a quick pull and we plunged out, alive to the air, my stomach in knots. I drove to Michael's. He'd been on an intense training schedule the last couple of weeks. *Be there, be there, be there*, I muttered. He wasn't. My head hurt as I walked up our porch steps. The puppies whined in the basement, and I had to let them be, had to count on deceit and patience, though their puny high-pitched cries ached in me. Bull's Eye thumped his tail as I opened the bedroom door, rubbed him. I grabbed a cold soda. Flicked on the computer. Two emails popped up:

From: Michael Gregorio <mikeatbat@yahoo.com>
To: Dirk Seward <ponchosboy@aol.com>
Subject: none
You haven't even told me what day you leave for Champaign, man. Wazzup?!
Michael

I replied:
McMinty's, tonight? Got to talk.

I called Nellie, spilling the whole long story; the fight, the photos. She had to insist to get a word in edgewise and when she did her voice came clipped and stern. "Let me talk to Wheeler. No one out there's determined, plumb crazy like you. He doesn't get it. Wait until he develops the film. You'll be able to stop playing everyone's superhero."

"You mean nobody's."

"Dirk, you have so many qualities. You're just the sweetest hero."

I laughed. "Yeah I feel like I'm doing a lot of good, I'm tremendous." One particular thought condensed in the bright daylight: "Hey, what if Wheeler publicizes the shots in the papers?"

"Catching a fight *in situ* will earn him much bigger accolades, trust me."

Later that night, I told Michael. His even-tempered face darkened, "Your dad's sick, man. I thought you were imagining things."

"I've postponed Champaign. Until January."

"Piss me off! Swear to me then you're going, though; you're the smartest guy I know. Know what? You'd make a great veterinarian!" The idea didn't sound half bad. Champaign had a Vet program. Too weird. Our cold glasses dimpled with water, leaving wet rings on the table. Michael shook his head. " If the police catch Russ, he'll expect you to bail him. Get the hell out of town for a while."

"Yeah, somewhere safe for the dogs, too. Until January." For a moment, I had a vision of Phoebe with me, both of us widening the distance from our homes. Traveling narrow country roads, stopping in unobtrusive towns. Until we had a better plan. I felt a rush of optimism, thinking of the possibility of her presence, her body close. *On the Road.* Or *Thelma & Louise*, where it hadn't worked out at all to drive state to state.

I stared tiredly out McMinty's big front windows. A neon Corona ad blinked a jaunty little lime. Commentators chattered behind us on TV. Michael muttered: "Do you know you seemed boring when I first met you?"

"Recognize yourself, huh?"

Michael tipped his throat back and drank. "This crap bums me out, man."

The front windows onto Devon Avenue absorbed the evening's purple light, light that turned the table surfaces shiny, liquidy. Headlights sparked and street lamps brightened. Scores of scissored legs hurried by. One of McMinty's TVs was playing a rerun of "All in the Family," the other some CNN interview in which Michael suddenly feigned interest. How busy the world was. How still I felt. There were things to be done that couldn't be avoided. The essential question was, now and always; are you a man or a sheep? Why had Nellie, Michael, Mr. Davario gone out of their way and more, taken risks, for me? My own mom hadn't. But they had; they didn't budge.

They had filled the void. But they hadn't had to live with Dad. Mom and I had. Turns out, Dad's central quality was to propel those near him to leave. I wondered about Mom, if we'd ever share this knowledge through a long-delayed bridge of words. Could she be found on the Internet? Safe in the knowledge Dad would never look, but I might. If I left, I'd look for her. Even if I never contacted her. Just to know, to ferret out the unnecessary unknown.

In the morning, I drove to Phoebe's house. I was tired of waiting, of caution, all its missed opportunities. Terry's car wasn't in the driveway. I rang the doorbell. Nothing. I rang again. Phoebe glanced out an upstairs window, "Oh! One minute!"

She appeared at the door, arms tightly clasped, looking nervously behind me as if I'd brought someone. Brazenly, I stepped inside. I touched her arm, and pulled her as gently as possible to me, "Oh Phoebe." She was crying, her chest pulsating in little jerks. I smoothed her hair, cradled her delicate frame. Her tears soaked a cold spot in my t-shirt. "Phoebe, I hope some day you'll come away with me."

Phoebe looked up, her green eyes wet-lashed and red-rimmed. She drew a heart on my chest. "I want to be with you so much." Tears continued to run down her face. I kissed her, her fingers on the nape of my neck, her tongue swirling like warm honey.

"I can help you be safe. Please don't cry." I bundled her in my arms, this small prisoner who made my heart beat loud. "How is it you're so pretty?"

Nellie burrowed right into Sgt. Wheeler's thick skull. "He's impressed. He wants *you* to call him. Doesn't want to call and get your dad on the line. *Call* him, Dirk. Be smart."

Poncho sprawled on one side of me, Bull's Eye's head heavy on my chest. We were still. Yet we were moving. Ahead. Bull's Eye's face wasn't any prettier, but he was almost well. His remaining life's wish seemed to be to sleep day and night on my bed. I wouldn't begrudge my sweet old boy. Poncho bothered him with nudges and licks and periodic encouraging barks, because Poncho was ever hopeful that Bull's Eye would rise up and play. Poncho who'd been able to recover, striking a lively pace when we walked, as if to say, *I take this young man out to give him some exercise. Who else would?* With humans as my only measure, I might have been forever stunted. But I'd been lucky.

Near the end, things took on a life of their own.

Michael hadn't been answering my emails, tired I supposed, busy. My work was cut out for me. I hung on, at home, dogged, unmovable, waiting for any hint of a fight. I prepared dinner religiously, waited and sat with Dad, pressed him to talk.

"We got off on the wrong foot, son," Wheeler had apologized. "I can't fly with every story that comes to me off the street, have to follow protocol. You got 20 or more identifiable guys here. The pics are grainy, but the profiles, the leering faces, oh they're clear. And the dogs – shit." He sighed, "We can set up a couple of undercover cops in Schiller Park, see what spying gets us. But you keep your ear to the ground, yeah?"

"I'm a full-time stay-at-home spy."

"Come anytime to see your pics. You ever consider a career in law enforcement? You got a knack for it. You should."

When he wasn't closing, Dad left Happy Mart around seven or eight. After supper, he worked the pups. They weren't fed at all until he opened their crates, swinging a piece of steak in the air. They lunged and snarled at each other, desperate to win the meat. When they were done and licking their wounds, Dad harnessed the winner to the treadmill, propelled to the reward of one biscuit per mile. The bitch usually went second, more agitated, more desperate. He called them: "A" and "B" to concretize his detachment. I'd offered to walk them, going out of my mind with my inability to do anything else, and he'd okayed this. I petted and washed them, too. But little more than that because they had to snap and growl for Dad. "Get them out in all weather. I don't want no seasonal-type dog."

Lawns crisped yellow-brown now in late August. The walls sweated. Passing pedestrians hunched peevishly, as if they could accordion-collapse their discomfort. Seconds crept sluggishly toward infinity. Half my classmates had already started college. There'd been a blaze of packing and good-byes. I had to trust that my present did not reflect my future. I worried, ever more sickened by this holding pattern.

Eyes closed, headphones on loud, I didn't hear the unexpected doorbell. Though moments later, when I did, it was ringing madly. I stumbled up. Gruffly unlatched the door to see Michael. We sat at the kitchen table, drinking iced water, the ceiling fan shuffling a lukewarm breeze. Michael recounted how his mom had gone shopping for his dorm room. "She picked everything color-coordinated, blue and white, man, like I'm some sailor. Hope it doesn't flip out my roommate. Be glad you're free of a hovering parent."

"Yeah, it's a real comfort zone around here." I looked out the window at the cracked stucco houses lining our street with their beat up steps. The puppies whined and I brought Michael to the basement. They growled, snapping their jaws, playing the warriors Dad taught them to be. The greater their display, the more treats Dad doled.

"I guess it's better they don't understand," Michael stuck his hands in his jeans' pockets, and tapped his big feet.

"I wonder."

"Someone's got to take them out of here."

"Well, you can't."

"You so get on my nerves." He jabbed me in the arm. "Couldn't I bring them to your crazy girl at the shelter? She's still there, right?" He high-fived me. "Tell me when, dude."

I wrote Phoebe.

From: Dirk Seward <ponchosboy@aol.com>
To: Phoebe Turrett <Phoebegrace@noahsark.com>
Subject: puppies

One thing, when Dad's arrested, Michael will spring the puppies. He'll bring them to the shelter. You'll have to rehabilitate them; they're already messed, but they're young. Don't let them be put them down, promise? Watch over them? I'm so grateful, pretty Phoebe.
    Dirk
    P.S. Thanks with all my heart.

Then it was the first week of September. My brain was harnessed, daily dragging more weight. Suddenly, Dad asked the obvious, though he'd ignored it like the plague, "When you going to Champaign?"

"Later this month."

Dad frowned, personally confronted: "One of my customer's kids left already."

"I'm skipping orientation, too expensive."

"Kids today think someone's got to hold them by the hand, at every step. We weren't like that." Some parents lived for their kids, I'd seen that. Forgave themselves their failures, their disappointed lives, put all the focus on their kids. These parents woke up mornings so they could follow after their kids. Bizarre. Coddling wasn't in Dad's make-up.

The more days passed, the more I developed insomnia. In the dark, I lay flat, rigid, like someone at his own wake. Alternately, I twisted my sheets, flailing and kicking, until they were knots my brain chattered to. Bull's Eye and Poncho awoke, being bumped around, dismayed. Sleep-deprived, I grew woolly, miserable, doubtful.

Then Tuesday Dad came home particularly late. He removed his shoes and set them side by side like compliant twins.

"Guess who stopped by Happy Mart?"

I shrugged, shoving meatloaf into the microwave.

"Fitzgerald."

I nearly dropped the pan, "Oh?"

"He's found a match for Midnight's brother, Speedo. Friday night, same place we went. You be around?" His blunt fingers furrowed his hair. He rubbed his glasses clean with his shirt.

"It'll be a going away present."

"Don't get mushy; you pay your own way in." Dad cut a slab of meatloaf. "Should be a smoking stud fight." He continued in an instructive mood, "Though don't think a bitch can't fight like hell. Especially if one bitch really gets on the other's nerves. Yowee!" He laughed.

And so did I.

I meant to lie awake, celebrating each bright passing second, right up until the morning drove Dad to work. Instead, I conked out like a baby. I shot awake like I was on fire.

Sgt. Wheeler answered my call right away. "We'll slip in on foot. Eight officers. Plus back-up cars, blocking all the preserve exits." This was Wednesday.

I almost said, "Sure this is the right thing to do?" Sgt. Wheeler was building his career. Dad was sharing his favorite event. And I was living out my choice. It would save Dad, this relative slap on the wrist, this shake-up, which stopped him before he got in too deep. But it had me feeling disfigured. Dad would never understand. It was the end of many things.

Thursday, Dad loitered over his bowl of Wheat Chex, "You still on?"

"What?"

"The dogs. Tomorrow."

"Right, right, same place?"

"Yep."

"I should bring cash."

Dad winced: "That's the point. Do I have to tell you everything?"

Friday, noon, Michael called according to plan. He was on stand-by.

I'd filled two suitcases, ready and slipped under my bed. I'd go to Champaign-Urbana, and lay low. With its thousands of students, classes, fraternities, I'd escape notice and learn the lay of the land while the dogs acclimated. I'd find a dog-friendly apartment building, establish new routines. I'd get a job, yeah, get a life. I'd be solid ready for school by January, chomping at the bit. I re-checked the dogs' records, tags and vaccinations, my own medical and school documents. Then I studied my room like an extended calculus problem, function upon function. Sun striped through my shutters; my swollen closet door was, as always, not completely shut; my desk was scuffed up and small. Piles of books, my old fortresses, punctuated the floor. I wondered if I'd come back. Or if this was an expiration. Once, Dad had been my North Star. Before exploding in space into a thousand pieces.

I'd gone to the pharmacy and bought a bottle of Ipecac to make me convincingly sick. That evening, after I'd swallowed half the bottle, Dad found the bathroom door flung open, me praying to the porcelain god. He snorted, "What the hay is this?"

"I'll be okay." I retched more.

"The hell you will. I can't take you!"

"Just wait, a few minutes." I played out the drama of desire. "I'll be fine." Retch. "One minute."

"I can't, Dirk."

"Damn, damn...." I moaned. "Please." Poncho nosed around.

"Just clean up after yourself. The whole damn house reeks." Dad walked away. I heard him scrubbing the kitchen sink, which he did when he got tense, swabbing the metal surfaces like they antagonized him.

I stumbled up. Dad was sponging down the counters. "Dad, I leave tomorrow."

"I forgot. Call when you get there." He slapped together a ham sandwich, and headed for the door, "Spray plenty of Lysol!"

I wasn't finished puking my guts out. Eventually, I staggered to my feet, put a washcloth to my stinking face and neck and hands. I phoned Michael, "Ready?"

"I'm coming right over."

I phoned Nellie, "Dad's left."

"Dirk, now leave this all behind you."

My mind flashed on Wheeler and his men, in the forest, tightening their circle before busting open the doors, everyone sealed in the basement, Dad, too. I could see his face, scowling, his face pushed to the wall. My stupid eyes burned.

Nellie said, "After you've settled in awhile, you may feel ready to find your mother."

"Why would I want to do that?" But Nellie knew, she always did.

"You don't know the whole story. Maybe she decided you'd have a roof over your head, if she left you with Russ. Running away, she would've had no business dragging a little boy around."

I couldn't incorporate this at all, "I can't— "

"Forget it. But one more thing— "

"Yeah?"

"A cause for celebration." Just like Nellie to find a silver lining. "I met with the Humane Society. Ready—?"

"Yup."

"Listen here:

The Humane Society of the United States offers a reward of up to $5,000 for information leading to the arrest and conviction of any person who organizes dogfights, participates in dogfights, promotes dog fighting, or officiates at dogfights.

"Wheeler's sending the paperwork in for you. Who knew?"

"I'm not doing this for money."

"Don't cut off your nose to spite your face, Dirk. College isn't cheap. This is their brave idea of how to spend money. You didn't ask for it. They offer. Let them. I'm proud of you."

"Nellie, I'm gonna miss you."

"You'll be seeing me. I'll drive down very soon. Go, go, go."

I leashed my boys and we stepped out. I patted my three hundred dollars, just to be sure. I closed the front door behind me. I studied the porch steps in the fading blue light, the dogs at attention. Michael hopped off the porch chair where he'd been quietly waiting, slapped my back, opened my car trunk, and shoved in my suitcases. Phoebe was standing by my car. Michael looked embarrassed, and not indifferent, "I brought her over. For the puppies."

Phoebe tilted her head, "He's pretty nice, huh?"

"It's your boy here, made me do it." Michael gave me another jab in the shoulder. "Hope you know he's nuts?" He paused. "They'll get your Dad, huh?"

"Yeah, I think. Misdemeanor. He won't go to jail, or anything. Scour the papers for me – don't forget! Call Nellie and get the scoop."

Phoebe said, "I'm going to miss you. But you're going to write, right? Promise?"

Anne Calcagno

"Cross my heart." I remembered her saying this.

Michael grabbed us round the shoulders, pulling us together, our three heads sheepishly bowed: "Group hug."

So I am driving southwest way into the wheat fields where, soon enough, education waits.   Out of the Windy City, streetlights shining through shadows, flicking on and off the dogs. Their attentive noses rub against the windows, leaving wet grey streaks.   Soon, they'll sleep.   I believe this much: life is not an addition problem; the future does not have to be the sum of the past.   One blessing is; you do not have to go the journey alone. What will come of this? I don't know, but I have just enough money, justice is being rendered, and a few bad claims to the world are being eradicated as we speak. Right now, that's plenty good enough.

Love Like a Dog

ACKNOWLEDGEMENTS

When I entered the fraught world of pit bulls and discovered those who work with them, I found that openness and generosity, without recompense, prevailed. For those who live with misunderstood breeds and difficult rescues, the desire to allay prejudice is strong and life-affirming.

I owe my greatest debt to Debbie & Rich Flude, who offered me their home, their expertise, and, finally, my Am Staff Terrier, Qalilah. Darlene Ueseling warmly welcomed my daughter and me into CARE (Center for Animal Rescue of Evanston) when we were new awkward volunteers. CARE opened my eyes. American Staffordshire and American Pit Bull Terrier owners thoughtfully answered my questions at dog conformations & weight pulls throughout the Midwest. That is, after my neighbors, Janice and David, taught me how to read competition logs. I thank ex-Lieutenant Jeff Wilson for leading me to Sgt Brownstein, former devoted head of Chicago's Animal Abuse & Control Team. Brownstein and his officers and their legal counsel Sandy Brode were most kind and informative, as was Sgt. Sue Trigourea of Evanston. I have the deepest respect for Cynthia Bathurst, founder of Safe Humane Chicago & D.A.W.G. D.A.W.G.'s Court Advocacy group is a remarkable volunteer group of men and women who tirelessly attend court hearings, countering any legal casualness to animal rights and dog fighting abuses. Watch Cindy Deir's Humane Society award-wining short film "Paisley Sky" for a deeply loving portrait of a pit bull (available on my website: www.annecalcagno.com). Remember: Punish the deed not the breed. Any factual errors in this novel are mine; no one else is responsible.

For stories shared, long hours of work, and creative spirit, I thank Patricia and Amy, B.J. Gregorio, Morgan Gliedman, Erin O'Neill, Hurmat Ulain & Michelle Sutherland.

This novel would never have shaped itself without my agent, my persistent literary guide Stuart Bernstein. Or without the intent critical readership of H. G. Carrillo, Lauren Iossa, and Jodie Ireland. You save my life.

Last but never least, my gratitude goes to Jessamyn, who started the story, Lucien who is the story, and Leo, always Leo, because you make imagination live.

FACT
There are twenty-five police districts in Chicago. Dog fighting
has been reported in twenty-two of those districts.

LINKS
There are wonderful informational and rescue organizations,
devoted to dogs of all breeds. A partial list of some organizations
devoted to the bully breeds are:

www.badrap.org
www.bestfriends.org
www.dontbullymybreed.org
www.forpitssake.org
www.mabbr.org
www.mariahspromise.com
www.outofthepits.org
www.pbrc.net
www.petfinder.com
www.pinupsforpitbulls.com
www.pitbulllovers.com
www.sulafoundation.org
www.thetruthaboutpitbulls.org
www.theunexpectedpitbull.com
www.vrcpitbull.com
www.workingpitbull.org

ABOUT THE AUTHOR

Anne Calcagno is the author of the story collection *Pray for Yourself.* Her honors include fellowships from the National Endowment for the Arts and the Illinois Arts Council. She is the recipient of the San Francisco Foundation Phelan Award and an Illinois Arts Council Literary Award. She lives in Chicago with her family, including two dogs and a cat. She teaches in the MFA in Writing program at the School of the Art Institute. Visit her website at www.annecalcagno.com.

To order *Love Like a Dog*, visit:

www.LoveLikeaDog.net
www.annecalcagno.com
www.amazon.com

You can also order copies at your local bookstore.

FOL
APR 0 2 2024

CPSIA information can be obtained at www.ICGtesting.com
Printed in the USA
241107LV00001B/110/P

9 781452 834986